FROM Russia WITH CLAWS

MOLLY HARPER
writing as JACEY CONRAD
and GIA CORONA

OMNIFIC PUBLISHING
LOS ANGELES

Omnific Publishing
1901 Avenue of the Stars, 2nd floor
Los Angeles, CA 90067
www.omnificpublishing.com

First Omnific eBook edition, August 2015
First Omnific trade paperback edition, August 2015

The characters and events in this book are fictitious.
Any similarity to real persons, living or dead,
is coincidental and not intended by the author.

Library of Congress Cataloguing-in-Publication Data

Corona, Gia; Conrad, Jacey.
    From Russia with Claws / Jacey Conrad and Gia Corona – 1st ed.
    ISBN: 978-1-623422-12-7
    1. Paranormal Romance — Fiction. 2. Werewolf — Fiction.
    3. Russian Mafia — Fiction. 4. Romance — Fiction. I. Title

10 9 8 7 6 5 4 3 2 1

Cover Design by Micha Stone and Amy Brokaw
Interior Book Design by Coreen Montagna

Printed in the United States of America

1

Say Cheese, Jackass

Galina Sudenko scanned the sea of vaguely familiar faces. The cream of the crop had turned out in full force at Katya Bulgakov's Sweet Sixteen party. Some of these people she hadn't seen in nearly a decade. Her father, Ilya Sudenko, held court at the round tables over by the bar with the rest of the elders of the *Volk Organizatsiya*, leaving the younger generations to mix and mingle. The DJ spun various abominations of Russian synth pop that made her want to gouge out her eardrums with a spork.

She was deeply bored.

She could feel the appraising looks of the young men in the room, both single and married, each of them eager to please her father and move up within the ranks of the Organization, to make their bones. If they could woo her, their lives would be made. Unfortunately most of them seemed cut from the same cloth as her eldest brother, Alexei, or her embarrassment of a brother-in-law, Sergei—either too hotheaded or too stupid. She wanted none of them.

Wishing her brother Nikolai were here, Galina snagged a glass of cheap sparkling wine from a passing waiter and tried to blend. Nikolai had been called out of town to fix a problem of Alexei's. It seemed that cleaning up Alexei's messes was all Nik did with his hard earned law degree, jetting here and there to work his magic and make the problem — or bodies — disappear. It also meant he got to miss out on joyous extended family celebrations like this.

Lucky him.

Galina ignored her father's summoning glare as long as she could, but knew she'd reached the end of his patience when he sent one of his underlings to fetch her to the table where he held court. Her sister, Irina, stood near the bar, wearing red and an expression of happiness so fake it made Justin Bieber's chest hair seem real. Irina blithely ignored the collection of other pretty *Volk* wives around her, choosing to watch the teenaged fits that passed for dancing on the ballroom floor.

"Papa," she greeted, kissing her father's cheeks. His face was flushed from all of the vodka he'd already imbibed, and he looked in no danger of slowing down. Galina knew that if her mother were here, she never would have allowed her husband to get so deep in the bottle. But Mama was dead these twenty-five years, from complications in birthing Galina. Papa had never remarried.

"Galya," he said, voice gruff with alcohol. He took in her short Alexander McQueen dress with a disapproving dip of his mouth.

"Little Galina, is that you?" Uncle Petyr, an old friend of her father's, pushed past Papa to envelope her in a massive bear hug. "Not so little anymore! I remember when I could pick you up in one arm."

"Hi, Uncle Petyr," she said when he returned her to her feet. "It's good to be home."

Her attention was drawn from her honorary uncle to an imposing figure crossing the ballroom to join a group of Rom. The man turned and Galina recognized the profile as one of the men in the group from the club she and some friends had visited the night before. It had been Sveta's idea to go out as a welcome home party for Galina. Their party had met up with a group of young men out for a good time. He'd been among them, keeping mostly to himself, but he'd caught her eye in a way she couldn't explain. Andrey Lupesco...that had been his name.

Galina stared at him across the room full of family members, hangers on, and business associates, unable to make her mind function properly. She could swear she knew him from somewhere other than the club last night, but it wasn't coming to her. His friends had bought drinks for her group, had danced with them. Hell, one of them had even given his number to Sveta at the end of the night. But

Andrey had hung back, watching, letting his friends make in-roads with her and her friends.

She could feel his eyes on her as she stood at the bar with Uncle Petyr. Andrey's steely blue gaze bore holes into her as she turned away to give Petyr her attention. She glanced over her shoulder and her eyes met his, sending a shudder of heat through her.

He stared at her like he wanted to remove her panties. With his teeth.

So it was probably good that she wasn't wearing panties, then.

Galina leaned closer to her uncle. "What's Andreyev Lupesco doing here?"

Petyr shrugged, signaling for another glass of Stoli. Galina pulled away. "Your father has business to discuss with him."

"At Katya's Sweet Sixteen?" she hissed, glancing up at the crowd of people surrounding them. "Last I heard the Rom usually weren't welcome at family functions."

Uncle Petyr made a face that told her exactly what he thought of their presence here. "Things change," he said sadly, following her gaze to the dark haired man that stood easily talking to a group of men only a few years younger than him. "He's head of them now."

Galina started, eyes darting away from Andrey. "What? How did that happen?"

Uncle Petyr smiled at her, looking like he wanted to ruffle her hair and send her off to the corner with a sweet. "I forget. You've been away at school."

When Petyr had too much to drink, he loved to gossip like an old woman. It was how, at ten-years-old, Galina found out the details of Irina's adoption even though she hadn't asked. She might as well use that to her advantage now. "So what happened?"

He leaned forward conspiratorially. "He staged a coup and took over leadership. Andrey runs all the shifter street drugs now. He's got more money than God and controls a huge section of the docks. Most anything coming through Seattle goes through him now."

Galina blinked in surprise. So her assumption last night, that he was just a bodyguard, was woefully incorrect. Most likely, the men her friends had been flirting with had been *his* bodyguards. Wonderful.

"He's a little young for it," she said absently. Andrey was only in his early thirties, if that.

"He's ruthless." Petyr's voice held a grudging respect. "He is not a man to be trifled with."

Papa interrupted their murmured conversation. "Galya, there's someone I'd like you to meet."

Uncle Petyr excused himself quickly. Galina gazed at her father, suddenly wary. She knew practically everyone here; hell, she was related to a good number of them. Who on earth could Papa introduce her to?

"Maksim!" He waved over a young man, probably only a year or two older than her own twenty-five.

He was tall in a rawboned way, almost as if he hadn't finished growing into his limbs. He had light brown hair, a bit too long, brown eyes fringed with thick lashes, the irises so dark they were almost indistinguishable from the pupil. His mouth was firm, with lips almost girlishly full. He was handsome enough, but looked unfinished somehow.

Galina slanted her gaze over to her father, standing beside her as proud as the proverbial peacock. He couldn't possibly be serious.

"Maksim Federov, this is my youngest daughter, Galina." Papa took her hand and placed it in Maksim's.

"A pleasure to meet you, Miss Sudenko," Maksim said, squeezing her fingers in his in a half-hearted shake. "You are lovelier than your father spoke." His English was passable, but he spoke with a thick Russian accent.

Galina throttled the irritation that rose inside of her chest, clawing its way up her throat. Instead she answered, "Those are kind words, Mr. Federov."

"Less kind and more true," Maksim returned, squeezing her fingertips again.

She extracted her hand from his, fighting the need to wipe her fingers on her dress. His hand was clammy, and she could still feel the sensation of damp fingers clutching hers. Her father put a heavy hand on her shoulder, his other clapping down on Maksim's. Papa's smile was wide and sloppy.

"The Federov family made a killing in caviar. They are looking to expand their operation. Maksim is here to discuss business." Papa pushed her closer to the young man. "I told him that you would be able to show him around Seattle—what the young people want to see."

Sliding out from under her father's grasp, Galina nodded once, just as her father expected. "I'd be happy to show Mr. Federov around." She eyed her father carefully, having a good idea of what he was up to with the sightseeing request.

"Please, call me Maksim." He tried to grab her hand again, but Galina stepped backward. She was not interested in holding hands with Clammy McSweatypalms ever again. Nor did she revel in making small talk with men whose idea of running a business had ossified somewhere around 1975.

"I should offer the Bulgakovs my congratulations," she told her father and Maksim, latching onto any excuse to escape. "I haven't gotten to say happy birthday to Katya yet. If you'll excuse me."

"Of course," the younger man said, a note of petulance in his voice. "One's familial obligations must be attended to."

Galina said her good-byes, happy to escape Maksim and whatever plan her father had cooked up. She was afraid she knew why Papa introduced her to the Caviar Prince, and it was part of why she dreaded evenings like these. Her father was going to marry her off to someone he approved of, someone who would probably bore her to death.

There wasn't anything particularly wrong with Maksim. He was handsome, came from a good family, had money, was Russian. A perfect young man for a woman with her pedigree. She should be happy that her father was interested in making her such a good match. She could have wound up with someone like Irina's husband, Sergei.

She told herself that she was jumping to conclusions, that the introduction wasn't about finding her a husband, but Galina wasn't an idiot. She was twenty-five — she should have been married with at least one pup by now, according to the unwritten rules of Russian families anyway. Papa had given her some breathing room while she'd been away at graduate school, but now that she was back, she knew he was not going to be put off for much longer.

Her gaze drifted over to Andrey Lupesco. He was staring at her, unconcerned with who might notice.

"Hey, Королева льда," came a voice from behind and to her left.

Ice Queen. Galina turned and saw her sister Irina's husband, Sergei. He leaned against the wall, smoking a cigarette, his eyes hooded. He was a total loss, an Omega with dreams of being an Alpha. Strictly small time, he would never rise further in their ranks, even with his marriage to Irina and his constant sucking up to Alexei. Galina noted that Irina had been avoiding her husband since they'd arrived. They'd probably had another argument.

She sneered at Sergei—a waste of werewolf DNA, as far as she was concerned. He knew that she hated being called Ice Queen. Some meant it as a term of endearment: she was statuesque, with white-blond hair, pale skin, and eyes the color of tumbled jade. She was also the only living biological daughter of the head of a powerful Russian crime family, and a werewolf. They were only giving her her due.

But Sergei didn't mean it that way and they both knew it. He used it as an insult, hurling it at Galina whenever he had the opportunity. To him, she was icy cold, a bitch who didn't know her place. She bit back a snarl, longing to take Sergei outside and show him what true werewolf royalty could do.

Unfortunately she couldn't. As Irina's useless excuse for a husband he was still, technically, family. And he wasn't alone. His regular group of knuckleheads formed a flotilla of stupid around him. His swagger and loud boasts broadcast exactly how drunk he was. Galina shifted her gaze to Irina, standing at their father's side, wearing what could only be called a stiff upper lip. Irina watched as her husband laughed and flirted with anything with a pulse, her face devoid of expression.

Galina's brother-in-law leered at a passing cocktail waitress who smiled widely at him. As he waved for his knot of admirers to continue on without him, Galina gritted her teeth, clutching the stem of the glass flute so hard it snapped. Sergei was an idiot. If he kept flaunting his dalliances under Irina's nose, he was liable to have parts of him lopped off. She was amazed someone hadn't done it by now.

Galina would happily volunteer.

Accepting a cloth from a server, she wiped her hands, giving the woman a grateful smile. The server took the broken glass from her, leaving Galina to watch Sergei walk out of the party after the waitress, an unlit cigarette in his hand.

Galina watched him go, torn between staying inside where she knew she should, and going after Sergei to administer a swift kick in his ass. No doubt he would find some place out of the way where he could dip his wick quickly, but maybe she could catch him before anyone noticed she was gone. He may have married Irina because Papa needed Volkov money, thanks to another one of Alexei's screw-ups, but that didn't mean he could publicly embarrass her sister with this woman.

Galina was willing to risk it.

She slipped out of the party, following Sergei's scent out to the loading dock. As she opened the door, the sound of voices stopped her. Removing her heels, she edged through the door, cautious. She recognized one of the voices and scents: Sergei. The second voice was a stranger's, but oddly familiar.

"Those weren't my people," Sergei was saying in a strangled voice. "And I don't have your shipment. Maybe it got lost in the mail."

The dull thuds of fists smashing into flesh carried to her sensitive ears. "Do you think I'm fucking stupid?" the strange voice said. "You're Alexei's lapdog."

Galina peeked out around some packing crates—Sergei, pressed up against the wall, being held a good foot or two off of the ground. He gurgled as the strong hand holding him up by the neck tightened. The man's other hand held Sergei's crotch in a white-knuckled grip. Those hands were attached to a very attractive, very dangerous looking man.

Andrey Lupesco.

Galina inched forward for a better look. How did he know Sergei? And why did he look like he might pummel her brother-in-law into paste? She had no interest in stopping him. She just wanted a better view.

Andrey released Sergei's privates and drew back his free hand, punching Sergei in the gut. Sergei tried to protect his midsection, but Andrey's hand on his throat kept him upright. Galina heard her brother-in-law cough and moan. Without giving him a chance to recover, Andrey's fist thudded into him again.

When Andrey let him go, Sergei fell to his knees in front of him. Andrey circled like a hungry shark, stopping behind Sergei. He landed four more punches, this time to Sergei's kidneys, before coming around to face him again. He grabbed Sergei's face in one hand and said in a voice as cold as the depths of the Pacific, "If you fuck with me again, Sergei, I will make sure they never find your body. Same goes for your boss." He leaned close. "Do you understand me?"

She drew back in surprise. Sergei worked under Alexei's crew. If he'd done something against Andrey's business, it was probably on her brother's orders. What had Alexei gotten them into this time?

Galina watched Sergei nod weakly as he tried to hide his gasps of pain. She felt a burn of satisfaction to see him like this. She only wished Irina could witness this. It might make her smile—a genuine Irina smile, the kind she'd offered regularly before her wedding day. She appreciated that Andrey hadn't messed with Sergei's face—it was Katya's Sweet Sixteen after all.

Andrey flung Sergei away from him. He strode back to the doors, catching sight of Galina on the way. He stopped for a moment, eyes searching hers. She nodded, doing nothing to stop him from leaving. There was no need to say anything.

After he was gone, Galina put on her shoes and took out her phone. She walked up to Sergei, who lay curled in a ball on the concrete of the loading dock. "Smile, Serg," she said as she snapped a picture with the phone's camera.

He stared up at her, a snarl on his face. "This will look great on Instagram," Galina told him, pocketing her phone. Then she left him to find her sister. The picture of Sergei on the ground in pain might be just the thing to put Irina in a real good mood.

2

Kitchen Confidential

Galina slipped back into the party, feeling immeasurably better than she had just a few minutes ago. Seeing her brother-in-law beaten to a bloody pulp had that effect on her. Maybe now that he knew how it felt, he'd be more careful around her sister. She looked around for Irina. She was still with Papa, watching the young people have fun on the dance floor.

Glancing around the room, her gaze came to rest on Andrey where he stood talking to a man she didn't recognize. She'd been attracted to Andrey last night, but hadn't acted on it. Something hadn't felt right. And now he—the head of the Romani contingent of the *Volk Organizatsiya*, gypsies—was here. Her father hated gypsies, thought they were nothing but liars and scam artists. Had he allied with them because they had power here in Seattle or because he knew about Sergei's massive fuckup?

Turning to back to the bar, Galina looked around for Irina, intending to pull her aside and show her the picture she'd taken. Instead, she saw her sister on the dance floor, in the arms of one of Papa's enforcers, a handsome Beta named Viktor. Galina glanced over at her father, still deep in conversation with the Caviar Prince and Uncle Petyr. He seemed unconcerned by Irina's dance partner.

The Botoxed she-wolves of the first circle, however, were another matter. They sat at their table, heads together, snarls curling their lips. All of them watched Irina as she swayed in Viktor's arms. The pair weren't doing anything untoward — it was just a dance — but from the looks on all of their faces, they couldn't wait to snipe at Irina for her daring to dance with a man who wasn't her husband. This, despite the fact that said husband had no qualms about going outside to get a piece under his wife's very nose.

Galina ground her teeth together, feeling the scrape in her jaw. If her mother were here, this never would have happened. Mama would have made sure these women knew their proper place, and that they respected Irina's. These women knew nothing of Irina's life or her marriage. They didn't have to deal with Sergei's moods, his anger, his abuse. Sergei knew how to hide the marks of his violence.

She looked over at her father once more. The fact that Papa ignored all evidence of his son-in-law's poor treatment of his daughter made the situation so much worse. He'd been the one to broker the marriage. Alexei had fucked up — again — a major deal with the Volkovs and Papa, still in the fog of grief over their mother's death, was short of cash. The Volkovs were long on money, but short on status, so he'd offered Irina's hand and future to them to cement the alliance. Papa's debt was settled and Irina got Sergei.

It wasn't much of a trade.

Galina wanted to march over there and slap each and every one of those bitches across the face until their eyes rattled in their skulls, but she knew it wouldn't help Irina. They weren't the problem. Sergei was.

She wished she could help. Irina had been like a mother to her, something much needed in a house full of testosterone. She'd been the one to talk to Galina about boys, about heartbreak, about being a woman. Irina deserved better after everything she'd done for her family. It infuriated Galina that she could do nothing to help.

Spinning on her heel, Galina walked away. The kitchen would be good, somewhere out of the way and moderately quiet. The food had been served long ago so it should be deserted at this hour. All she wanted was a bit of space for a few minutes, so she wouldn't drag Sergei out to the middle of the dance floor by his ear and slam her perfectly manicured fist into his arrogant face.

Her Papa wouldn't have appreciated that. Women were ornaments to be dangled on the arms of powerful men, looking beautiful and keeping quiet. Galina knew she had the beautiful part down—why deny what the mirror told her every time she looked in one—but the "keeping quiet" part gave her a lot of trouble. And tonight, she didn't want that trouble to carry over to her sister, who looked a little more miserable every time Galina saw her.

She pushed through the swinging doors and retreated to the back of the prep area. There was no one left back there. Everything had been cleaned up and put away neatly. The stainless steel countertops gleamed under the bank of low lights above. It was all cold steel and blissful silence. Even the sound of the party was muted in here.

Her feet were killing her. Already tall, Galina loved sky-high heels. Tonight she'd gone with a pair of four-and-a-half inchers, in a finish called "devilfish"—black with pale tiny circles. They reminded her of the back of a manta ray she'd seen in one of her childhood ocean life books. They were beautiful, but after several hours of standing and mingling, her calves were beginning to cramp.

Galina hopped up onto the counter, lifting one leg across her knee so she could massage her calf. Her short dress rode up her thighs as she dug fingers into the muscle, but no one was there to see. Not that she cared if there were. Embarrassment was for other people.

She heard the swoosh of the swinging door opening—probably a server or kitchen staffer coming in to pick up something they'd forgotten—but didn't turn around. She wasn't immediately visible from the door, so there was a good chance she'd be left in peace. She had too much to think about, and she just wished the party would end so she could go back to her apartment and start picking apart what was bothering her.

She'd been away for too long, that much was clear. While she'd been working on an advanced art history degree in California for the past several years, things up here had become unstable. Her eldest brother, Alexei, was agitating for family leadership, urging their father to step down. Her other brother, Nikolai, was the family lawyer, and more interested in finding a less violent solution to the endless conflicts between warring families as everyone jockeyed for an ever shrinking slice of the pie. But lately most of his time was spent keeping Alexei out of prison. And Papa just seemed content to sit back and do nothing.

She felt that special skin prickle that came with the sensation of eyes on her. Galina raised her head to find Andrey standing at the opposite end of the countertop, watching her. His silvery blue eyes were hooded, giving nothing away. The strong bones of his face stood out in a wash of shadows and highlights from the lighting above him. He looked like a contrast photograph come to life.

Her nostrils flared, taking in the scent of him. He smelled of both man and wolf, and it lit something in the base of Galina's spine. Her werewolf sense of smell recognized another like her. It also recognized the scent of Alpha. She raised her eyebrows in surprise. Petyr hadn't been kidding. Andrey really was the head of the Romani side of things.

He stepped forward. Galina watched him lazily, still digging her fingers into her sore calf. He didn't frighten her, not even with the slow stalk he was doing now. She was more than able to take care of herself, even when not in wolf form.

"I've been watching you," Andrey said, stopping a few steps away from her. His voice was like a good cabernet—rich, sensual, and full of blood and darkness.

"I know." She kept her voice pitched low, just for the two of them. "I've watched you too. Nice work with Serg."

"You don't remember me, do you?" A bitter smile quirked the side of his mouth.

He obviously wasn't talking about last night. She wasn't forgetful nor had she been so drunk as to ignore a face like his. Galina cast back, trying to remember where else she might have seen him. When he cut his eyes to check the door, she remembered.

"I was eight," she answered, dropping her leg. "My older brother was holding you down and punching you. It was in our backyard, so I guess you were visiting with your father."

Galina remembered now. Andrey had been a serious boy of perhaps ten who'd come to her house one autumn afternoon. He'd been with his father, Nazur, who'd come to see her Papa in order to pay his respects and talk business.

Alexei had loved lording his status over any other child unfortunate enough to cross his path. Galina had been playing tag in another part of the garden with Nikolai, when she'd come upon Alexei sitting atop a smaller boy. His face was already bloodied and Alexei had his fist raised for another strike. The younger boy's eyes cut to her, showing no pleading or fear.

"Stop!" she shouted, breaking into a run.

Alexei turned toward her without lowering his fist. Galina plowed into him, throwing him off of the boy. She punched him in the ribs and they tumbled together in a mess of limbs. Her brother quickly gained the upper hand, jerking her arm up painfully behind her back. He wasn't allowed to hit her — Papa wouldn't stand for anyone touching her in anger — but he could hurt her in a way that wouldn't leave marks.

Galina had leaned forward and sunk her teeth into his other wrist. Alexei yelped and let her go. She scrambled to her feet, balled her hands into fists and stuck them on her hips. "You are such a jerk, Alexei. You know you're not supposed to hurt our guests!"

Her brother snorted, an angry sound, as he clutched his wrist in his other hand. "Shut up, you little bitch." He climbed to his feet, shoved her to the ground, and ran off.

A hand came into her field of vision. Galina looked up at the boy who only moments before had been beaten. His black hair was in disarray, standing up in wild tufts. His cheekbone was already beginning to darken with a bruise, and there was blood on the side of his mouth. But his blue eyes were calm, like two still lakes.

"Thank you," was all he said, helping her to her feet.

Galina had put her hand to his face, wiping away a smudge of dirt. "My brother is a bully," she said by way of explanation.

"I know." His lips twitched in a smile.

"Yeah, guess you do." She took his hand. "Come inside and I'll wash your face. I'm Galina."

"Everyone knows who you are," he said. "I'm Andreyev."

Present-day Andrey raised his brows in surprise. He obviously hadn't thought she'd be able to recall their first meeting. He'd hoped to stump her. Galina saw all of this, even as his face smoothed into a pleasant mask. She hopped down from the counter and took a step closer to him. What kind of game was he playing with her?

"You stopped him," he said, as if that explained everything. "He hurt you and you still fought him. And then you took me inside and cleaned my face."

She nodded. "So I remember you. That doesn't explain why you've spent the whole evening staring holes in the back of my head." He was tall. She was six feet in these heels and he still topped her by several inches.

His answer was to wind his fingers in the hair caught up at the back of her head in a loose up-do and pull her into him. Her eyes widened, just before his mouth dropped onto hers in a soft kiss. Galina felt his lips on hers, soft and demanding at the same time, and the fire at the base of her spine ignited, spiraling flames shooting through her belly and down her legs.

He pulled away slightly so he could meet her gaze. They stared at each other for a few moments, eyes wide, as if daring the other to speak. Galina felt the tension ratchet up inside of her.

She reached forward with both hands, grabbing the sides of his neck and pulling his mouth down to hers again in a bruising kiss. She kept her eyes open, as did Andrey, watching each other as their mouths went to war.

His hands slid around her waist and to her back, pulling her to him so that she was pressed against the length of his chest. Galina wrapped her arms around his neck, dragging him closer as she slid her tongue into his mouth. He bent her back over his arms, forcing her chest even closer to his so that her breasts rose and fell against him.

Galina sighed into his open mouth, so happy to be touched again that she thought she might lose her mind. She hadn't felt this attracted to someone in years. The feel of his hands on her was a reminder of how much she'd missed the sensation of a broad hand spanning her back, of being physically moved by another person. When he pulled her upright once more and backed her forcefully into one of the massive refrigerator doors, she moaned against him, the sound swallowed up by his lips and tongue.

She slid her tongue against his, wrapping around it, sucking hard. She felt an answering spasm in his pants. Galina smiled, deepening the kiss still further. Andrey's hands skimmed up her hips to cup her breasts through her tight dress. She pushed into him, the blossom of heat in her belly moving lower, until she felt like she might die if he didn't touch her skin directly.

Her hands worked at his plum colored tie, loosening it so she could get at the buttons and then at his flesh. She growled against his mouth as the fastenings frustrated her, her hands clumsy with lust. She heard him chuckle low in the back of his throat and she growled again.

Andrey broke their kiss, pulling away from her slightly. Again they stared at each other. Galina could only imagine what she looked like now: hair falling down from her up-do, face flushed, lips swollen from kisses, eyes hungry and wanting. Her sex throbbed with the need to be filled. Why was he stopping?

"Galina," he whispered, his eyes a dark blue. He ran his thumb over her bottom lip lightly. She nipped at it, drawing it into her mouth and swirling her tongue around it. His nostrils flared as he looked down at her, and she knew he could smell that she was ready. His eyes, if possible, grew darker.

"Galya," he said, even lower, using the diminutive form of her name.

She hummed in response, releasing his thumb. Galina stared up into his eyes, her green ones meeting his blue. "Andrey."

They were quiet for a moment, their harsh breathing the only sound. Then he spoke. "I'm glad to see you again."

In answer, she slowly dropped her hand to the front of his pants, palming his erection through the cloth. "I would never have guessed."

His eyes flared with a wicked light and he laughed softly. Andrey's hand wrapped around hers and he brought it to his lips so he could press a kiss to the inside of her wrist. Galina drew in a sharp breath, feeling her knees turn to liquid at the warmth of his mouth on her flesh.

She threaded her free hand through his dark hair, feeling the thickness wind around her fingers. Andrey stared at her, his eyes watchful as he bent over her wrist like a supplicant. His long fingers wrapped around it, pulling her into him. Galina allowed him to do so, not resisting, even raising her chin so he could press a kiss to her mouth.

His hands wrapped around her waist, lifting her up and back onto the countertop. He stepped forward, urging Galina to wrap her legs around his waist. His mouth was a warm, wet heat against her own, his tongue sliding against hers. She moved her hands into his shirt, feeling the hard planes of his chest, the muscles in his shoulders, the strong line of his collarbone. She dug her fingers into his ribs, urging him closer.

Andrey's hips bucked involuntarily against her. Galina's skirt had ridden up when he'd lifted her and now it barely covered her ass. His strong hands kneaded her thighs, urging them to open wider. She let her head fall back, reveling in the feel of his hands on her. This is what she'd been missing when she'd been in California, something she could never get with regular men. There was something about being with another wolf, someone like her, that was intoxicating.

She sighed in pleasure when he licked a line of heat down her carotid with his tongue. Her hands fumbled at his belt, her fingers ungraceful and stupid as his mouth slowly undid her. A passing thought caused her to smirk bitterly. If Sergei could see her now, she sincerely doubted he'd call her Ice Queen ever again. Of course, that was if her father didn't kill her first.

Andrey's hands rested on hers, stilling her fumbling. Then his hands returned to her thighs, sliding over them and pushing them farther apart. He stepped even closer to her, holding them open with his body. Galina caught his mouth with hers once more, pulling his bottom lip into her mouth so she could suck and nibble. His hands crept beneath the hem of her dress, strong fingers digging into the tops of her legs.

Galina slid her hands against his chest, skimming beneath his shirt and ghosting over the hard muscles of his shoulders. She moved forward, lifting her legs and wrapping them around his waist. There was a part of her that wondered vaguely what would happen if someone walked in on them. She smiled against Andrey's lips, imagining the scene that would probably play out.

He pulled away, his hands hot against her ass as he held her close against him. "What's so funny?"

"I was just thinking of what would happen if my father walked in here." She smiled sweetly at him.

Andrey pushed a lock of nearly white hair from her face. "I imagine things wouldn't end well for either of us."

"You have a gift for understatement." Her father would probably drag her out of the kitchen by her hair and leave his enforcers to teach Andrey a lesson wrapped in pain. He'd done something like that before with her other sister, Elena. "Does the thought of it make you want to stop?"

"Not really." Andrey nipped at her nose. "What about you?"

Galina breathed deeply, her breasts pressing against him. "Not even a little." She dragged his head back down to hers.

Their tongues warred, twisting around each other, tangling together. He sucked on hers and she moaned against his mouth, her fingernails digging into the back of his neck. She felt a melting sensation starting in the bottom of her stomach, tightening the muscles there. Galina wanted to move, she wanted clothes off, she wanted the feel of his flesh against hers.

Andrey had grown into a powerful man. The dark hair that tumbled into his eyes when they were children had been carefully styled, but it was crisp and thick beneath her fingers. His eyes were still the same intense steely blue, but they were harder; they were the eyes of a man who had seen and done dangerous things. The promise of height when he was younger had been fulfilled. He was all firm muscle and silken flesh, strength and softness under her hands.

Galina had felt a pull toward him from the moment she'd seen him in the club last night. She'd thought he was familiar then, but hadn't known his position in the hierarchy of the Organization, not that it would have mattered to her. He was Rom. She knew that made him unsuitable, both as a mate and a bed partner. Galina found she didn't particularly care.

She traced the strong line of his jaw with her lips, feeling the beginnings of stubble against her mouth. He tasted delicious, so tempting that she wanted to open her mouth and bite, wanted to feel his blood spill against her lips and drink her fill. Galina continued her explorations, licking a stripe up the side of his neck, before fastening her mouth over his pulse point. She nipped lightly at his neck, sliding her hands back down his chest.

The pops of what sounded like fire crackers broke them apart. Andrey almost dropped her, steadying her before she could fall. Galina's heels hit the floor unsteadily, and she hastily pulled her skirt down. She knew what those sounds were: gunshots. From outside.

Andrey quickly buttoned up his shirt and tucked it back into his pants. Galina tried to fix her hair, tucking what she could behind her ears. She spritzed herself with some of the wolfsbane perfume she always carried. The herbal concoction would mask the scent of Andrey all over her. When she looked at him, she saw her red lipstick smeared across his mouth. She pulled him closer so she could wipe it off with her fingers. He placed a kiss on each of her fingertips.

The sounds of feet running and growing chaos carried to them as people in the main ballroom streamed to the outer doors. They only had a few more moments before someone would inevitably burst into the kitchen. Galina straightened Andrey's tie, then rested her hands against his chest before pushing away.

"How do I look?" she asked, sliding her hands down her dress in effort to look less mussed.

"Like someone who needs me to drag her against the wall and make her sob with how good I make her feel." Andrey's teeth flashed white against the darkness of the kitchen.

Galina took a deep breath, suddenly feeling like all of the air had been sucked from the room. By looking at her like that, Andrey was making it nearly impossible to leave. But now shouting and screams filtered in to where they stood. She had to go.

"Some other time," she said, before turning on her heel and hurrying to the swinging doors.

"Count on it," he said, grabbing her hand to prevent her from leaving. "You should stay here, where it's safe."

"Like hell," she shot back. "I'm a Sudenko. I can take care of myself." She jerked her arm free and burst through the kitchen doors.

3

Party's Over

Galina nabbed her purse from the table and spritzed herself again with her wolfsbane perfume to blot out whatever remained of the scent of Andrey all over her. Then she ran through the ballroom, following the sounds of screaming. A crowd filled the front of the hotel, blocking the entrance. It was chaos. Galina pushed her way through the screaming women and the mass of people. She finally managed to shove her way through to the entrance only to be blocked by her father.

"Galina," he said, grabbing her arm as she tried to pass. "Where were you?"

"The ladies room," she answered quickly. "What happened?"

Her eyes scanned the parking lot and the stairs that led up to where they all stood. She caught sight of her sister being held down by Viktor. *"Irina!"* she screamed, breaking away from her father to plunge down the stairs to her.

She didn't get far. The man Andrey had been talking to before he'd followed her into the kitchen grabbed her around the waist and hauled her out of the way. Galina found herself pressed against the rough brick of the wall, shielded by a body in a dark suit. She shoved backward, but it was like trying to move granite.

"What the hell do you think you are doing?" she seethed. "That's my sister down there!"

"I have my orders," the young man said.

Galina glared at him. He had dark hair and eyes, a chiseled face, and a no-nonsense manner about him. "Fuck your orders," she snapped, ignoring Andrey as he walked over to them. She pushed against him. She had to get to Irina.

"Konstantin," Andrey called, gesturing for his man to release her. His eyes were scanning the parking lot, alert for signs of further danger, but it seemed that the threat had passed.

Galina ran down the steps, dropping to her knees beside her sister who was being held by her father's bodyguard. Sergei lay bleeding on the ground, four bullet holes in his chest. Black blood—a sign of silver poisoning—was slowly seeping into the red already staining his shirt. Her brother-in-law's eyes stared into the night sky above them. Even now he wore a mean little smile, but he was barely breathing. This couldn't have happened to someone who deserved it more. Galina dismissed the thought—she had to see to Irina.

Her sister's hands were red from having pressed them against her husband's chest wounds. Irina's eyes were closed, shutting out the sight of her dead husband. There was blood on her chin, but she didn't seem to be harmed. Viktor held Irina carefully in the circle of his arms. When Galina reached for her, he pulled away. "Was she hit?" she demanded of the man.

"No, I made sure of that." Viktor's voice was low. "I know my job."

"Thank you."

Galina relaxed a bit, taking a moment to look around her. Uncle Petyr was holding back Papa, while another bodyguard corralled their aunts. A number of Papa's retinue handled the crowd. Sirens sounded in the distance. As her eyes swept the gathered crowd, she spotted Andrey, standing with Konstantin by the back door that led to the kitchen. He would have taken a different way out just in case anyone could have seen them exit together. Smart.

That didn't mean she wasn't still furious with both of them.

Galina took Irina's hands in hers, not caring about the blood. If she was going to be picky about blood, she'd been born into the wrong family. "Irina, talk to me."

Biting her lip, Galina asked Victor, "Are you sure she's okay?"

He shook his head. "Her husband was just wasted in front of her. She's in shock."

"Take care of her," Galina ordered, meeting Viktor's blue bombardier's gaze. She slipped her hands out of Irina's limp ones, brushing the back of her hand over her sister's cheek.

She got up and stalked over to Petyr and her father. "What the hell happened?" she snapped. "Who shot Sergei?"

"We didn't see, we were inside," her father began. "One minute they were both inside, the next Sergei was dragging Irina outside. I am glad that Viktor followed them. He's the one who'd know anything." He looked her up and down suspiciously, and Galina was glad she'd had to push through all of those people. It explained her mussed hair and dress. Her perfume should take care of the rest. "How is Irina?" He grabbed her arm in a bruising grip, fear making him harsh.

She hid a wince. "I don't know, Papa. She's fainted. Viktor thinks she's in shock," she explained, gently breaking his hold and pulling her arm from his grasp. "I would have gotten to her sooner but I had to get through the moron brigade all crying at the door."

"Nikolai should be here," Petyr said softly.

Galina nodded. Unfortunately for all of them, he'd been dispatched to mop up the latest mess Alexei had made with one of his girlfriends. Her eldest brother made Tony Montana look like a model of calm and restraint. Of course, if Alexei had been present, the shootout probably would have resulted in a much higher body count.

An ambulance came roaring up to the traffic circle at the front of the inn. "Go with your sister," her father told her, giving Galina a push in that direction. "Make sure she is taken care of."

"Yes, Papa."

The quiet after the ambulance drove away was devastating. Irina was revived when the paramedics plied her with smelling salts. She was still in shock, but at least she was awake. Galina had handed Irina off to the EMTs and they had bundled her sister up into a blanket and then put her in the ambulance with Sergei. Galina had wanted to ride with her, but Irina insisted she take care of Papa.

Galina went to the bathroom to clean the blood from her hands, then collected their things from the inn, keeping an eye on Papa, Maksim, and Petyr. She took the time to observe Viktor. New to the stable of muscle that usually surrounded her family, Viktor was lean, with a strength evident in the way he moved and stood. His blond hair was shorn close to his head, and his blue eyes blazed with vitality. His features were sharp and his skin tan, the polar opposite of Sergei, who had been dark in both manner and appearance.

Feeling her eyes on him, Viktor turned his head and met her gaze. There was nothing cowed or submissive in his eyes when he looked at her, rare considering who Galina was. She nodded, hiding her surprise.

"I'm going to the hospital," she said as she walked to the small group of men.

Uncle Petyr put his arm around her, pulling her close. "Hell of a welcome home, Galya." He kept his voice soft so that only the two of them could hear.

"I shouldn't have expected anything else," she whispered back. Her family worked with criminals, was made up of criminals. To expect something different was to live in fantasy land.

The sound of footsteps approaching made Galina pull away from her uncle. Her heart stuttered as Andrey walked over to them, looking as cool and nonchalant as if he'd never had her legs wrapped around him back in the kitchen. She gritted her teeth at the memory that sent heat racing through her core and forced a placid, absent look on her face as he approached.

Andrey first approached her father and shook Papa's hand. He was careful not to exert too much pressure, but his grasp was firm. Andrey knew the civilities he had to maintain when dealing with the Sudenko family, Galina observed. But that wasn't the same thing as knowing his place.

Just one of the things she found fascinating about him.

Andrey introduced himself to Maksim when Papa hadn't bothered. Galina stared at the two men, unable to resist comparing them. Maksim did not stack up well beside the older, more accomplished Rom. From everything she'd heard of the Federovs, Maksim would inherit his fortune, having to fight for none of it. Andrey was a self-made man.

Galina still recalled the boy from the garden who had taken Alexei's abuse with a kind of pride that her brother could never hope to understand. Andrey was the quiet, smiling threat, not the open aggression that was her older brother.

And so was she. Perhaps it was what had drawn her to Andrey in the first place.

Galina knew she'd been sent away to learn, but mostly to keep her out of the way of the family business. Women were still thought of as ornaments, pretty dolls kept high up in pretty boxes, trotted out when their owners wished to show them off or trade them away for an alliance. But Galina had used the opportunity away from the rules and expectations of her family to learn everything she could that might one day be of use in the family business. She'd majored in art history—something her father thought a useless, if societally impressive pursuit—but she'd also graduated with another degree: one in business. She planned to be more than just an accessory on some man's arm. She had brains, ambition, and the breeding to take a leading role in her family's business, and nothing would stop her.

"If there is anything I can do to help," Andrey was saying as he gripped Papa's hand once more, "call me. My people will be at your disposal."

"Thank you, Andreyev," Papa said, his eyes clear and sober. He must not have been hitting the vodka as hard as she'd thought. Either that or seeing his adopted daughter covered in her husband's blood had sobered him up real quick. "Have you met my daughter, Galina?"

She kept her face neutral as all eyes turned to her. Andrey released her father's hand with a smile. "We haven't been formally introduced."

"Not true," she replied, skating a glance at the men—loyal to Alexei—who flexed in frustration behind her father's shoulder. Alexei despised Andrey, not that it came as a shock. Andrey had Alpha written all over him. The best label Alexei could hope for was "Psycho."

Galina stepped forward, extending her hand. "We met when you were still a boy and your father was visiting mine."

"Ah, I remember now." A small smile played around the corner of his lips and Galina ached to smack it off of him. He was still playing games. "The garden, wasn't it?" He glanced at Ilya. "You've grown up since then." He took her hand in both of his.

A condescending little comment. Well, she could play too. "Nice of you to notice," she answered, her gaze sweeping over him. "As have you." She smiled coldly when she felt his fingers tighten around hers.

She dared him with her eyes to say something else, knowing that he couldn't risk it. Still, it disappointed her when he merely said, "A pleasure to meet you. Again." He pressed a chaste kiss to the back of her hand, then ran his tongue quickly over her knuckle.

"Likewise." Galina felt herself flush at the feel of his tongue on her skin and hoped that her high color would be attributed to the events of the evening and not the fact that Andrey made her insides twist and jump. She removed her hand from his, staring at him, daring him to look away first.

His brief smile was the barest flash of sharp, white teeth. "If you'll excuse me?" Galina inclined her head, a queen giving a courtier leave to go. He returned his attention to her father and she used that distraction to leave. She needed to get to the hospital and her sister. It wasn't right that Irina should be there alone with only Sergei's family for company.

Nobody should be subjected to Sergei's family. They were worse than he was.

4

You Make Bathtime So Much Fun

Galina let herself into her condo, disabling the alarm system. She was in a secure building with a doorman, but she didn't believe in taking chances. The first thing she'd done when she knew she was moving back to Seattle was search out separate living quarters from the rest of her family. Her father practically had an aneurysm, but she'd made him see sense. Spreading the family among different locations meant more targets to hit if someone wanted to take them all out. If they all lived together, it would be ridiculously easy to wipe them all off the map in one fell swoop.

Besides, her brothers had their own places and Irina had her house with Sergei. Why shouldn't she have a place of her own, pack or no pack? Galina needed both privacy and space, and living under her father's roof would afford her neither.

Shucking off her coat in the foyer, Galina kicked out of her heels. She nearly cried with relief when her swollen feet hit the cool travertine stone of the floor. God, she wanted to burn the dress she was wearing; it reeked of hospital. Those places terrified her — her childhood fear of being hooked to machines, kept alive and studied like a bug in a jar had never left her. She shuddered. The only reason she had gone was to support Irina. She didn't give a damn about

Sergei and she hoped he was now boiling in the fiery pits of Hell or wherever douchebags like him went when they died.

Galina had gone because her sister had needed her. Even if the werewolf side of her cringed at all of the gleaming white surfaces and cold overhead lights and the chance of exposure and experimentation, Galina's human sister needed someone to hold her hand and run interference with Sergei's mother. Plus, Galina would have to bribe the medical staff to "forget" about the strange nature of Sergei's reaction to the silver bullets…and the fact that the bullets were silver. She'd already arranged for a morgue attendant to switch normal spent ammo with the bullets taken from Sergei's body.

Surprisingly, Maksim had insisted on accompanying her. He and his bodyguard had followed her to the hospital, sitting with her as she supported Irina through the nurse's, and then the police's, questions. While her sister had answered questions in a dull voice, he'd looked bored, making her wonder why Maksim had even bothered to come. Most of the time he'd wandered around, looking for a decent cup of coffee. Had Papa told him to go with her?

When Anya Volkov, Sergei's mother, arrived, Maksim took the opportunity to flee. Anya had gone into hysterics when the doctor emerged from surgery to give them the news that Sergei hadn't made it. The old she-wolf had verbally attacked Irina, only stopping when Galina had threatened her with the Gauntlet, the werewolf equivalent of a trial by combat, for nearly exposing them to humans.

Galina had never been happier to leave a place in her entire life. At least Sergei had shuffled off this mortal coil before he could hurt Irina any further. That was some small comfort.

Her phone buzzed at her from inside the pocket of her discarded coat. Galina fished it out, saw that it was her brother and sighed. Her bath would have to wait. "Hi, Nikolai."

"Pop just wanted to make sure you got home okay." His voice was the best thing she'd heard in hours.

"Yeah, I'm in and I'll set my alarm after I get off the phone with you." She walked down the hall to her bedroom, holding the phone to her ear. "So you heard? When are you getting in?"

She could hear loud voices speaking in Russian on Nikolai's end but it was too muffled to make out exactly what they were saying. "We're on our way back as quick as we can. Should be in by morning."

"Anything else?" She passed through the sitting room and her bedroom to get to her bathroom. Her feet slapped against the marble tile.

"Nothing yet. Pop did say he's sending a detail over to your place. And Irina's."

"Why do I need one? I'm not the one being shot at!" But Galina knew why. Papa was scared. Someone had killed a man—his man—on his turf. He was going to be in lockdown mode now. He was going to protect his own. "Are we in a war that nobody told me about?"

"No!" Nikolai exploded. He lowered his voice. "Pop's just being careful."

"How did everything go with Alexei?" She turned on the taps to her massive clawfoot bathtub, filling it with steaming water.

Nik lowered his voice. "It's a mess. Again." He sighed. "I can't keep doing this—we can't keep hiding dead girlfriends."

"I'm sorry," she said, putting the phone on speaker so she could shimmy out of her dress. "I wish I could help."

"It's fine. You were there for Irina." Nikolai sounded concerned. "How is she holding up?"

"Okay, all things considered." Irina had been quiet when Galina walked with her and Viktor to his car. The bodyguard had practically been carrying Irina, she was so exhausted from the night's events. "I'm glad Papa's got someone watching out for her. I'm going to head over in the morning." She looked at the clock and saw it was nearly three o'clock. "Well, later in the morning anyway. To help her with arrangements and things."

"Be careful, Galya. I don't know what's going on but there wasn't even a hint of a hit out on Serg anywhere in our information network. It came out of nowhere."

She assured Nikolai she'd be careful, and then ended the call. She put her phone on the teak table next to the tub and lowered herself into the water. The hot water hit her like a welcoming wave, making Galina realize just how tired she was after a night spent in the emergency room. She sank into it gratefully, pulling the pins from her hair. She felt like she was covered in blood and grime, like she might never be clean.

Ducking her head beneath the water, Galina soaped her hair. She was rinsing the shampoo from it when her phone rang again. With a sudsy, tired hand, she hit the Send button. "Hello?"

The voice on the other end of the phone made gooseflesh rise along her arms. Andrey's deep voice. "Hello, Galina."

Galina swallowed, her mouth suddenly dry. "How did you get my number?" It was private and she kept her direct number as guarded as she could. Short of asking her family or employer for it, he should not have been able to get it.

A deep, throaty chuckle was answer enough to her question. "Your friend, Sveta. She called one of my men. He got your number from her."

Galina remembered her friend Sveta getting the number of a guy they'd been drinking with at the bar. She would have to have a talk with her friend. Giving out her own number to anyone who asked was one thing, but Galina didn't want hers handed out, no matter how handsome the guy asking for it might be. She knew Sveta was just trying to help find her a mate — Galina's friend despaired of her ever finding someone who was "boyfriend" quality — but that didn't excuse this breach of trust.

She let the matter drop for now. "Why are you calling me?" She peered at the clock sitting on the marble vanity. "And why at three in the morning? Why not call at a decent hour?"

Again the throaty chuckle. It made her insides liquefy with want. "But you and I aren't decent people, are we, Galina?" he said and Galina clenched her thighs together.

He had a point there. She knew she wasn't decent in the traditional sense of the word, but traditions weren't made for people like her. "No, I suppose we aren't."

He changed tack suddenly. "How is your sister?"

Galina nearly got whiplash from the conversation switch. "She's holding up okay," she answered, though how one could be okay with the events of the night was anyone's guess. "I don't think it's hit her yet."

There was a pause. Then Andrey spoke. "And you?"

Galina slid further down in the water, until it was up to her neck. "I'm fine. Just tired."

"Where are you?" Amusement colored his voice. "It sounds like you're in a tunnel."

"I'm taking a bath." She splashed some water for effect. The sound echoed off the walls of her cavernous bathroom; the size and the tub was why she'd chosen this condominium.

When he spoke again, his voice had gone low and even deeper, like smoke given sound. "You mean to tell me you're in the bathtub right now? Naked? And wet?" Galina felt her body tighten as heat rushed through her.

"Yes," she said, surprised when her answer was so steady.

Andrey growled. The sound seemed to reverberate throughout the bathroom. Her nipples hardened painfully. God, how could he possibly affect her like this over the phone? It wasn't normal, even if they were both werewolves. He was ridiculously good looking, with a body built for sin, but she'd had lovers before. None of them had made her this turned on just by speaking. Granted, none of them could actually growl like that either.

Galina trailed a hand across her breasts, before dipping it down to follow the line of her sternum to her stomach. She heard Andrey take a deep breath and slipped her hand between her thighs. Her body throbbed at the sound, and her memories of his searing kisses in the kitchen flooded her with heat.

"I wish I could see you now," he said, his voice hoarse.

"Maybe next time. Good night, Andrey." She ended the call and turned her phone off. She didn't want to be disturbed for the next few minutes.

Her fingers pressed into her flesh beneath the water, the warmth of the bath rivaled by that between her legs. Her eyes drifted closed as she called up the memories of the sensations that she'd felt with Andrey. Her breathing was shaky as she recalled the feel of his hands on her back, of the way he'd lifted her up to him, of the way her legs felt wrapped around his waist. Her fingers moved faster beneath the water and she could feel the world spiraling down to a point as her body tightened into that familiar coil of need.

Galina sighed, remembering the heat of Andrey's mouth, the way the callouses on his hands felt against the smooth skin of her inner thighs. She was close to the edge now, arching up as her fingers pushed her to her climax. She cried out as her release hit her, leaving her shuddering in the hot bathwater. She lay still for a few minutes, feeling the shakes in her legs subside.

This thing with Andrey might be a problem. Especially since she still wanted to march over to wherever he was and demand they finish what they'd started in the kitchen. Galina finished cleaning her hair and rinsed out the conditioner. She stood, grabbing a towel from the stack she kept by the tub and wound herself in it.

Andrey was a Rom. He might be the Alpha of his organization but her father would still have pups if he found out she was anywhere near him. Galina was a rare she-wolf, not to mention the youngest daughter of the Sudenkos. There were expectations. And slumming with a Rom—because that's how her family would see it—wasn't one of them.

Galina didn't give two figs about him being Romani. She thought the old ways were just that: old. People should rise through the ranks of the *Volk Organizatsiya* based on merit, not on birthright or were-status or family background. It was ridiculous how many talented and capable people were shunted off into lesser jobs just because they didn't bear the Sudenko name or carry the were-gene. It was stupid and wasteful.

She dried herself and pulled on her bathrobe. The feel of the soft chenille on her over-sensitized skin made her sigh with relief. It had been a long day and an even longer night. Wrapping her towel around her wet hair, Galina got into bed. In a few hours, she had to be over at Irina's house to check on her, and then she wanted to talk to her father. He wasn't going to leave her in the dark about the shooting. She would make him include her.

Her eyes grew heavy, sleep dragging her down into comforting darkness. Before she was lost to it completely, she remembered Andrey's growl of desire on the phone and smiled. She hoped to see him tomorrow too.

5

The Morning-After Blues

Galina and Franny Valenti, Irina's very human best friend, walked up the stone steps that led to Irina's front door. Two men sat in a black car directly across from the house, one man inside — Papa's security detail. She stopped at the large wood and glass front door and used the coded knock that would alert the guard inside that she was family so he didn't blow her head off her neck as soon as the door opened. Papa's guards tended toward the over-reactive.

Stepping inside the house, Galina's nose was hit with the smell of strong coffee brewing. Heels clicking across the stone tiles, she led the way to the cozy white-and-blue kitchen.

She heard voices and called, "I'm here! And I brought Franny! And cinnamon rolls! But mostly Franny!"

Irina and Viktor turned to them, the conversation they'd obviously been having forgotten. It almost seemed like they'd been arguing. Galina cocked her head, eyeing her sister and Viktor carefully.

"It's good to know where I rank compared to breakfast pastries," Franny muttered, giving Irina a hug. "How you doing, kid?"

Her sister glanced at Viktor, who excused himself to the living room. Galina raised an eyebrow but said nothing. There was an energy between Irina and Viktor, but perhaps she was reading into it. He had been there when Sergei was shot, maybe that was all it was.

"Would it be wrong to say I'm relieved?" Irina asked, wincing.

"Not to anyone who'd met Sergei," Galina deadpanned, pouring coffee for herself and Franny. Franny toasted her with the mug.

"Galya," Irina admonished her. "We can't talk like that. It's too soon."

Galina pursed her lips. Just because Sergei was dead didn't mean he was suddenly less of an asshole in life. "Why the hell not? Do you think Viktor's going to tell on us?" Galina jerked her head in the direction of the living room, where Viktor stood.

"Look, Irina, whoever shot Sergei did you a big favor. I know you have to put on a proper public show and be the tragic widow for a while. But in private, here with us, we expect you to actually have feelings."

She took Irina's cool hand in hers. "Sergei was horrible to you. You were miserable. Now he's dead, and you have the chance at being happy. If you waste that because you're feeling guilty, I'm going to have to beat your ass like when we were kids."

Galina knew her sister would need time to grieve, maybe not for Sergei, but for the life she had made with him. But that didn't mean Irina had to forget what being married to him had been like. It was possible to be sad and relieved at the same time.

"Okay, first of all, you had werewolf strength on your side," Irina sniped, pointing her finger in Galina's face. Galina snapped her teeth lightly, a mock warning. Irina flicked her nose and she growled playfully at her sister.

"And second, I don't feel guilty right now. I feel sad and numb, like I shouldn't feel anything. Not because I'm in mourning, or because I'm going to miss Sergei. I'm sad because the last few years of my life seem like such a waste. Scared because I don't know what my role is now and I'm afraid of how that might change. But mostly, I'm grateful because it's over…Wait, no, I lied, there's the guilt."

Galina reached casually over the counter and smacked Irina's arm. She needed to stop with the feeling bad for having feelings.

"Ow!"

Franny nudged the cinnamon roll on Irina's plate in front of her. "Eat."

When Irina balked, Galina gave her a mock glare, watching as her sister began to take apart the roll in a semblance of eating.

"It's all over the news, Rina," Galina continued, digging into her second cinnamon roll. Good God, Franny could bake. These things were like heaven on a plate. "And Papa's beside himself, worrying about you here alone. Unless you're willing to move back into your old room, you better just accept whatever muscle he sends your way."

"If the muscle looks like that one, I would just say thank you and send your father a gift card or a fruit basket or something," Franny said, with a grin and a gesture toward Viktor.

Galina laughed. Viktor was attractive, but he didn't hold a candle to Andrey. As soon as she thought it, she wanted to smack herself. She did not need to be thinking of him right now.

"Franny," Irina hiss-whispered. "Werewolf hearing!"

"Oh, come on, a man like that knows he's hot. With his werewolf nose, he can probably smell the pheromones rolling off of us." Franny gave Irina a *get real* look and dug into her cinnamon roll.

"Anyway," Galina said, tossing Franny a grin, "the next couple of days are going to be a cavalcade of nitwittery. The funeral will be held on Friday. Mama Anya has already called Papa to let him know the arrangements have been made at Kandinsky's."

"Wow, she works fast," Irina said softly. Galina watched her sister's expression turn thoughtful. Irina seemed to come to a decision after a few moments. "Let her have it. A man should be buried by someone who loves him, even an asshole like Sergei. I'm not going to fight it."

"I figured you'd be all noble about it." Galina nodded. "And it does give Nik and Alexei time to get home. Nik says he loves you and as soon as this shit-storm passes, we are going to party like it's New Year's."

"That seems so wrong." Irina sighed. "But I have the feeling I'm going to need it."

"Well, now that we've discussed the trivial stuff, let's focus on what's important." Franny sniffed. "What are you going to wear to the funeral?"

Irina grinned and Galina glimpsed a hint of the not-so-good sister that she remembered from her youth poking through the *volk zhena* shell. "Well, Sergei always did like me in red."

Viktor was in the kitchen when Galina came back downstairs from Irina's bedroom. "How's Mrs. Volkov?"

"She's picking out a scandalous dress for the funeral," Galina answered, going immediately to the coffeepot and pouring herself a fresh cup. She doctored it with sugar and cream before turning to stare at Viktor. While Irina was occupied, she might as well try to get some answers. "What did you see last night?"

"I've already told your father." His blue eyes met hers, his face set in a neutral mask.

"And now you're going to tell me." Galina narrowed her eyes, watching him over the rim of her cup as she took a sip. He glanced away, then returned his gaze to hers. She raised her eyebrows at him.

"I didn't see much. A car. Late model sedan in burgundy. I only got the last two numbers of the plate. Forty-nine." He rubbed a hand across the top of his nearly shorn head. "And then I was on top of your sister."

"I'm sure my father loved it when you put it like that," Galina answered, lips lifting in a wry smile. He had the grace to look briefly uncomfortable before his usual lack of affect returned.

"You didn't get a look at the trigger man?" When Viktor shook his head, she sighed. "Something about this seems very wrong," she said, turning her coffee cup in her hands.

Viktor regarded her with something like surprise. Galina knew that look. Everyone assumed that because she was the Sudenko's youngest daughter she'd be a pampered princess without the mental acuity to string two thoughts together. People always seemed shocked to find she actually was possessed of a fully functioning brain.

At times, it was something she cultivated; it was easier to deal with men who dismissed her out of hand. They were always so surprised when she got the better of them. It was delightful when it wasn't patently infuriating. Because she was a woman, and pretty, and blond, no one expected her to be intelligent or to be savvy about the family business.

"Why do you say that?" Viktor asked her, leaning a hip against Irina's kitchen counter.

"Sergei was a joke. Papa gave him the simplest assignments because he couldn't manage anything more complicated. Half the time he couldn't even manage those. He wasn't a power player — he wasn't on the board. Hell, he wasn't even board adjacent." Galina drummed her fingers on the counter absently.

"So this wasn't a hit carried out to cause a power vacuum. Unless Sergei wasn't the target?" She raised a brow at Viktor.

He shook his head. "No. The shooter was aiming at Sergei. Four shots to center mass. Irina would have been an easy kill if whoever it was had actually wanted her dead."

"And the bullets were silver. Meant for a werewolf." So the shooter knew what he was, or perhaps thought Irina was a werewolf. She dismissed that. Sergei had to be the target.

"What on earth did they hope to gain with his death? There's no profit in it, no chaos to sow." She finished her coffee. "It doesn't make sense."

She watched Viktor watching her. He was good at the poker face, but he had a few tells. Galina had given him something to think about. She could tell she'd surprised him again with her careful reasoning.

"I have to go check in with my father," she told him, placing her cup in the sink. "Tell Irina I'll stop by again later." She stepped around him and walked out of the kitchen. Before she left, she gave him one last thing to consider. "If you think of any compelling reason why Sergei would make a worthwhile target, you be sure and let me know."

She already knew of one reason why Sergei might have been shot and it had everything to do with Andrey Lupesco and his missing product.

The gates to her father's property swung closed behind her black Mercedes. She listened to the tires crunch against the loose stones from the paved drive as she followed it the half mile up to the main house. It was a mammoth Victorian structure, a turret topped with an onion dome taking up the west side of the house. Another wing jutted from the back of the east side. A wraparound porch flanked either side of the gabled entryway. Gingerbread trim followed the roofline and decorated sills and arches. It would always be the most beautiful place she'd ever seen.

It was also the saddest.

Galina pulled to a stop in the circular drive before the house and got out of the car, feeling a heaviness in her chest. She had good memories of this house, but all she felt now was a sense of dread to be back here. Her father had built this house for her mother. And this was where her elder sister, Elena, had died.

Squaring her shoulders, Galina stalked past the two guards stationed either side of the front door. She didn't bother acknowledging them—it would only distract them. Instead she opened the door and continued down the corridor until it branched. She took the left hall, pausing outside a closed door to gather her thoughts and breathe deeply for calm.

She pushed the door in and stepped through to greet the gazes of her father, her two brothers, and her father's closest and most trusted advisors. "Gentlemen," she said, as she closed the door behind her, "I trust I'm not interrupting." She looked at each of them in turn. "Pray, continue."

Her father looked like he was in danger of blowing out the vein in his neck that was throbbing with anger. Alexei's dark eyes had gone distant, as if he was imaging what her head would look like if it were no longer attached to her neck. Nikolai merely looked amused. She caught his grin before he ducked his head to hide it.

Alexei strode over to her, grabbing her upper arm roughly. He glared down at her. "What the hell do you think you're doing here?"

Galina kept the pleasant smile on her face, even though Alexei's grip was painful. She looked around the room and saw all eyes on her, waiting to see what she would do next. She had to show strength. "I came," she began, putting her hand over her brother's where he held her arm, "to speak with *our* father about what happened to *our* sister last night." She dug her fingernails into the top of his hand, gouging his flesh. The smile never left her face.

She felt her brother's hold on her loosen and she gently disengaged his hand from her arm. His face flushed with rage but he held his tongue. She stepped around him and walked to her father, kissing him on the cheek. "Morning, Papa."

"Galina," her father said, a note of warning in his voice. "I didn't call for you."

"I just came from Irina's. I thought you would want to know," she answered simply. She moved away, finding an unobtrusive place beside Nikolai, allowing the conversation to resume.

The men remained guarded. They weren't used to having a woman at their meetings, noting their posturing, measuring them with her eyes. Galina forced herself to keep silent, no matter how much she wished to interject when one of Papa's advisors said something so patently wrongheaded, she couldn't believe he was still allowed to remain in a position of power.

Eventually, they seemed to relax with her presence in the room. All but Alexei, who watched her like she was going to make off with the family's china and pets. His eyes bored into her, making her feel like he would love nothing better than to open up her skull to see what made her tick. Galina kept her eyes downcast, attempting to look unthreatening. She'd already accomplished what she came here to do: get them to accept seeing her face at the table.

Alexei could not be allowed to follow her father as head of the family. Galina knew that; anyone with eyes and a brain knew that. He was volatile, unstable, and violent. If he took over control of the Sudenko family, he would usher in an era of bloodshed and death the likes of which hadn't been seen in decades. Originally, Galina's plan had been to put Nikolai in the running. He was level headed and smart, not one to allow his emotions to rule him. He'd be a good leader.

But Nikolai was gay, something the family never spoke about. It made her sad that Nik could never be who he really was in public, but it was safer for him this way. The *Organizatsiya* had very strong feelings about homosexuality, and Papa was right to protect his younger son from that kind of backlash. If he was found out, the leaders could order Nik to face the Gauntlet—something they would make sure he didn't survive.

So if Galina wanted to save the family fortunes, it was up to her.

6

Art Appreciation Lessons

Galina drove up to the Seattle Art Museum, happy to finally be at work. She'd been lucky to secure a job here, which she attributed more to her stellar recommendations and hard work than to her family's criminal connections. She'd actually used her mother's maiden name when applying for jobs and graduate programs because she hadn't wanted to risk her father's name and money influencing anyone.

Pulling her Mercedes into her parking space at the Russell Investment Center garage, Galina made her way to her office. She'd planned to take the afternoon off to sit with Irina, but she wanted to pick up a few articles and auction catalogs so she could get some work done in her down time. Her security detail hadn't followed her in. They'd find somewhere else to park or sit outside until she left. Her errand wouldn't take long. Galina wanted to get back to Irina quickly to help with anything her sister might need. Or to be there in case the police had more questions. She knew her father was using what contacts he had at the local level to keep the details of Sergei's murder under wraps, but that didn't mean they could overlook the murder of a man in public.

Her small work space was dark. She was alone in the warren of offices, her few coworkers out at installations or on travel this week. It was rare for the curators and assistants to all be in the office at the same time. Flipping on the light, Galina walked to her desk, heels clicking lightly on the wood floor.

She was bending over to unlock the lower drawer of her file cabinet at her desk when she caught the scent of someone she didn't recognize. Her nostrils flared, and Galina could feel her teeth elongating inside her mouth. She reached into her purse lying on the desk and gripped the handle of the .40 automatic she always carried. She switched off the safety.

There was a knock at her open door. Galina turned smoothly, keeping her hand in her bag. Maksim stood in the doorway, looking somewhat abashed. "Your father suggested I take you to lunch. Perhaps it is not a good time?"

She smothered her irritation behind a polite mask. How had her father even known where to find…her security detail. Of course. Not only was Papa able to keep her safe, he was also able to keep tabs on her as well. Perfect.

Galina slipped her hand from her bag. If she didn't get this out of the way now, he'd just keep coming back until she did. And her boss hadn't expected her to come in today anyway due to the family tragedy. Still, that didn't mean she wanted to make a day of it.

"I do have a meeting later," she lied pleasantly, "but I can step out for a quick bite."

He looked caught between disappointment and relief, as if even he wasn't sure he wanted to pursue her. "I wouldn't want to inconvenience you."

"You're not an inconvenience, Maksim," she told him because she knew it was expected. "We'll go to Pike Place," she said, swinging her purse over her shoulder. "It's a quick walk from here and I can show you a little of downtown."

She led him out into the watery light of the city. It wasn't raining, but it was overcast, the sun's light filtering through cloud cover. There was a brisk wind off the water, snarling Maksim's dark hair as they walked. His security detail followed about ten feet behind.

"How do you like Seattle so far?" Galina asked, hoping to find out more about this man Papa seemed intent on throwing at her.

His lip curled in an expression of disgust. "It is not Russia."

She stared straight ahead. Really? That was his answer? She decided to lead the conversation in a different direction since she couldn't think of anything pleasant to say in response. Her father would never let her sit in on a meeting again if she alienated a potential business partner.

"Tell me about the caviar business," she said. Most people enjoyed talking about themselves; she hoped this would keep him occupied until they had ordered their food.

He launched into a long winded history about his family's caviar fortunes. By the time they reached Piroshky-Piroshky, Galina knew more than she thought possible about the price of sturgeon eggs and the harvesting thereof. She ordered a beef and onion *piroshky* and a *vatrushka* and waited while Maksim debated the choices at the counter.

"How long are you planning on staying in Seattle?" she asked as they strolled the market with their lunch.

Maksim glanced over at her, shaking his brown hair from his eyes. "I am not sure," he answered around a mouthful of smoked salmon pate piroshky. He made a face. "My mother's are superior."

Galina handed him a napkin. "I'm sure they are." Of course. Everything was probably better in Russia.

"Do you cook?"

Galina snorted, and then realized he was serious. Maksim raised his eyebrows, shocked at her reaction. "My mother died giving birth to me. We always had Magda who did the cooking."

"My mother can teach you." Maksim threw away his half eaten piroshky. "A woman should know how to cook."

Galina bit back a snarl. She was done humoring Maksim and his "old country" mannerisms. If nothing was as good as Mother Russia, perhaps he should take the next flight back. She certainly wouldn't miss him. She was going to have a good, long talk with her father.

"What is that over there?" Maksim asked, gesturing to a large crowd of people gathered under a clock.

She looked where he pointed. "That's Pike Place Fish." She grinned, an evil idea springing to mind. "Come on."

Leading him over to the raucous crowd of tourists and local alike, Galina pushed him forward. She signaled one of the fishmongers, and told him that her friend from out of town wanted the full experience.

"Get ready!" she called to Maksim.

Perplexed, he opened his mouth to say something when a silver skinned salmon came flying through the air at him. He raised his hands, but the tail still caught him in the face. Stumbling backward, Maksim pulled a handkerchief from his pocket to wipe fish juice from his face.

The two bodyguards sprang into action, pushing laughing bystanders aside. Galina took his elbow, doing her best not to burst into hysterical laughter. She should learn to cook indeed. He should learn to catch.

"It's a tradition," she explained, shooing his guards away.

Red-faced, Maxim drew himself upright. His eyes snapped with insult, not mirth. He mopped his face with the handkerchief once more before snarling. "It is barbaric." He tucked the handkerchief back into his pocket.

Galina stood next to him, ready for this lunch date to be over. "I should be getting back," she said, checking her watch.

Maksim cleared his throat. "Yes, I too need to attend to business matters." Offering her his arm, he turned his back to the fish counter.

A tuna slapped him in the back of the head, sending him staggering forward. Galina grabbed his arm, keeping him on his feet. She turned and saw one of the fishmongers shrugging, a wide grin on his face.

"Sorry!" he called.

Galina bit back a laugh. He totally wasn't. And neither was she.

The two security men surrounded him, ushering Maksim away from the fish market. She followed more slowly, happy to be done with that particular trial. When Maksim was out of earshot, she let loose with a barking laugh that startled a few people nearby. The look on his face when the fish blindsided him had been priceless.

Walking back, Galina enjoyed the time to herself. It was nice to just wander the streets without an agenda. A light drizzle began to fall, misting the sidewalks and turning the world softer, as though the rain was feathering the edges of the city. She loved days like this one.

She'd only been back at her desk for a few minutes when an intern appeared at her door.

"There's someone at the front asking for you."

Nodding, Galina waited until he turned to go back to wherever it was interns sprang from before dropping her head to the desk with a groan. It couldn't be Maksim again, could it? God wouldn't be that cruel. She checked the calendar on her blotter to see if there was a meeting scheduled that she'd forgotten about. There was nothing written under her appointments. Odd. The tension in her neck increased as an image of Sergei's body lying on the concrete flashed into her mind.

As soon as she entered the open rotunda of the museum's entrance, even with his back toward her, Galina recognized her guest. Andrey. If she'd been struck blind, she would still be able to pick up the scent of him. The dark grey suit he wore did amazing things for his shoulders. She clenched her fists at the sight of him.

In the time since their last meeting, she'd done her homework on him. The son of a small-time drug trafficker, Andrey had forced his way into the higher circles of the organization by working smarter, not harder. He always seemed to know exactly what people needed, before they knew themselves, and he always found a way to get it to them first. He'd risen to prominence while several of the older families, like Sergei's, could barely hold onto their few bankable operations with tooth and claw. These proud families were forced to do business with Andrey out of necessity, but they despised him for his "filthy, Gypsy roots."

Andrey turned when he heard the sound of her heels clicking on the stone floor, though he'd surely scented her well before that. "Miss Sudenko," he greeted politely, even as his eyes danced with wicked mischief.

"Mr. Lupesco." She held out her hand for him to shake and when he instead raised it to his lips, she murmured, "What do you think you're doing here?"

He lowered her hand from his mouth, but kept hold of it. His head dipped close to her ear. "I plan to donate a large sum of money to the museum. I wanted to stop by and get an idea of what my money would be paying for."

"And I'm here because?" Galina wasn't wild about someone just showing up at her place of employment, huge donation or not. She was in Acquisitions. She wasn't involved in soliciting donors.

"The curator suggested I speak with someone who might show me the collections." He grinned, and Galina felt her toes curl inside her expensive heels. "I'm just fortunate that someone turned out to be you."

"Fortunate, my ass," she whispered into his ear, and then stepped back to address the curator who was watching their exchange with questions in his eyes. "I was thinking I could show him some of the restorations, Bob," she said to the curator, before leading Andrey deeper into the museum. "If you'll follow me?"

She didn't wait for an answer before making her way to the largest of the collections. She felt Andrey keep pace with her, his body just a touch too close for her peace of mind. Her nerves felt raw, jangled, and she didn't know whether she wanted to kiss him or bite him. It was possible she wanted to do both. But in what order?

She swept into a room full of fine examples of nineteenth-century portraits. Stopping in front of the first, Galina began to give Andrey the history of the painting, keeping it as boringly dry as possible.

He stood close to her, the heat from his body radiating off him in intense waves. She was in the middle of describing the ornate details on the dress, when Galina felt his finger trace a path down the back of her arm, leaving a line of heat in its passing.

"So if you'll note here," she continued, ignoring the ripple in her stomach at his touch, "you'll see the fine brushwork in the background and clothing—this is a mark of the period."

"Fascinating," Andrey whispered, his lips mouthing her ear.

She stepped away, but he followed. "This painting is an excellent example. If you'll look here, you can see the way the shadows and light play off each other."

"Yes, it's quite impressive." Andrey nuzzled the side of her neck, pressing down the collar of her jacket so he could press his lips there.

Again, Galina stepped away. She could keep this up all day if she had to. "Are you going to tell me what you're really doing here? And don't give me that line about donating a metric ton of money to the museum."

His chuckle was low and throaty. Galina felt heat build between her legs, but kept her gaze steady. "You don't believe me? I'm disappointed."

Galina smiled slowly, lowering her eyes so her lashes swept across the top of her cheeks. She stepped up to him, until they were almost nose to nose, then locked her eyes with his. His nostrils flared and darkness danced in his eyes. "And I think you're full of shit," she said softly.

Andrey threw back his head and laughed, a loud snap of sound that was out of place in the quiet of the gallery. A few patrons turned to look their way. Galina grinned at his response. Then she continued. "We have an exhibit of Miro's works that I'd be happy to show you."

Galina felt him press against her back. His head dipped down, his mouth again at her ear. "Are they as incredible as what I'm seeing right now?" She felt the length of him pressed against her backside. If he was thinking that would distract her, he was underestimating her.

"Yes, they are." She ground her hips back against him, enjoying the sound of Andrey's indrawn breath. "See something you like?"

"Very much." His breath was hot against her neck. "When can I see a private collection?"

"Soon," Galina said, stepping away from him to point at another painting. "Now this one here…" she began, hiding a smile at his groan. "Come now, you're the one who wants to donate to the museum. Don't you want to see what your money would be paying for?" She took pity on him and walked through the other doorway, beckoning for him to follow. "Or is that not really why you're here?" She smiled as she led him deeper into the museum.

Opening the wooden double doors to one of storage rooms on this floor, Galina waited for him to step through. Then she closed them, turning the lock. She had a feeling she wouldn't want to be disturbed. She felt the liquid heat between her thighs and she wasn't sure she'd take an interruption with good grace.

Andrey gave her no time to turn around. In one move he'd fastened his hands in the hair at the base of her neck, pulling her head backward so he could ravage her throat with his lips. His free arm wrapped around her waist, pulling her back tightly against him.

Fire flared in her pelvis, skimming up her spine in an electric arc. Galina made a sound that was half-sigh, half-moan as the heat of Andrey's mouth sent her senses spiraling. She couldn't explain why he affected her this way. She was a creature of logic, of rational thought. But one touch from Andrey made her panties combust and made her want to throw all of her careful plans out the window.

Not that she would, of course. But she wanted to, and that was bad enough.

"This is a storage room," she gasped, gamely continuing the "tour." He laughed against her throat, the deep rumble of his chuckle against her flesh making her knees nearly buckle. She braced a hand against the door. "You'll note the packing materials…and…" She trailed off as teeth lightly bit along the skin over her pulse point.

"Galya?" He kissed along the edge of her jaw, nipping lightly at the spot just below her ear.

"Yes?" Her voice came out huskier than she meant it to.

His free hand, the one not wrapped in her hair, skated down the front of her black pencil skirt. It slipped beneath the hem of it, dragging the fabric upward as his hand moved back up, his fingers fluttering over the tops of her thighs. "I don't care about art."

His finger breached her suddenly, making her cry out. She felt his lips curve into a smile against her neck. He removed his finger, only to return with two. When he pushed inside her, Galina put her other hand against the door, gritting her teeth. She was so close to orgasm that it was going to be embarrassing. Her hips began to move, circling and rubbing against his palm.

She wasn't going to last long at this rate. Her breasts felt heavy and full and they ached for his mouth and tongue's attention. But she didn't want him to stop what he was doing.

"What was Federov doing here?" he asked, his lips moving against her throat.

Galina went still. "How did you know he was here?" She yanked his hand away from her. "Were you following me?" Because that wasn't creepy at all.

He stepped back, giving her room to move past him. "No," he began, slowly licking the taste of her from his finger. His gaze scorched her. "My offices are near here and I was out for a walk. I saw you and Federov at Pike Place."

"And then you decided to follow me." She adjusted her clothing until she was set to rights. It took all of her willpower not to yank him back, especially when he smelled so delicious to her.

Andrey shrugged. "It amused me to see you with him." His expression darkened. "And I would never have let you walk back to your building unprotected like that young idiot."

A lock of dark hair fell across his forehead, and Galina itched to brush it aside. Instead, she stepped over to an empty stack of pallets and leaned against it. "You wouldn't have had anything to do with the flying tuna to the back of Maksim's head, would you?" She narrowed her eyes in suspicion.

He grinned. "I got the idea after watching you with the salmon."

They stared at each other for a moment, then both laughed. "I didn't even see you there!"

Andrey's laugh tapered to a chuckle. "I'm good at not being seen when I don't want to be." He waved it away like it was no big deal.

Galina frowned. That was a Rom trick, a way to get the eyes to slide right off them. It made it easier for them to steal, to con, to escape.

He paced, his presence filling the small space nearly to the bursting point. It would be impossible for anyone to ignore him; he drew eyes to him as easily as breathing. How had she missed him at Pike Place, Rom or not? Galina allowed herself a short moment to appreciate the sight of him before getting back to the business at hand. "Why?"

"What do you want me to say, Galina?" He stopped his pacing and looked at her, his generous mouth quirked upward at one corner in a wry smile. "That I've thought about you while waking and sleeping since that night at the club? That I wanted to see you again?"

"Pretty words," she replied, crossing her arms over her chest. "But that doesn't explain what you thought to gain by coming here."

"Do I have to have something to gain?" He frowned, turning serious.

She smiled bitterly. Everyone had something to gain. It was the way their world worked. Galina had gotten that lesson through her mother's milk. "Most people usually do," she noted absently, tucking stray hairs behind her ear. "At least that's how it is in my family." She shrugged.

"So should I be asking what you hope to gain in all of this?" There was darkness in his eyes now. She'd put it there.

"You'd be a fool not to." She tapped her fingernails against the wood of the pallet.

Andrey crossed his arms across his chest. "Well then. What do I have to offer?"

Galina pushed off from the pallets and walked over to him. "You want to know what you offer — besides the obvious?" She waited for her compliment to sink in, smiling at him when he raised his brows in surprise.

"Nothing. I just want to be Galina. Not my father's daughter or my brother's sister. Just me." She'd said it. And meant every word. When he'd approached her in the kitchen they'd just been a man and a woman. Two wolves. Names and families and plots hadn't mattered.

She wanted that. Even if just for a little while.

She wasn't stupid. She knew what she'd been born for: an alliance, power, a marriage contract. The fact that she was a rare female werewolf only made her more valuable to her family. They'd tried to run her life from the moment she emerged from her mother's womb. She knew her choice of mate would not be left up to her. They didn't see her as a person, just a piece to be moved around the board as they wished. And her father was already brokering a deal for her marriage with Maksim. She felt it in her bones.

So she would choose to be Galina now. While she could.

Andrey was looking at her like he didn't know what to do with her. He was doing an admirable impression of someone who'd been hit upside the head with a flying tuna. Walking past him, she whispered, "And now you know."

She unlocked the door and disappeared through it. It had been fun while it lasted.

Galina walked to her car, eyes scanning the garage for signs of trouble. Sergei's shooting had rattled her. She didn't want to believe it was the first salvo in a turf war, but she wasn't going to stick her head in the sand. If someone was gunning for her family, she'd be a target. It was why she was carrying a loaded gun, its hollow point bullets packed with silver.

As she unlocked her car, she had the strange feeling that other eyes were on her. Unfriendly eyes. Galina had lived in large cities all her life and she knew to listen to the voice in the back of her head that warned of danger. Something was most definitely not right.

Turning the key in the ignition, Galina put the car in reverse and backed out of her space. In the rearview mirror, she thought she saw someone walk between the two buildings behind her, but then a car rounded the corner, its lights momentarily blinding her. She blinked away the glare, and when she could see again whoever had been there was gone.

She pulled out of the parking lot, the black sedan of her security detail pulling behind her as she drove up First. Her mind worked on the problem of Sergei's shooter, whatever he'd stolen from Andrey Lupesco, and how Alexei was involved in any of it. She was missing pieces. Maybe Irina would find a clue when she was going through Sergei's things. She made a mental note to ask her sister to keep an eye out.

Galina pulled into her garage, feeling the weight of the past two days crash into her. Her work at the museum had kept her busy all morning, she'd visited with Irina in the afternoon, and she'd stayed late to finish up some research in the SAM library. All she wanted to do was fall into bed and sleep for the next ten hours. Her eyes felt gritty and she stifled another yawn. She wasn't even sure if she could make it to her apartment. The backseat of her car looked awfully tempting.

With a tired sigh, she slammed the door and circled behind the car to open the passenger side. Galina pulled her leather satchel from the floor of the front seat and slung it over her shoulder. She caught the barest whiff of a strange scent before someone grabbed the back of her head and slammed it into the roof of the car.

Galina cried out, stunned. Her bag thudded to the concrete. There was a hand at the back of her neck and she stiffened her muscles, fighting with all of her strength against the force that wanted to smash her face against the metal once again. Fire rushed through her limbs, energizing her, giving her access to her were-strength. She lashed out with an elbow, feeling something give as she connected. She scented blood.

The hand holding her neck dropped and Galina whirled, her arm snapping out. The back of her fist connected with nothing. She saw a figure running away, heading toward the garage's exit, his gait uneven. Kicking off her shoes, Galina took off after him, feeling the change rising inside her. But the garage swam in her vision and she stopped to try to clear her sight.

She wasn't in any shape to chase her attacker. Her heart thundered in her chest, and her sight was darkening around the edges. She needed to get somewhere safe.

Unsteadily, she made her way back to the car, staggering a little when she scooped up her shoes and bag. There was no sign of her security detail, but Galina would worry about that once she was behind the door of her apartment with the alarm set. She made her way to the elevator, hitting the up button on her second try. She fell inside gratefully when the doors slid open.

Bracing herself against the wall with one hand, she pressed the button for her floor. The lurch as the elevator began its slow climb caused her stomach to churn. She fumbled her phone from her bag, intending to call Nikolai to find out where her damn detail had got to, but it rang before she could do so.

"What?" she answered. She was clearly not at her best; usually she waited to find out who was on the other end before being so rude.

"Galina?" Andrey's voice echoed strangely over the line.

She swallowed, feeling bile rise in the back of her throat. She should have finished her change; now her body was in revolt from the shock of it. "Yes?" she asked, trying to pull it together. She breathed deeply in through her nose, hoping she wouldn't hurl all over the elevator.

"What's wrong? You sound strange."

Galina laughed, and then had to stop when it made her head ache. She could imagine the angry flare of his nostrils, his dark brows drawing down in a scowl. It was ridiculous how much she wished she could see him right now. "I'm fine." She staggered as the elevator lurched to a stop.

The doors opened to let in a few people. Taking one look at her, a young woman said, "Oh my God, are you okay?"

"I'm on my way," Andrey said, hanging up before she could stop him.

Closing the phone, Galina put a hand to her head. A lump was already rising on her forehead where it had connected with the top of her car. "Just a little accident," she assured them, trying to look like she wasn't dead on her feet. "I'm fine."

"Do you need us to call the police?" the woman's date asked. "Or the hospital?" He looked into her eyes. "No offense, but you don't look fine."

Which was a very diplomatic way of saying she looked like hot buttered crap on toast. Galina groped for a smart ass response, but then decided to save her energy. "It's okay. I just want to get home." The next floor was hers and it felt like the elevator was taking a decade to traverse the distance. The walls of the compartment were moving in and out, like the breathing of a great beast.

This was not good at all. She should probably look into lying down.

The doors opened, allowing Galina to stumble out into the hallway. Putting her key in the lock was nearly beyond her, but eventually she managed to get the key into the correct one. The door swung inward, taking her with it. She managed to get it closed before dropping onto the couch in a graceless heap.

She drifted — she didn't know for how long. Her head ached and all she wanted to do was sleep, but she knew it was better if she didn't. Her were-healing would kick in soon, but until she felt better, she needed to stay awake.

The muscles in her neck screamed when Galina tried to turn her head. Instead, she stared at the ceiling and tried not to whimper. Once again, she wondered where her security detail had gone. And who it was who'd attacked her.

The insistent ringing of her doorbell brought her back to her surroundings. When she didn't move fast enough, whoever was on the other side began to pound a fist against the door. Galina pushed herself up with a groan just as Andrey began to shout, "If you don't open this door right now, I'm kicking it in!"

Galina managed to lurch over to the door, opening it just as Andrey was prepared to bang on it again. "Not so loud," she admonished, wincing.

"Galya," he whispered, and then swept into her apartment, closing the door behind him and locking it. Then he picked her up as if she weighed no more than a pup.

"I'll be fine," she protested sourly.

He cut her off. "No. Not another word out of your mouth."

Galina closed her eyes, feeling exhaustion pull at her. The scent of him washed over her and her tense muscles began to relax against the warmth of his chest. He was a wall of muscle beneath an Armani suit. She rested her head against his chest, listening to his steady heartbeat. It should be illegal for anyone to look and smell this good.

Andrey set her gently down on her bed. "Stay there," he ordered when she moved to get up. He disappeared back into the living room of her apartment.

Galina unbuttoned her jacket and slid it off, then did the same with her skirt. She stripped down and pulled on her old Clash T-shirt that sat at the foot of her bed before crawling under the covers.

"I thought I told you not to move," Andrey said, his voice a dark rumble from the doorway. She barely heard his footsteps as he crossed the room to help her lie down.

"I've always been shit at listening." Galina lay back against the pillows with a tired sigh.

"Shocking." He held a towel filled with ice up to her forehead. When she put her hand up to hold it, Andrey swatted it away lightly. "Still."

"You are a very bossy person."

"That's why I'm Alpha."

"You're not *my* Alpha," she countered, but she subsided into the bed.

One side of his mouth lifted in a small smile. "Will you please be quiet?"

Galina heard the laughter in his voice. "You're making fun of me."

He shook his head, making minute adjustments to the home-made ice pack. "Never," he said, his voice a soft sound in the darkness. "I couldn't possibly make fun of you."

She turned her head and hissed out a breath of pain. "I find that highly doubtful." Her voice sounded strained as she tried to find a comfortable spot for her neck.

Strong hands pushed lightly at her shoulder. "Let me see."

Galina rolled over onto her stomach. Andrey set the ice pack on her nightstand and laid cool hands against her neck. He began to lightly knead at the knotted muscles. "You want to tell me what happened?"

She sighed, cracking open one green eye to look at him. "I am perfectly capable of taking care of myself," she warned him.

"Of that I have no doubt," Andrey answered, his voice soft. "Still, I would like very much to know what happened." His hands stroked the sides of her neck and the tops of her shoulders, fingers only barely digging into the painful collection of tension gathered there.

"I was getting some stuff out of my car and someone came up behind me and slammed my head into it. Hard. So I elbowed them somewhere soft and chased after them." She luxuriated in the feel of his hands on her. "You could do that forever, you know."

Andrey laughed, a quiet puff of breath. Galina felt him gather her long hair in one hand and push it aside, giving him better access to her back. She heard him moving and turned enough to watch him remove his jacket. He undid the buttons on his cuffs and rolled up his sleeves, before returning to the place beside her on the bed.

"And?" he prompted, going back to massaging her shoulders.

"And, that's it. I was a little dazed, understandably," she added, finding she was too tired to be more than slightly defensive, "so he got away."

"Did you recognize him?" There was something dark in Andrey's voice, the threat of violence lying just beneath the pleasant sounding surface.

"I really only got an excellent up close and personal look at the roof of my car—you know, when my forehead was being introduced to it—so I didn't get a good look."

Andrey lay down next to her, his fingers tucking a lock of hair behind her ear. "You are entirely too sarcastic, has anyone ever told you that?"

"No," she answered, voice deadpan. "I have never heard that before in my life."

He chuckled. "Did he smell familiar?"

Galina tried to nod, thinking better of it when her neck muscles rebelled. Andrey began to knead them again. "That was one of the strange things." She bit back a yawn, not wanting to do it in his face. Because nothing said sexy times like yawning into a blazingly, mind numbingly hot man's face. "I didn't smell him at all until he was right there. And even then, his scent was faint, like he'd masked it somehow." She had wolfsbane perfume that operated in much the same way.

"Didn't your father assign a bodyguard to you?" He smiled at her indrawn breath when he hit a particularly sensitive spot. "You're carrying quite a bit of tension."

"I can't imagine why." She smirked when she said it. She was beginning to feel a bit better, although whether it was because her were-healing was finally kicking in or Andrey's presence she wasn't able to say. "And yes, he did."

"So where were they?" He traced a finger down her jawline.

"That's an excellent question. And one I intend to ask my father tomorrow." She paused. "I don't think I'm carrying tension there," Galina observed, feeling a rush of heat to her face.

His blue eyes sparked with his impish grin. "Just trying to be thorough."

"Hmm," she hummed. Her eyes drifted closed. She needed to sleep. And with Andrey here, she felt it safe to do just that. But she fought it to try to think more about the attack. Too much about it didn't add up. Was it related to Sergei's shooting? It didn't feel that way.

A light touch on her brow at the spot between her eyes snapped her out of her sluggish thoughts. "You get a wrinkle right here," Andrey said, before dipping his mouth to place a soft kiss to the spot. "It means you're thinking." He brushed his fingertips down her cheek. "Rest now. Whatever you're thinking about can wait until you wake up."

"Will you?" She hadn't meant to ask, but it slipped out. Galina blamed the head injury.

A slow smile spread across his face and Galina shut her eyes, mortified. Stupid attack.

He leaned in closer. "There's nowhere else I'd rather be."

Galina snuggled deeper into the covers and tried not to smile.

7

Water Conservation Measures

Galina awoke slowly to the feel of arms around her. She stayed still, letting her sleep-dulled mind catch up to the waking world. Andrey's scent wrapped around her, like his arm clung to her waist. It made her feel protected, a new feeling for her. None of her partners had been long term and she'd never let one spend the night. She preferred her space to stay *hers*.

Even when she'd been growing up, she'd never felt this way. Her father cared about her safety, of that she had no doubt, but it was a sort of absent care due to what she was. Being a rare female Alpha made her a valuable commodity, treasured by her father for what she could bring, not for who she was.

And then there was Alexei. Galina was positive that if her elder brother could have gotten away with hurting her more when they were kids, he would have. He'd been the oldest and had attention, love, and care lavished on him. But when Galina was born, some of that attention was transferred to her. He'd never forgiven her for it, and had made her pay for existing in a hundred different little ways. Her father turned a blind eye to his elder son's torments.

But lying here with Andrey, Galina felt like nothing could touch her. It was a dangerous feeling, and a strange one. She didn't want to get used to this. Relying on anyone just led to disappointment. And she knew she couldn't have this, not really. Andrey was Romani. Despite being an Alpha, or maybe because he was, Galina knew her father would never allow her match to be wasted on someone he thought unworthy.

It didn't matter that Galina might think otherwise.

She brought a hand up and touched her forehead. The lump was there, but not nearly as large as it had been. She imagined she was bruised, but it barely hurt when she pressed on it. She tried moving her neck and felt only a faint twinge.

Andrey's hold on her tightened. Galina rolled over slowly so she could see his face. His eyes were open, watching her, his grey-blue gaze open and frank. "Good morning," he said, his voice a low rumble in his chest.

"Morning," she murmured. She lifted a hand to his face, feeling the stubble beneath her palm. He turned his head into it and pressed a kiss there.

"How are you feeling?" Andrey carefully touched her forehead.

"Better than expected," she admitted, feeling herself flush. "Thank you for staying."

He nuzzled her hair. "Like I said, there was nowhere else I'd rather be."

Galina slid her palms against his chest and stared at the buttons on his shirt. She wanted him, more than anyone she'd ever met. It wasn't something she could explain. And it wasn't something she should pursue, no matter how much she may want it.

"I'm going to put on some clothes." That was probably the safest course of action. Galina was keenly aware that she was wearing nothing but a pair of panties and a ratty T-shirt.

Andrey dropped flat on the bed. "Now that's a damn shame." He pillowed his head on his hands.

Galina climbed out of bed, taking a moment to stare at Andrey. He looked good lying there in her bed, even if he was fully clothed. Plus it gave her a moment to make sure her legs would support her without going all bendy as they had the night before. When she was sure she could walk without staggering, she headed to the bathroom, closing the door behind her.

In the mirror, she surveyed the damage. A small bump decorated her forehead with lovely purple and yellow bruising surrounding it.

She had dark circles beneath green eyes that were still dull from sleep. Galina leaned forward, pushing back her hair to get a better look. She could probably cover the worst of it with some carefully applied makeup. She'd heal up completely in a day or so.

She turned on the shower. She brushed her teeth as the water heated, desperate to get the morning breath taste out of her mouth. Steam soon filled the bathroom and Galina stripped, tossing her clothes into the hamper. She wanted to feel clean.

The water was just shy of skin blistering and Galina sighed in pleasure as the heat of it went to work on tired and sore muscles. She soaped her hair first, then reached for the body wash and bath poof. Cool air hit her back and she turned around in surprise.

Andrey closed the glass shower door behind him, joining her in the steaming water. It glistened on his tanned chest and stomach. Galina's eyes traveled over his body, learning it by sight before she even thought about touching him.

His torso was well-muscled, broad shoulders tapering down to a lean waist. His stomach was flat, and the planes of his chest held a smattering of dark hair. Her eyes dipped down, following the line of hair down to his cock. He was half erect already and a more than adequate size. Galina swallowed and continued her perusal.

Everything about him was perfect. His legs, his ass, even his feet. It was like he'd been designed just for her. She finished her mental inventory of his parts, sweeping her gaze back up to his face.

"Mind if I join you?" Andrey asked, a slow smile sliding across his lips.

"If I said yes, would you leave?" Galina countered, tilting her head up to look at him when he stepped closer.

His arms reached out to wrap around her waist, pulling her into him. "But you're not going to say yes," he whispered before capturing her mouth with his.

Galina leaned into the kiss, opening her mouth beneath his. Andrey's tongue slid along hers, drawing it into his mouth. She wrapped her arms around his neck, pressing herself against him until they fit together without any space between them.

His mouth left hers only to press kisses across her jaw to the spot right above where her pulse beat. With the flat of his tongue, he licked a line from the base of her neck up to that pulse point, and stayed there, pressing against it as if he wanted to taste her heart. "No bites," she managed to gasp out around the heat coiling inside her that was making her stupid. As much as Andrey turned her on, there was no way she was risking a mating bite right now.

Werewolves mated for life, and in order to have viable offspring, they first had to administer the mating bite. Even a were/human combo needed the bite in order to have children, but the subject had to be willing to accept the bite. And that was a complication that Galina didn't need in her life now.

Andrey growled against her throat but relented. "Fine," he said, "and the same goes for you."

"I have no interest in *biting* you," she answered, shoving him back against the tile wall of her shower. He allowed her to move him with just the pressure of her fingertips on his chest, giving her a dark chuckle as she did.

"What, pray tell, do you have an interest in?" The smile stuttered off his face when she gripped the base of his cock.

"I think you can figure that out for yourself." Galina slowly lowered herself to her knees, keeping eye contact with him while she did so. "You're a smart boy."

Galina didn't take him in her mouth right away. She pressed kisses to the outside of his shaft, then licked it from the tip to the base. He grimaced and she grinned up at him. "Don't tease," he ground out, hands clenching against the tile wall.

His words ended on a gasp as Galina took him in her mouth. He tasted of man and musk and something indefinable that was uniquely wolf and uniquely Andrey. She lowered her head further until her lips met the hand that was holding him. She fell into a rhythm, sucking on the upstroke, her tongue teasing the head of him.

Andrey moaned deep in his chest. Galina felt hands in her hair, lightly holding her but letting her set the pace. She placed her free hand against his thigh to better brace herself. She hummed around him, earning another groan in response. She increased her pace, lingering on the downstroke when Andrey's hands tightened in her hair.

Galina heard the faint noises he was making, felt the involuntary twitches in his hips. She slid her hand from his thigh to cup his balls, fingering them lightly. When she sucked hard on the upstroke, Andrey cried out as if he couldn't help himself, banging his head against the wall. Her jaw ached—she hadn't done this in a while—but it was nice to see she hadn't lost her touch. She wished she could watch him as he came undone.

A spasm passed through him. Galina felt him shudder. He was always so serious, so buttoned up in his dealings—she'd seen him out and heard the talk about him. Always so controlled. It was a joy to see him lose himself in her like this, that he allowed her to do this to him.

"Galya," he gasped out, his voice hoarse.

She hummed in encouragement, wanting his release. Andrey's hips thrust forward as he cried out, spilling himself down her throat. Galina swallowed everything. His fingers flexed and released against her head. When he'd spent himself, he dropped his hands to her arms and pulled her upright.

"Jesus, woman," he said, after swallowing heavily. "I'd ask where you learned to do that, but I'm not sure I should ever know. There have to be state secrets involved." He pulled her into his arms, then stepped them into the stream of hot water.

Galina laughed, nuzzling his neck. "As much as I'd love to stay here all day, I have to check on my sister." *And talk to my father*, but she didn't want to say that aloud while naked in the shower. Her father would kill her if he knew what she was doing with Andrey.

Andrey slipped his hands under her ass and lifted her up. He wrapped her legs around his waist. "If I didn't have a previous appointment, I would take you back into your bedroom and let you know just how much I appreciate your oral skills." He kissed her deeply. "But since it sounds like we both have prior engagements, I will have to wait."

Digging her fingers into his hair, Galina bit at his earlobe. "Damn shame." She unwrapped herself from around him and stood on her own two feet once more.

"It is," he said, eyes roving over her appreciatively. "I wish I had more time to properly acquaint myself with your naked body." His hand skimmed down her side, lightly brushing her breast before coming to rest on her hip.

Galina stood on her tiptoes and kissed him, sucking his bottom lip into her mouth. He tasted of mint and she wondered if he'd brushed his teeth in the guest bath using one of the spare toothbrushes and toothpaste. She'd kept them there in case Irina had needed to spend the night. She supposed her sister wouldn't have need of a safe haven any more.

Andrey pulled away, blue eyes dark with lust. "If you keep doing that, we'll be in here until the hot water runs out."

"And I wouldn't want to make you late," Galina countered slyly, knowing the devious look on her face turned her words into a lie. But she had an appointment of her own to get to and so she stepped back and finished rinsing her hair. She handed Andrey a bar of soap and then stepped out of the shower.

She dried herself quickly, and then pulled out a towel for him. Galina found she didn't mind him in her space first thing in the morning, which was an odd thing. She typically hated sleeping with anyone beside her, hated being touched or held at night. But he'd spent the night and had joined her in the shower and instead of the expected warning bells and tension in her gut, all she felt was a sort of low grade satisfaction that he was still here.

She pulled on a robe and squeezed out the excess water in her hair. When Andrey exited the shower, she was waiting, ready with the towel. He thanked her with a light, wet kiss and then began to dry himself. When he was finished, he wrapped the towel around his waist and turned to her. She'd watched him the entire time, enjoying the sight of his naked body. Again, she marveled at just how well he was put together. And she was reminded of how much she wanted to explore him with hands and mouth.

He stood in front of her, the towel riding low on his hips. Galina's hands itched to remove it, meetings and responsibilities be damned, and just enjoy the gift that he was. But she did have responsibilities and so did he, and the easiest way to get caught was to forget that.

"Galya," he said softly, his hand brushing her chin. "When can I see you again?"

She met his eyes, studying what she saw there. She had several very great reasons to stop this right now, her father's anger and disapproval chief among them. All of the families had heard the rumors, dark gossip really, of what Papa had done to her elder sister. No one talked about Elena, but Galina had been listening to what people didn't say as much as what they did. Elena had rebelled and she had been punished for it.

Then there were her brothers. Alexei was a loose cannon, unfit—at least as far as she was concerned—to run the Sudenko family. He'd have a field day if he found out she was…doing whatever it was she was doing with Andrey. Her plans to oust him from his position and put someone more suitable in his place would be ruined if he had that kind of leverage over her. And Nikolai was wonderful, but she doubted he would understand what it was like to go against their father's wishes for them. He was loyal and dutiful and intelligent: the perfect son. He would never dream of disappointing their father.

Galina shook her head, at war with herself. "I don't know," she said. The part of her that wasn't a slave to her familial obligations didn't want to let him go. Andrey was a secret that was hers alone. She didn't know how long she'd be able to keep him, but she did know that she wasn't ready to end things yet.

"Can I call you later?" she asked, making up her mind, at least for the moment.

He nodded, pressing a finger against her lips. His black hair hung in his face. "If you promise me something."

She raised one pale eyebrow at his words. His face was serious, no half smiles, no mirth snapping at the back of his blue eyes. Galina waited for him to continue. She wasn't going to promise anything until she heard exactly what he wanted from her.

He put his knuckles beneath her chin, lifting her head up and holding it there so he could stare down at her. "I want you to tell your father about what happened last night and to accept whatever protective measures he offers."

Galina tried to draw back, but his hold on her chin tightened. "I'm serious, Galya. I know you think you can handle this yourself, but you need to tell your father what's going on. It may be related to your sister's husband's shooting."

She narrowed her eyes, feeling a complicated surge of emotion flow through her. She'd already thought that the two attacks might be related. And her protection detail going missing was something that needed an explanation. That was the first item on her agenda for the day.

When she didn't reply immediately, Andrey frowned. "Promise," he ordered in a tone that made her thighs clench. "Or I'll put a detail on you myself."

"Do you have a death wish?" Galina countered, not bothering to keep the annoyance out of her voice. "You're right, I do think I can take care of myself. And you know how I know that? Because I've done it before." She pulled away from him, not liking being told what was going to happen in her own life.

"I'm trying to protect you," he ground out, his voice getting deeper as his temper flared to life.

"Here's a newsflash: I don't need your protection." She inhaled sharply, picking up his prickly scent of pine and amber. "You don't get to dictate what I do just because you've seen me naked."

Andrey's nostrils flared and his eyes turned even darker. He stormed out of the bathroom. Galina sat on the edge of the tub, listening to the sounds of him getting dressed. The urge to go out there and apologize to him was nearly overwhelming, but she stayed where she was. This was the problem with the males within the *Volk Organizatsiya*. They had that unbending habit of thinking they knew what was right for everyone else, most especially their women. Well, Galina had been away from the family for years and had experienced how good it felt to make her own decisions.

Andrey didn't say good-bye. The sound of his shoes on the wood floor, followed by the click of the front door as he closed it behind him told her he was gone. Galina sat for a few moments, missing his presence with a dull ache that surprised her. Then she pulled herself up and began to get ready to face her father.

8

How to Succeed in Smuggling
without Really Trying

She drove up to her father's house, her detail—suddenly reappearing after their conspicuous absence—following her through the gates. They'd been waiting for her when she drove out of her garage. The question of where they'd been the night before still required an answer. She intended to get one when she spoke with her father. And then she intended to replace them with guards that could be trusted.

Galina had dressed carefully this morning. For ten minutes, she'd sat in her car, steadying her breathing. On the outside, she looked cool and untouchable, but that wasn't how she felt on the inside. She was getting ready to do something no Sudenko woman had done before.

She was going to ask for a line of business of her own. Not a business like the Red Crown, the jewelry shop where Irina worked, passing along stolen gems. What she was asking for was a venture of her own, that she would run, from planning to execution. Leading, eventually she hoped, to voting rights within the *Volk Organizatsiya* itself.

Not right away, of course. These things had to be approached delicately. But she intended to lay some groundwork, to prove that she was more than just a pretty face and breeding stock. She knew her father's organization needed to diversify and she had some ideas.

Now she just had to get her father to listen.

Nikolai would help. He didn't want to see Alexei in power any more than she did. If Papa was old school, then Alexei was living in the Mesolithic age. His ideas for furthering the family business involved more gunfire and a lot of dead bodies. He'd drown the family in blood if he were left to run the business unchecked.

She stepped out of the car, brushing imaginary lint from her tailored Armani pants. She'd gone with what she hoped was corporate chic—nothing outwardly sexy but still feminine enough to remind everyone she was a woman. She didn't want to disguise or hide her gender in the hopes of running the business, but she didn't want to be taken lightly either. She'd chosen a dark cashmere sweater and a patterned wrap over one shoulder. The only jewelry she wore were her favorite onyx earrings and a huge steel cuff chased with heavy Celtic engravings of wolves. Might as well remind them of who and what she was.

She passed by one of Alexei's bodyguards on her way to her father's study. The bruising around his eyes and the swollen top of his nose were consistent with a recently healed broken nose. Galina stopped.

"Looks like you caught yourself a good one, Timur," she said by way of greeting. A hollow feeling settled in her gut. Had one of Alexei's men been the one to jump her last night? She knew he wasn't happy about her presence during the last meeting, but would he have been able to call off her protection detail?

With a sinking feeling, she realized he could do exactly that. Papa was the only one who could have countermanded his order, and if Papa hadn't known…Galina swallowed nervously.

Timur grinned lasciviously, displaying a gaping hole where one of his front teeth had been. "Got hit with a vodka bottle when I wasn't looking," he answered.

She tried to get a scent read off of him, but without much success. He smelled a little nervous, but the same could be said for many who spoke with her. She continued on down the hall.

Nikolai, Alexei, and their father were already gathered around a table that would eventually seat the other powerful families within the Organization. "What are you doing here?" Alexei's voice was just shy of a sneer.

Galina smiled sweetly at him, and then ignored him completely. She turned to Papa. "Did you call off my security detail last night?" she asked him as he stood to greet her with a kiss on the cheek.

"No," Ilya replied, his sharp eyes searching her face. "Why do you ask?"

"I just didn't see them when I pulled into my garage. They were probably there and I just didn't notice." She kept her eyes on her brothers. Nikolai was saying something to their brother. Alexei's gaze flicked over to her, but otherwise he didn't react to her news. Galina sniffed the air to see if she could catch a whiff of nervousness or fear, but the room smelled as it usually did.

Galina took a seat next to her father. He looked confused, but that was nothing compared to Alexei's response. Breaking off his conversation with Nikolai, he snapped, "What are you doing?"

"I would think that would be obvious," Galina said, keeping her voice pleasant and even. "I'm going to sit in on the meeting."

"The hell you are," her brother said, taking a step closer to her. "Women don't come to meetings."

"Well, this one is, so you'd better get right with the idea." Galina sharpened her tone, a verbal baring of teeth. This was the first step. She had to gain permission to be there.

"What do you know about the business anyway?" Alexei stood over her, hoping to threaten her physically. It might have been frightening if he hadn't been doing this for her entire life.

Oh thank you for such an obvious opening, brother dear, she thought. Containing a grin, she began to list off points on her fingers. "I know our holdings are not what they once were. I know that the other families are hesitant to continue alliances with us because we're perceived as weak, as failing. I know that if we don't further diversify our interests, we'll be left in the dust, running numbers and selling dope at a stop sign. I know that we need to move into the twenty-first century or we're sunk."

Her father opened his mouth, and then closed it again. He looked shocked. Then he turned to Nikolai and Alexei. "Do you both agree with Galya's assessment?"

Nikolai nodded slowly, face serious. Alexei looked to be in danger of spitting, he was so angry. Galina leaned forward, taking Ilya's hand in hers. "Papa, I don't say this to hurt you. I love our family and I want to keep us safe. But if we continue doing business in the same old way, we'll go the way of the dinosaurs."

"What do you know about anything?" Alexei's voice was all snarl and snap. "You've had your head in books for the past five years!"

Galina gave him a withering glance before turning back to her father. "And when I had my head in those books," she said, dismissing her brother, "I was learning things." *Unlike you* went unspoken but clear to all of them.

Alexei made a move behind Galina's back, the scuffle catching her attention, and then her father was standing, his face thunderous. "Enough!" The old man's voice was hard, the sharp bark of an Alpha calling his pack to heel. "You will remember where you are!"

Turning her head, Galina saw Nikolai holding back Alexei. She came to her feet in one smooth motion, baring her teeth. Ilya jumped between them, holding his arms out to keep them separated. Alexei's face began to morph as his anger got the better of him.

Papa moved faster than someone his age should have been able to, backhanding Alexei across the muzzle. A high whine escaped her brother's lips, and his face slowly reverted back to human. "You will *not!*" their father shouted. "You will control yourself. We have guests coming!"

"Come on, Alexei," Nikolai said, giving Galina a significant look. "Let's go for a walk." He took their brother's arm, forcefully steering him toward the door, but Alexei shoved away from him with a growl and stalked out of the room.

Ilya walked to the bar and poured himself two fingers of vodka. He downed the drink in one gulp, throwing the liquor back with practiced ease. Galina got up and poured one for herself. She smiled when Papa frowned at her.

"You are too young," he scolded.

"I've been legal for four years, Papa," she chided him gently. He needed to stop seeing her as a little girl in blond pigtails. She'd been grown up for quite some time. She sipped at her drink, smiling at him over the glass.

Sitting down with a sigh, Ilya rubbed at his forehead with a heavy hand. "I do not know what you want, Galya. You embarrass Alexei, you do not know your place. I want to find a nice husband for you, but you fight me at every turn. What am I to do with you?"

Galina tried not to bristle. Alexei was the embarrassment, not her. How many times had Nikolai had to clean up one of his messes? Ten, twenty times? More? And "knowing her place"? It was that kind of hidebound thinking that would keep them from utilizing all of their assets to the fullest extent. It was stupid and wasteful.

Taking a deep breath, she let all of her frustration and anger go. She was close to getting what she wanted, and she needed to remain calm. In a soft voice, Galina asked, "What if I could prove that my ideas have merit?"

Ilya took another swig of his vodka. When he spoke, his voice was harsher than she was used to hearing. "Tell me."

She wrapped long fingers around the rocks glass in front of her. It kept her from fidgeting as she met his gaze. "There are plenty of people who would pay handsomely for art and artifacts that can't be acquired through the usual means."

"Smuggling."

"If you want to call it that," Galina conceded. They had a number of smuggling operations, but none that dealt in the fine arts. She had the knowledge and contacts. She just needed the infrastructure already in place at her father's operation to make it work. "I have a number of buyers just waiting for the right product. It's got minimal risk."

"Galya, you know that women and business do not mix." But there was a hesitation in his voice that she knew she could capitalize on.

"Papa, you sent me to school to learn. And I did." She leaned forward, eyes on his face. "I've been watching you run the business since I was old enough to walk. I can help our family. Let me have this so I can show you what I can do." A chance, that's all she wanted.

"And after that?" Her father stared at her as if he knew the inner workings of her mind.

"You can see my results and make your own decision." She smiled at him, as if this was of the least concern to her. "And I will accept whatever you decide."

Ilya's eyes narrowed. "You should have been born a boy," he said with a frown.

Galina kept the calm mask on her face through an effort of will. She would not show her father how much his words had stung. "But I wasn't," she answered softly. Then she smiled, "And besides, you have two sons already."

She didn't say that one of them was too busy stroking his own ego to be able to run the family and the other was too busy cleaning up the other's mistakes to be effective in his own right. "I can do this."

Ilya pushed up from the table, the small jowls along his jaw line shaking slightly. "Very well, Galina. You have your wish. I will give you a few men to use in your operation. Don't disappoint me."

I'm not the disappointment, she almost said, but kept it to herself. Because she knew that she was a disappointment to him. What good was intelligence and drive when they were housed in a woman's body? Galina didn't feel like she lacked anything, but her father certainly did, and she knew that others of the old guard felt the same as he did.

She stood with him. "Can the men be of my choosing? With your approval, of course," she added quickly. She suspected that her father would select the most recalcitrant and unbending of his people if she let him in the hopes that she would fail. And if Alexei had a say in it, he'd make sure she worked with idiots and psychos. She needed young men, eager to make a name for themselves and with the ability to think for themselves.

"And I want a new set of guards. I'm not impressed with the ones I've got."

Her father's eyes narrowed, sweeping her from head to foot. "Did something happen?"

Andrey's words came back to her. "I went to lunch with Maksim yesterday. He had to leave early and took his guards with him." She thought it best to leave out the assault with flying fish. "I had to walk back to the museum by myself. I didn't see the car or either man anywhere near me." That Maksim came out sounding like he'd been unconcerned for her safety too was a mark in the "win" column.

Papa's face turned red. Taking her shoulders, he peered at her face. "Are you all right?"

Resting her hands on his, she said, "I'm fine, Papa. But I want different guards."

He sighed, dropping his hands from hers. "You are a good girl, Galya. Why don't you want to settle down and have babies?"

"Who says I don't, Papa? I just don't want to do that *right now*." She winked at him.

Ilya threw back his head and laughed. He wrapped an arm around her shoulders and pulled her into him. She smelled his cologne—a cloying scent that made her wrinkle her sensitive nose — and alcohol leaching from his pores. He must have tied one on last night. "Come now. I will introduce you to the rest. If you are going to be working for me, you should meet them."

"Have you thought of who will replace Sergei yet?" It wasn't a high ranking position, but a competent person could make something happen in it.

"Alexei wants Vasily." Her father guided her down the hall, leading her toward the front parlor where her father always met with his lieutenants when he was home. He usually preferred to meet with them at one of his businesses, but with the death of Sergei, everyone was being more circumspect.

Galina frowned. "What does Nikolai say?" She knew what Nik would say. Vasily was a cocky thug with about as much sense as a rock — although Galina wondered if rocks might be insulted by the comparison. He was hired muscle, nothing more, but he was one of Alexei's long standing confederates and he was loyal only to him. He backed Alexei on every play he made, even the disastrous ones that got people killed. Usually the wrong people. Vasily was a menace. Which made him Alexei's perfect choice.

"He thinks Vasily to be unseasoned." Her father's eyes snapped with mirth and Galina grinned at him. Trust Nik to be diplomatic and understated in his disapproval. "I agree with him. He suggested the Demidov boy."

She fought back a laugh. Everyone under the age of fifty was still considered a boy in her father's eyes. She knew vaguely of the man he was talking about — at least Andrey's age if not a bit older — and he'd be a good fit. Much better than Vasily anyway.

"And what do you think?" she asked him, curious as to which way her father was leaning.

"I've already spoken to his father."

Galina smiled. Perhaps her father wasn't as blind as she thought he was.

9

The Merry Widow

Everyone who was anyone came to Sergei Volkov's funeral. It was like the damn Oscars for Russian criminals who embraced questionable fashion choices. The Kandinsky Funeral Parlor had been reserved for the occasion; Anya Volkov had spared no expense for the send-off of her beloved Sergei.

Galina smoothed her black dress over her hips one last time and looked over at Irina. The only word that came to mind when she saw her sister was resplendent. Irina was wearing a fiery red dress and the diamond necklace that she'd worn at Katy's Sweet Sixteen party. Her makeup and hair were flawless.

Mama Anya was sending Irina death glares as she hovered over the casket that held her son's body. They were all gathered in the private viewing room — the Sudenkos and their bodyguards, and the Volkovs. The Volkov contingent consisted of Mama Anya, her remaining son, Gregori, and their two men. Irina stood out like the proverbial rose among thorns.

Mama Anya wept openly, sobbing over Sergei's body. Galina watched Irina step over to Anya, her hands out to comfort the woman. Before she got within a foot of her, Irina's mother-in-law snapped upright and whirled around to face Irina.

"Don't touch me!" she shrieked, eyes wild in a face contorted by grief. "You never loved him. If you had, you would have given him children and he might have had something to fight for! Just look at the way you're dressed, like a whore on her way to a party. No respect! No modesty! No heart! You were always a cold, unfeeling woman! You didn't deserve my Sergei!"

Galina had to agree with her. No one on earth deserved Sergei. Galina thought that Mama Anya might be done, but she was mistaken.

"You pack your things and get out of my son's house. It is mine now, by right! Go back to your father's house, you useless little human bitch!"

"You're right," Irina said, her voice quiet but forceful, "I didn't deserve your son."

Galina interposed herself smoothly between the two women before someone drew blood. Viktor, who was shadowing Irina for the funeral, looked as if he was going to use Anya as a chew toy. Galina couldn't blame him. After the spew of insults that the woman had hurled at Irina, she wanted to smack Anya until her hand hurt — after she'd toughened it up beating on a tree for six months. "Okay, why don't we all just give Irina a moment alone? Give her the opportunity to say good-bye to her husband."

She snagged Anya's arm in a firm grip, tightening it when the older woman began to struggle. "My baby! I won't leave *that woman* alone with my baby!"

Galina had had quite enough of this fuckery. She leaned down and whispered in Anya's ear, "Listen to me. You can either walk out of here, or you can be carried out of here unconscious. It makes no damn difference to me, but let's at least try to have a modicum of decorum in the funeral home."

Mama Anya stopped her keening long enough to stare at Galina in horror. At the same time, Galina signaled Nik and Viktor over to help Mama Anya out of the private viewing room. The other body-guards helped usher everyone else out. When Anya had been safely conveyed to somewhere that wasn't there, Galina walked over to Irina.

Her sister stood stone-faced before the casket. Galina lightly touched her arm to get her attention. "Take your time. We'll meet you at the receiving line." She squeezed her sister's arm, kissed her on the cheek, and left her alone with her dead husband.

Galina closed the door behind her to give Irina some privacy, resting against it as she gathered her thoughts. This was a farce of the highest order. The casket Mama Anya had picked out was the Elvis Presley of caskets: gleaming white, gilded to within an inch of its life, and covered in huge swaths of white roses. She'd hired a horse and carriage to carry the abomination to the cemetery.

Franny walked up to her. "How's Irina doing? I just saw Mrs. Volkov having the vapors in the receiving room."

Galina grimaced, rubbing at the bridge of her nose with her thumb and index finger. She was getting one hell of a headache from all of this nitwittery. She wanted to take Irina, go back to her house, and watch stupid movies for two days.

"Mama Anya is a giant pain in the ass," Galina gritted. "Irina's hanging in there, but it hasn't been an easy day."

"Gotcha. I'm on it." Franny disappeared back down the hall, a woman on a mission.

Galina followed more slowly. She dreaded standing in the receiving line, but she'd do it for Irina. She wasn't sorry Sergei was gone, and she wasn't going to pretend she was torn up over his death. She was happy her sister was rid of her albatross of a husband. It wasn't particularly nice, but Galina didn't think you got anywhere as a woman — at least not in her family — by being nice.

The number of people in the receiving room was staggering. Mama Anya must have strong-armed the entire *Volk Organizatsiya* to attend. Galina knew that half of those here despised Sergei, but a lot of business was conducted at funerals. She was hoping to corner one of Sergei's old lieutenants and see if she could glean any information about what Sergei had stolen from Andrey.

Maksim Federov stood near her father, shaking his hand and offering condolences. His suit was tailored, but it still looked a bit too big for him, giving her the impression that he was playing dress up in his big brother's clothes. Galina ducked behind a knot of mourners, not ready to make small talk with the Caviar Prince.

"My sincerest apologies for the loss to your family, Miss Sudenko." Andrey's voice was rich and warm. Galina turned to see him watching her, a sly smile on his face as if they shared a private joke.

She extended her hand, feeling the now-familiar tension twist within her. He took her fingers in his, pressing his lips to the back of her hand, deliberately nipping at each knuckle. His eyes never left her face and Galina felt herself growing warm. She pressed her thighs together, cursing Andrey to the lowest hell possible. He knew what he was doing to her and he knew he was doing it to her in the middle of a room full of werewolves. If she had to leave to change her underwear, everyone would know why.

He smirked at her in a way that made her insides melt. She could have killed him. Twice.

"Thank you for the kind words, Mr. Lupesco." She gave him a tight smile. Andrey's silvery eyes snapped with mirth. Konstantin, the bodyguard who had grabbed her at Sergei's shooting, stood directly behind Andrey's left shoulder, and his usual blank mask was marred by the amusement dancing in his eyes.

Oh, this was just lovely. She wondered how much Konstantin knew about her and Andrey's extracurricular activities.

She took her hand back from Andrey's grasp. "If you'll excuse me, I should go and check on Irina." Galina searched the room and found her father deep in conversation with another high ranking member of the *Organizatsiya*. "I believe my father wished to speak with you." She inclined her head in his direction.

"Of course, Miss Sudenko. Again, my condolences."

Galina smiled wickedly at him, an idea forming in her head. It wasn't fair that he got to have all of the fun making her uncomfortable. She stepped to his side, intending to go around him. Konstantin moved back a pace to allow her room, conveniently blocking her from sight for just a moment. As she walked behind Andrey, she ran her hand down his ass, feeling him jerk in surprise. "Good-bye, Mr. Lupesco."

Once she was free of the room, she used her sense of smell to guide her to Irina. Her sister wasn't in the private viewing room, but she was nearby. And Irina was clearly feeling something she hadn't felt in *quite* some time if the scent of arousal was any indication. Who knew that funerals could be hotbeds of inappropriate sexual encounters?

Galina followed the scent to a nearby coat closet and flung open the door. She managed to keep her jaw from hitting the floor, but just barely. Irina and Viktor — *Viktor* — were tangled against the wall of the closet, and her sister wore the look of a woman who'd quite possibly gotten a glimpse of Heaven during an earthshaking orgasm. The smell of sex hung heavy in the air.

"Oh, for the love of fuck," she said as she stepped in and closed the door behind her.

Viktor spun, arms braced around Irina as if protecting her from danger. He growled—actually *growled*—at her! She crossed her arms over her chest and raised one blond eyebrow at the two of them. Things had just gotten *very* interesting.

"You fucking *reek* of him, Rina. What were you thinking? I mean, I don't blame you for hopping on that train, but at your husband's funeral? That's a little tacky. Not to mention there's a fucking werewolf cabal out there who will smell that mess under your dress."

She turned on Viktor, wanting to smack him for being so careless. She didn't care who her sister got her rocks off with, but a large number of people in the next room over would care a great deal. "And *you*, you fucking moron! I know why she's not behaving rationally, but you're supposed to be thinking with something other than your junk."

Viktor looked abashed, glancing over his shoulder at Irina as if he only just fully grasped the danger they'd put themselves in. Galina couldn't help but roll her eyes. At least she tried to be a little circumspect in her dealings with Andrey. "There's a break in the receiving line, go out the back way, get my car and bring it around. I'll take the merry widow here and meet you at the employee exit."

Viktor nodded, then leaned in to press one last kiss to Irina's swollen mouth. Galina smacked his shoulder. "Damn it, cut that out and get out of here, you hormonal dumbass."

Huffing at her, Viktor walked out of the closet. Why didn't he just get a goddamned plane and skywrite that he'd just finger fucked her sister in a coatroom? Dazed, Irina slumped against the wall, trying to pull her clothing back to rights.

"Rocked your world, did he?" Galina asked her.

Irina nodded, still stunned. "Why are we going home?"

Galina adjusted Irina's clothes, pulling everything back in place. She explained again about the werewolves gathered in the next room, preparing to mourn for Irina's dead husband while she'd been getting busy in the closet. When it looked like Irina understood, she draped her sister's arm over her shoulder and opened the door.

The hallway was thankfully empty, so Galina stepped out of the closet, holding Irina up as she walked them toward the exit. She spotted a little blond boy coming out of the area that passed for the private lounge for the family. Pulling a twenty out of her purse, Galina waved it at the kid. "Find Ilya Sudenko and tell him that Galina had to take Irina home because she's taken ill."

The little boy nodded eagerly, snatching the bill out of Galina's hand. "What if I can't remember all of it?" he asked. "Another twenty might help my memory."

"I don't know whether to smack you or hire you, kid," Galina muttered, taking another bill out of her purse and handing it to him. "Now get out of here before I decide to feed those to you."

The boy grinned, tucking the bills into his jacket. He turned and ran down the hall to deliver the message. Galina glanced at Irina, still leaning against her in a daze. "Greedy little Volkov."

Galina pulled into Irina's driveway to find Franny already waiting for them. She'd gotten Irina into her car with little problem, although for a few minutes she thought she might need to pistol whip Viktor with his own gun to get him to leave Irina and clean himself up.

Irina had begun to feel the guilt of her coat closet sexy times on the way home, so it was good that Franny came prepared. While Galina burned her sister's funeral dress — on Irina's order — Franny rolled a massive joint with the ease of long practice.

The flames were burning quite nicely, the dress just ash in the grate. Irina sat beside her on the couch, freshly scrubbed and wearing comfortable clothes. Franny grinned at them over the rolling paper. Galina heartily approved of Irina's friend and her idea to get Irina properly and truly relaxed.

"I don't know if this is a good idea," Irina fretted. "For one thing that was an awfully phallic gesture, so I don't know if I want to smoke your surrogate penis."

"Oh would you just lighten up," Franny told her. "I have been trying to get you to smoke since college. This is going to be funny as hell."

Galina snorted, because she agreed with Franny. It *would* be funny as hell to see Irina finally high. Her sister was wound way too tight, not that she didn't have a reason to be.

Irina glared at her. She said, "I never smoked in college because I had to go home every weekend to my family of werewolves, who will smell this shit from a mile away."

"Oh, just blame it on me," Galina said airily, checking the messages on her voice mail. "Everybody will believe it. Besides, you're thirty years old. If you want to get high, you should be able to get high." She excused herself to make a phone call.

Galina dialed Stepan Pleshenko's number. He was a collector of Estruscan art, on the board of several museums, and a huge mover in the Seattle arts scene. He was also not afraid of acquiring artifacts with questionable provenance. She'd met him when she'd been home last summer. They'd discussed art during the intermission of *Rigoletto*.

As soon as her father had given her the go ahead, she'd put the word out to those art collectors who were known to use black market methods of acquisition. Mr. Pleshenko was the first to contact her.

She made her way to Sergei's old office as she waited for Pleshenko to pick up. "Good afternoon," she greeted when he answered her call. "It's Galina Sudenko, returning your call."

"Ah, Ms. Sudenko! A pleasure to hear from you." He launched into rapid-fire Russian, telling her about his purchase from a local art gallery Galina often frequented.

She closed the door to Sergei's office. The last thing she wanted was to involve Irina in anything else illegal. Bad enough that her sister already dealt in Papa's stolen gemstones. Galina didn't want to drag Irina in any deeper.

"What can I help you with, Mr. Pleshenko?" she asked, speaking Russian as well.

"I have a hole in my collection," he began. "You know how distressing that can be, I'm sure."

"Of course. Can you give me the specifics on what you are looking for?" As he rattled off his wish list, Galina made mental notes. She would put the word out to her contacts who worked in areas with recently discovered historical finds. There were also a few other collectors who might be interested in similar items; she could contact them as well, in case Pleshenko backed out.

She hung up a few minutes later, feeling flush with success. Since crowing from the rooftops wasn't an option, Galina returned to the living room to snag the joint from Franny as it made the rounds. Irina's eyes were already glassy.

She passed the joint to Franny. Pot didn't really hit her like it did regular humans because of her werewolf metabolism. She usually wound up feeling a little sleepy, and that was if she felt anything at all.

Franny slid a nine-by-thirteen pan of chocolate frosted brownies across the table. "And because I know that we're dealing with varying metabolisms, I brought special brownies for milady."

"Are these what I hope they are?" Franny would know to make it with twice the normal amount of hash oil to counter Galina's high metabolism.

Two hours later, Galina was on her second order from Hunan Palace. Having demolished the entire pan of brownies, she'd begun suffering the werewolf version of the munchies. So she'd called the Palace and ordered everything on Column A to be rush delivered to Irina's house. She'd polished it all off in much the same way that typhoons destroyed coastal villages, not sharing a single grain of rice for the others. Then she called to order everything on Column B.

Galina met Nik at the door as she accepted the second load of bags from the delivery guy. He was pulling off his tie and looked like he hadn't slept in three days. He eyed the bags with hunger as Galina began unloading the cartons on the kitchen island, and said, "Papa sent me to check on you. I'm starving."

When Nik tried to grab a crystal prawn from one of the little paper cartons, Galina snatched it out of his grasp with a throaty growl.

He raised his eyebrows and rubbed at his hand in mock hurt. "You're not going to share?"

Galina shoveled a forkful of beef and broccoli into her mouth. "I ate an entire pan of Franny's pot brownies," she said around her mouthful of food. "I'm hungry."

Nik sniffed, his sensitive nose picking up the burning tar aroma. "There were special brownies?" Galina nodded. "And you didn't save me any?" Again she nodded. "You bitch."

"Not sorry," she said with a grin.

Galina gathered up as many of the cartons as she could reasonably carry and followed her brother into the living room. Nik wrapped his arms around Irina, who was plowing through a bag of nacho cheese Doritos and a piece of chocolate bobka. "Wow, you smell like weed," Nik said, nose wrinkling. "A lot of weed."

"I got a lot high," Irina said with a lazy grin. "It was Galina and Franny's idea. They are a very bad influence on me. Always have been."

"And we're not even sorry," Franny said, echoing Galina's earlier statement. She continued smearing peanut butter all over an Oreo.

The doorbell rang. Everyone looked at Galina. She shrugged. "I don't think I ordered anything else. Maybe the delivery guy forgot something."

She dragged herself off the couch, taking a carton of food in each hand. Before she left, she speared her brother with a look. "If you so much as touch a bite of my lo mein, you will draw back a nub."

She padded to the door, upending one of the cartons of fried rice to get another mouthful before answering it. Konstantin stood on the front step holding what was, quite possibly, the largest floral arrangement ever created by human hands. Galina stared at him for a moment, then turned up the other carton into her mouth.

"Mr. Lupesco sends these for Mrs. Volkov." Konstantin stood there awkwardly, obviously waiting for something.

Galina chewed absently. He had that same leashed power that Andrey had, but he was wearing the most amazingly tailored suit she'd ever seen. His dark hair was neatly trimmed, his designer shoes polished to a high shine. Everything about him was calm and neat except his brown eyes. There was a wildness in them that reminded her very much of Andrey. When he just kept standing there, she raised her brows and said, "What?"

"Can I come in and put these down?" He watched her strangely.

"Oh, yeah. Sure." She held the door wide so he could get the floral monstrosity inside. "Just put it in the kitchen, I guess." Galina lifted a carton to her mouth again and followed him.

Nik met them in the hallway. "I was just coming to see what was taking so long," he said, then caught sight of the flowers. "Christ, who sent the flower shop?"

"That would be Andrey Lupesco." She took the giant vase of lilies, orchids, and various other heavily scented blooms from Konstantin and placed them on Irina's kitchen table. When she turned back to her brother, she found him staring unabashedly at Andrey's bodyguard. She ducked her head to hide a smile. Her brother didn't usually stare so openly, but it had been a strange day.

"Nik, this is Konstantin. He works for Mr. Lupesco." She crossed to her brother so she could gauge Konstantin's reaction.

Nik put his hand out and the two shook. Nik was more relaxed than he was normally, probably due to Franny's kind bud. Konstantin's brown eyes lit up when their hands touched and the two men stared at each other for several very long seconds. Galina was beginning to wonder if she was going to have to get the jaws of life to pry their hands apart, when Nik abruptly let go.

"Hey, Irina," he called, a nervous edge to his voice. "You got some flowers."

Galina raised her eyebrows. Very interesting. Her brother was hardly ever flustered. He was now. Being gay in a family and organization that prized masculinity above all else wasn't something you wanted to become public knowledge, and Nik was careful to make sure nary a whiff of his sexual orientation was discovered. If you didn't know Nikolai, you'd never know it, but Galina knew her brother very well.

Irina arrived in the kitchen, her eyes a little glazed. "Holy shit," she said when she spotted the arrangement that towered atop her kitchen table. "Well, if there's a lily shortage along the western seaboard, we know why." Then she realized that Konstantin was standing there, looking at all of them like they were escapees from a mental institution.

"They're from Andrey Lupesco," Galina helpfully supplied, enjoying the awkwardness of the situation probably more than she should.

Irina straightened her Seahawks jersey and yoga pants. "Please send Mr. Lupesco my thanks. The flowers are lovely."

"He's sorry he missed the opportunity to speak to you at the funeral. He was hoping to pass on his condolences personally." Konstantin's eyes skipped over to Galina. She raised a Chinese food carton as if toasting him and then shoved the remaining food in her mouth with a pair of chopsticks. She saw his lips twitch as he tried to hold back a smile. She could only imagine what this scene looked like to an outsider.

"I'll be going," he said as a way of making his escape. "Mrs. Volkov. Miss Sudenko." He inclined his head to Galina. She waved her fingers at him. "Mrs. Volkov's friend."

Konstantin took a step closer to Nikolai and held out his hand. "Mr. Sudenko."

Nik looked around the room, as if he didn't know what to do. "Call me Nik," he finally said, taking Konstantin's hand and shaking it.

"I'll see you out," Galina interrupted, curious about something. She wanted to get Konstantin away from all of the competing scents in the kitchen. She waited for Nik to release his hand, then led the bodyguard back to the front door.

She opened it wide, following him out to the front step. The air was clear here, uncluttered by the stink of pot smoke and lilies.

Galina sniffed lightly, not wanting to make Konstantin aware that she was trying to get a scent-read off of him. What she smelled made her smile. "Tell Mr. Lupesco thanks again," was all she said as she walked him to his car.

"You can be sure I'll tell him," Konstantin replied, looking like he was fighting to keep from laughing.

She waited until he turned out of Irina's driveway before running back into the house. The others had gathered around what food remained from Galina's Column B order and were scarfing it down as quickly as possible. She couldn't even find it in her to be mad.

"He *likes* you!" she shouted at Nik, who was cleaning the meat from the bones of a tin of Chinese spareribs.

"What are you talking about?" Irina asked, dusting Dorito crumbs from her T-shirt.

Galina whooped, grabbing Nikolai and giving him a huge hug. "Konstantin." She grinned up at her brother. "He totally has the hots for Nik!"

"How can you possibly know that?" Franny asked, popping a shrimp into her mouth.

Galina looked at Nik. He was staring at her, a gobsmacked expression on his face. A rib hung forgotten in his fingers. She plucked it out of his slack grip and cleaned it of meat in one smooth motion. "Oh, these are really good." She turned back to Franny. "I smelled it on him."

Nik stood up, wiping his mouth with a napkin and licking the barbeque sauce from his fingers. "I'll see you guys tomorrow." He dropped the napkin into an empty carton and grabbed his jacket from the end of the couch.

Galina shared a confused look with Irina, then went after their brother. "Hey, what's the matter?" she said as she caught up with him at the door. "I thought you'd be happy about it."

"We're not having this conversation," he said, pulling the door open.

Galina put her hand out, pushing the door closed. "Why not?" She met her brother's dark eyes. "Nik, this is a good thing!"

He put his large hand over hers, a small, sad smile on his face. "How is it a good thing, Galya? I can't see him publicly. He works for the head of a competing family. If I were going to pick someone to be with, he'd be at the bottom of my list."

Galina pulled her hand out from under his. She knew why he couldn't go public with Konstantin, and she wasn't suggesting that he do so. It was kind of like the way things had to be with her and Andrey. But that didn't mean he couldn't have a little fun. "Do you not like him?"

"I don't know him. But it's not about whether I do or don't like him. I'm the son of Ilya Sudenko. It's just not something I can do." He leaned down and gave Galina a light kiss on the cheek, and then disappeared out the front door.

When Galina returned to the kitchen, she threw up her hands and rolled her eyes. "Our brother is a stubborn horse's ass…wolf's ass…mule."

Franny emptied the last of the shrimp carton into her mouth. "Okay, now you're just naming random animals."

10

Sex Bomb at the Black Swan

Galina pulled into the parking lot of the Black Swan Inn and stepped out of the car. The meeting at Papa's house hadn't been productive and Galina couldn't help wondering if it had been because she'd been seated at the table. She imagined it had made some people uncomfortable.

Too bad. They may as well get used to the idea of her. She was there to stay.

Predictably, Alexei shunned her as if she was a plague carrier. Her reception by the other leaders was lukewarm. At best. The Volkov representative seemed confused by her presence, but she didn't expect much from a family that was neither bright nor particularly bold. They preferred the status quo to anything that required effort. The head of the Oniayev family eyed her cautiously. They would wait for everyone else to decide if they accepted her or not before throwing in with the winning side. The Demensky family representative welcomed her, if not warmly, then at least without immediate derision.

Support had come from Andrey. While not overly warm, he was polite and civil, allowing her to express her opinions and giving her thoughts consideration as if she were an equal. He didn't have to do that and she hoped it wasn't just because she'd given him a stellar blowjob.

At least Maksim hadn't been invited. He was still considered an outsider. Galina wondered what would happen if she did have to marry him. Would she be cut out of the business entirely, even the art smuggling line that she had started? Or would Maksim be given a spot in the Organization? She couldn't decide which would be worse.

Now that the funeral for Sergei was over, Galina had some headspace to think about the circumstances of his death. She hadn't yet had a chance to examine the scene of the shooting. Everything had been so crazy after Sergei was taken away, and she'd wanted to get to Irina at the hospital. Now that the crime scene tape was gone, she wanted to poke around to see if she could find any clues to who might have been behind it. She didn't expect to find any scents, certainly not at this late date.

But things weren't adding up. No one had heard about a hit, there was no one moving in on Sudenko territory, and none of the usual bravos were bragging. The only one who had a problem with Sergei, at least as far as Galina knew, was the man she was hooking up with behind her family's backs. He certainly could have ordered a hit, but the timing was off. Why assassinate a man you've just beaten to a pulp?

The police had questioned everyone at the scene. She'd given them a statement when they'd come by to question Irina again. No one had seen anything other than the color of the car. The police had no leads, and even if they'd been able to come up with anything, Galina was certain that her father and the other leaders would block anything from coming to light. A random murder involving silver bullets? That was a good way to start tongues wagging and garner attention none of them wanted.

She studied the tire marks, tracking the car's progress by the tracks. Lining up with where the shooter must have first fired.

"Galina." Andrey's voice sounded behind her.

She turned from her study of the scene of the shooting, arms crossed over her chest. "What are you doing here?"

"I followed you from your father's house." He stopped several feet from her. "What are *you* doing here?"

"That doesn't sound stalkery at all." She narrowed green eyes at him.

"Galya." The sternness in his voice sent a thrill through the core of her.

"Andrey." They stared at each other for several minutes. When the silence became too great, she said, "And now that we've proven that we know each other's names, are we going to stop with the staring contest?"

"Are you going to answer my question?" He took a step toward her, running a hand through his hair in frustration.

Not deigning to answer, she presented him with her back. Rude, perhaps, but she didn't have time for this. She'd managed to ditch her security detail, but she didn't know for how long. When she left her father's house after the meeting, Andrey, as well as the other heads of the families were still talking to Papa. She'd wanted some time alone at the Black Swan.

She felt Andrey approach, looming over her shoulder. His voice was soft, but there was a threatening edge to it. Instead of scaring Galina, it sent a shiver of desire down her spine. She clenched her thighs, feeling heat pool in her belly. It was obscene how easily he turned her on.

"I'll tell you what I think." His breath was a blast of heat against her neck. "I think you're sticking your nose in something dangerous. I think you're out here, trying to track down Sergei's killer." His hand snaked around her waist and he inhaled into her hair. "And I think you could get yourself into serious trouble if you're not careful."

Galina spun, breaking away from him, a sliver of fear sliding through her. Had he just threatened her? "Duly noted." She began to climb the stairs to the entrance of the Inn. "But I have work to do."

She walked past the front desk and into the bar. There were only a few customers scattered around the room, nursing their drinks. As she approached the bar, she saw the lone cocktail waitress adjusting the short black skirt she wore that barely covered her ass.

Galina stopped. It was the same waitress who had left with Sergei at the party. Same heart-shaped face, same black hair, same doe eyes. She was, at most, twenty years old. Taking a seat, Galina waved the young woman over. The waitress sauntered to the table, a worried frown on her pretty face. Taking a fifty out of her wallet, Galina gestured for the other woman to sit.

"You were working a party here—a Sweet Sixteen birthday party maybe five days ago. Do you remember?" Galina caught and held the waitress's eyes with her own. The woman nodded reluctantly. "Do you remember the man who went outside with you?"

The woman's eyes widened. She moved to get up, but Galina caught her wrist, squeezing it tightly. The waitress blanched and sat back down. "Yeah."

Galina released her wrist and subsided back into her seat. "You're not in trouble. I just want you to tell me the truth." She paused and waited for the woman across from her to nod. "So you remember the guy, right? Did he say anything to you?"

The waitress shook her head. "Not really. I was told to find the guy and get him to go outside with me. That's all."

Galina sat up straighter. "You were told? Who told you?"

"Just some guy. Tall. Dark hair. Hot. He gave me a hundred bucks to get the guy alone." Her hands twisted around each other on top of the scarred wooden table.

"Anything else you can tell me about him?" Galina leaned forward slightly.

The waitress's eyes widened. "If you turn around, he just walked in."

Galina did so, her heart sinking. Andrey stood at the threshold of the bar, glaring at her. "Him?"

"Yeah." The waitress stood. "He gave me the money and told me to get the guy alone. So I did and then I came back inside." She looked nervously at where Andrey still stood. "Can I go now?"

Galina nodded, feeling a churning in her gut. The timeline still didn't add up, but Andrey had threatened Sergei. And Sergei had stolen something from him. Would he have been angry enough to call in a hit? How would he get it done so fast? And what was he doing, hanging around with her if he had?

She got up, intending to walk out the other side of the bar. She stepped into the hallway, moving quickly, but Andrey caught up to her in two steps. "Galina, wait." He tried to put his hand on her arm, but she brushed him off.

"No." Galina didn't want to be there anymore. She wanted some space to think.

"Damn it," Andrey cursed. He grabbed her upper arm and half-walked, half-pushed her toward the elevators. He pushed the up button, hustling her into it when the doors opened.

"I'm going to talk. And you're going to listen," he warned, scowling at her. His eyes snapped blue sparks as his brows lowered in a fierce frown.

"Oh yes," Galina snapped, yanking her arm away from him and putting her back to the wall. "Because shoving me into an elevator and ignoring what I want is a great way to get me to do that."

"I swear to God, Galina," he began, then stopped when the doors slid open. He took her by the arm again, leading her to a room. He stuck the key card into the reader, then pushed open the door.

She stalked inside, torn between anger and curiosity. She did want to hear what Andrey had to say, but she did not approve of his methods. "If you ever touch me like that again, I'll make sure you never have to worry about laying hands on a woman because you won't have them." Her words were even and calm, but the undercurrent of rage was plain to hear.

Andrey closed the door and tucked the key card into his jacket pocket. "I didn't kill Sergei."

"I never said you did." Galina walked farther in the room, keeping well clear of the king size bed that dominated much of the space.

"You're thinking it." Andrey ran a hand through his hair once again. Galina recognized this was his tell when he was frustrated. She was inordinately pleased that she had gotten to him.

"No, I'm not thinking you killed him." She swept a piece of her long blond hair behind her ear. "I'm wondering if you hired someone to *have* him killed. Completely different things." Galina smiled at him. She wasn't worried that he'd hurt her, not if he wanted to stay on the good side of the Sudenko family.

Andrey made a noise that was part sigh and part growl. He crossed the room in three quick strides to stop so close to her that she could feel the heat coming off him. "You are the most infuriating woman I have ever met!"

"And I'm pretty cute too."

She was pretty sure that Andrey was *this* close to a face palm. She couldn't help herself. He smelled absolutely delectable when he was angry.

"If I swear to you that I was in no way responsible for Sergei's death, will you believe me?" His blue eyes locked with hers.

Galina tuned her senses to him. His heart beat was steady, no spike to indicate he was lying. His scent was the same spicy-pine scent that she liked. It had no sour tang that came when someone lied. And he met her eyes, not blinking, holding hers. "I believe you."

"Good," he said. Before she could think, he'd taken her upper arms and pulled her to him, his mouth covering hers in a bruising kiss.

Galina felt her insides ignite when her lips met his. Blazing heat curled around her pelvis, skimming across her nerves. Her mouth opened beneath his, lips parting to allow his tongue to meet with hers. He tasted like the bourbon he'd had in the meeting at her father's house. She sucked at his tongue, lightly scraping it with her teeth.

His mouth left hers only to trail down her throat, nuzzling as he went. Galina let her head fall back, closing her eyes so she could revel in the sensations of wet heat. He nudged away the collar of her blouse to continue to trace his lips and tongue along her collarbone. She made a thin noise in the back of her throat when his teeth closed over the flesh and bone there, worrying it lightly. The smell of her arousal hit her nose, a heady scent when combined with his.

Andrey slipped off his jacket and threw it on a nearby chair, then kissed her again. This kiss was harsh, powerful, all heat and need. He sucked her tongue into his mouth, his own stroking it. Galina felt her pussy clench and release, throbbing with want.

Her hands traced the line of his shoulders. She worked at loosening his tie, their mouths still connected as they both fumbled with each other's clothes like they were inexperienced teenagers. All Galina wanted was to feel his naked flesh pressed against hers, his cock inside of her making her feel full.

Andrey broke off their kiss to yank his tie over his head. Galina unbuttoned his shirt, yanking it down off his shoulders as soon as she had it free. A leather necklace with a series of charms rested against his skin. His chest was taut muscle and smooth flesh with a dusting of dark hair. She lowered her mouth to his nipple, swirling her tongue around the peak.

His hands clenched in her hair. "Galya," he whispered in a hoarse voice.

She loved that sound. She wanted to hear his voice break in pleasure. It sent a pulsing deep inside of her. She sucked hard on his nipple feeling it stiffen even further in her mouth, before scraping her teeth across it. He hissed, pulling her head up and away from his flesh.

Claiming her mouth, Andrey's fingers went to work on the buttons of her blouse. He cursed when the cloth coverings made unbuttoning them difficult.

"Rip it," Galina said against his mouth.

Andrey's head drew back. "You sure?" His blue eyes were hooded and sleepy looking with lust.

"Rip the fucking shirt," she growled, wanting his hands on her and not caring about fabric at a time like this. She could buy another shirt. What she did not have was him inside of her.

His big hands grabbed the lapels of her blouse and yanked, tearing the fabric as if it were newspaper. Galina shrugged out of the sleeves, dropping the scraps of cloth that used to be a shirt to the floor. Her panties were soaked as the heat inside of her threatened to combust.

She wriggled out of the camisole top and stood before him in bra and pants. Andrey's gaze slid across her, so intense she could almost feel it, like a caress. They stared at each other for a moment, then Andrey reached out, pulling her bra strap down and pressing a kiss to the top of her shoulder.

"You are gorgeous." He lapped at the hollow of her shoulder.

She reached for his belt, but he stopped her hands. Instead, he undid the button and zipper on her pants, pushing them down to pool around her feet. She slid her feet out of her heels and then Andrey was lifting her out of her clothes, his hands wrapping around her waist. He placed her down next to the bed, pulling her against his body.

"Andrey," she whispered, looking up at him, wondering what he was thinking.

He brushed his lips against hers. Galina tried to drag his head down to deepen the kiss, but he pulled her arms away. Then he dropped to his knees. He pressed his face to her mound, pulling her panties aside with one finger. He inhaled deeply. "God damn, I love the way you smell."

Galina throbbed with want. She didn't know what she wanted more, his mouth on her or his cock inside her. All she knew was that she thought she might die if he didn't hurry it up and fuck her properly. Every touch of his lips, his hands, his tongue was making the tension at the base of her spine ratchet up another notch. She was fairly certain her head might pop off if he didn't make her come soon.

His fingertips skimmed up to her hip, tugging at the string of her panties. His mouth followed the same path on the opposite leg, stopping when he reached the string on that side. Slowly he began to drag the lacey cloth down her body, using his teeth and fingers.

Galina inhaled sharply, wondering if it were possible to spontaneously combust from lust.

When he reached her feet, Andrey looked up at her, grinning around the waistband of the black lace panties caught in his teeth. Galina's breath caught in her throat. The look he was giving her was so…wicked. She felt her pussy throb in response and moaned low in the back of her throat.

"Andrey." Her words strangled in her throat.

He surged up, pressing his mouth to her mound, his clever tongue spearing her. She cried out, clutching at his shoulders, back arching as he licked and teased her overheated flesh. "Oh God," she whispered, digging her fingers into his back, not caring if she drew blood.

Stopping what he was doing, Andrey stood until he was nose to nose with her. "God has nothing to with it," he murmured, his voice like dark thunder. Then he picked her up and threw her on the bed.

Galina licked her lips as she watched him undress. He was beautiful, all sleek flesh and lean muscle, dark hair and smoky blue eyes that pierced her to the core. Andrey stood before her, his naked body glowing in the filtered golden light from the window. Galina's eyes devoured him, wanting to commit every part of him to memory. Her eyes lingered on his cock, wanting to feel it inside of her. He pulled a condom from his pants, unwrapped the foil pack and rolled it over his erection. Galina watched in fascination, tongue swiping over her bottom lip.

He climbed on the bed, crawling up her body slowly, kissing as he went. He lapped at her stomach, tongue swirling around her belly button. She dug her hands in his hair, trying to yank his head up to hers, but he would have none of it. He continued to take his time, his hand spanning her ribs as he worked his way up to her bra.

He nosed first one breast and then the other, nuzzling her through the lace cups. Galina felt the heat and wetness between her thighs and didn't know whether to weep or scream in triumph when one of his fingers finally entered her. She writhed on his hand, urging him to get on with it. Andrey chuckled, biting at her nipple through the fabric and she cried out with longing. She clenched around his finger, arching into his mouth.

"Does this feel good?" he whispered, laughter in his voice.

"You know damn well it does," she answered, alive with sensation and want.

He slid another finger inside her and moved them over her g-spot. Instantly she was arching off the bed, vision whiting out as waves of pleasure crashed over her.

"How about this?"

"Son of a…" She trailed off into a moan as the pleasure spiked deep within her, twisting up through her core and rising through her spine. She gasped as the pressure built. Her legs tightened around his hand.

"That's not very nice," he admonished, biting down a bit harder on her other nipple. She cried out, bucking up into his mouth again.

He pulled his fingers out of her, licking the taste of her from them. Galina tried to push herself up on her elbows, but Andrey pushed her back down. He moved against her, the head of his cock teasing against her entrance. She dropped her head back, trying to move onto him, but he held her still. He ghosted inside her, the very tip of him entering her before he pulled out again.

She hit his shoulder and growled at him. "Fuck me properly already."

He grinned at her, hips thrusting so that he sheathed himself deep in one stroke. Galina shouted in pleasure at the stretch, the feeling of fullness deep inside of her. Andrey lifted one of her legs to the top of his shoulder, sliding in even deeper.

His hands found hers, lifting them up to the pillows at her head. Twining his fingers through hers, he set the rhythm, his hips pumping against hers as they moved together. "Andrey," she gasped, unsure what it was she wanted to say, only knowing that this was possibly the best sex she'd had in her life. There was something in him that called to her, that attuned her to his body.

He buried his head into her neck, forcing her leg even higher, driving deeper into her. "Galya. Beautiful, Galya."

She squeezed his hands, moving her hips to meet his thrusts, wanting everything he could give her. She felt like she'd never get enough of him: his lips, the feel of his skin against hers, the smooth hardness of his cock inside of her. As she shifted her hips, she made sure that her clit made contact with his roughness. She felt the heat inside her move like lava, filling her limbs with fire as she rushed toward her peak.

His hips moved faster, slamming into her, drawing cries from her with every stroke. Galina twisted on the bed, close now, so close that she wanted to scream. Andrey made her feel amazing, like she was going to erupt into flame like a phoenix until she was consumed and burned to ash.

Andrey lifted his head with a groan, thrusting even faster as his climax approached. His eyes were an amazing blue, and Galina leaned up to claim his mouth. Her tongue fought with his and then she had to wrench her mouth from his as her climax hit her with the force of a cruise missile. His hands clenched around hers as she thrashed, her body shuddering as everything turned to heat and light inside her. It rolled through her in waves as the muscles in her body tightened and released and tightened again with the force of it.

Crying out with her, Andrey increased his pace, pounding into her as he sought his own release. He gave one final thrust that sent her senses reeling, then he came with a hoarse shout. He fell forward on top of her, panting out as his hips slowed, then stopped.

Galina smiled, removing one of her hands from Andrey's grasp so she could comb fingers through his dark hair. He was so beautiful, a study in contrasts: dark, crisp hair, smooth skin, pale blue eyes like cut gems. She heard him rumble sleepily against her chest, then his head lifted so he could look at her.

"Did that meet with your qualifications for a proper fucking, then?" His lips quirked into a satisfied grin.

She stretched, feeling him slip from her. "It was…adequate," she replied, mouthing at his chin.

He rolled off of her enough to remove the condom and deposit in the wastebasket by the bed, then moved back so he lay next to her. Galina turned so they were facing each other. "Only adequate?" He pulled her over to him so they were flush against each other. "I'll have to try harder next time." His hands slid down the small of her back, fingers digging in to the muscles there.

Galina sighed, relaxing into his body. Already looking forward to next time, she rubbed her palms across his chest, lightly scoring it with her fingernails. She plucked at his necklace.

"What do all these mean?" she asked, touching each charm one by one.

Picking one up, he held it so she could get a better look at it. "They are Romani charms. This one wards off the evil eye." He dropped that one and took up another. "This one brings good luck." Another. "This one diminishes bad luck." Another. "Protection."

She touched the protection charm. "Do they work?"

"I'm still alive." He brushed a strand of hair from her face. Andrey breathed in, then ducked his head to her neck. "I love the smell of me all over you."

She laughed, relaxed and sated for what felt like the first time in ages. She would get up and leave in a few minutes, but for right now she was content to lie beside Andrey and enjoy the feel of his body against hers.

He trailed kisses up her neck, stopping to nip at the sensitive place just behind her ear. Galina felt her toes curl and heat flared once more inside her. "Mmmmmm," she hummed, bone deep pleasure making her lazy and slow.

"Do you plan to tell me what you hoped to find out here?" His voice was low, almost a purr that sank deep into her spine.

"Aside from your bribery of a waitress so you could hand Sergei his ass — which thank you, by the way — I got a great picture of him after you were done. I didn't find much." She pulled away so she could watch his expression. "So you didn't order the hit on Sergei. I believe you." Galina rested her hands on his shoulders, brushing at the stiff hair at the nape of his neck. "What shipment did he take from you?"

Andrey went still beneath her hands. His dark brows drew down and his generous mouth turned down in a frown. "It's not your concern, Galina."

At his words, she rolled out of his arms, climbing out of bed. Andrey made a grab for her. "Where are you going?"

"It's pretty obvious I'm leaving. Has the blood flow to your brain not resumed?" She rummaged on the floor, finding her still wet panties and pulling them on.

Andrey got out of bed and snatched her pants. Galina tried not to admire his body, but she wasn't made of stone. "I would like my pants back, please." She held her hand out for them.

"Not until we finish talking."

"You just said it wasn't my concern. I don't see what else there is for us to talk about." She kept her hand out, this time making the gimme motion.

"Why are you always so difficult?" He stood there, radiating affront, holding her pants.

"It's my default setting. Pants. Now."

"No."

"Fine." She scooped up her camisole and shrugged into it, then snagged his blazer and threw that on. It wasn't great, but it was better than walking out in just her Agent Provocateur underwear.

"You are *not* leaving like that." Andrey's voice had dropped to an angry rumble.

"You bet your fine ass I am," she said, pulling on her heels. "And I'm sure no one will notice that I look like a sex bomb went off in my vicinity as I walk to my car *sans* pants wearing only a *man's* jacket. I'm sure that won't make it back to my father *at all*." She strode to the door, snatching her purse as she went.

Galina thought she heard Andrey say *fuck* under his breath, but she didn't stop. She could probably make it to her car without attracting too much attention. The blazer at least covered up all the important parts.

"It was Bullet." Galina froze where she was at Andrey's words. "The shipment was Bullet."

She turned on her heel slowly, letting his words sink in. "Sergei ripped off a shipment of Bullet?" At Andrey's slight nod, she shook her head. "That man was the dumbest man in all of Dumbonia."

Andrey cracked a smile at her turn of phrase, despite looking like he'd just swallowed a porcupine. Bullet was the street name of a powerful stimulant for werewolves, its effects akin to what cocaine did to humans. Galina had heard of it, though she never had any desire to try it herself. Bullet was a designer drug specifically created for werewolves after ordinary street drugs caused a number of unfortunate public "incidents." The heightened were-metabolism had interacted strangely with human stimulants, processing the drugs too quickly and causing violent and unpredictable behavior. Some enterprising souls decided to capitalize on this turn of events and developed a special drug — Silver Bullet. It had been steadily released into the streets for the past six months or so.

With Andrey controlling the distribution of the drug into Seattle it was no wonder why Alexei and Sergei would want to break off a piece of that action for themselves. It explained a great deal of Andrey's seemingly meteoric rise within the Rom's organization, as well as his high standing with her father.

And Sergei had decided to shit on it. Thank God the man was dead or she would have killed him herself.

She thought quickly. If she could find where Sergei stashed the drugs and return them to Andrey, it would be a huge help in securing a place at the ruling table. She'd be in good with the Rom and she would have saved face for Papa before he was even aware that there was a problem. Galina was sure she could accomplish it, so long as she was careful and Alexei didn't get wind of what she was after.

Galina met Andrey's eyes, serious now. "What if I can find out what Sergei did with the Bullet? *Without* involving my father. Would you support my request for a permanent place as my father's right hand?"

Andrey's face grew thoughtful. She could see him assessing her and the possibility of her succeeding. She would have felt better if she'd been fully dressed. She might not be projecting the proper image of professionalism, but since he was the one who'd contributed to her current state, he'd have to give her a pass.

His gaze raked her up and down, as if he were having similar thoughts. He shook his head, as if he were arguing with himself. Finally he seemed to come to a decision. "If you can do it, then yes. I'll back you."

Galina tried not to wilt in relief. She held out her hand so they could shake on it. Andrey took it. "Excellent," she said. "But if you want your drugs back, I'm going to need my pants."

II

Woman Who Runs with the Wolves

Galina had noticed the white panel van following her for the past two days. She'd been able to pick out a tail since she was eight years old. The van was too new, too obvious. It wasn't Seattle PD, which meant it was probably FBI. A redheaded woman in her late thirties usually manned the driver's seat, while a blond man sat in the passenger side, usually hiding a long-lens camera where he thought she couldn't see. She'd gotten close enough to them to get a scent-read just so she would know if they were nearby.

It made getting in touch with her growing list of clients a bit more difficult, but avoiding the law and covering tracks was second nature to a Sudenko. She used burner phones and messenger services to communicate to her buyers. She kept to her schedule so that nothing would seem out of the ordinary. She went to work, to Irina's house since her sister wasn't allowed out because of the traditional seclusion required by widows, and back to her condo. She'd gotten approval from her father to hold her buys at his compound for the security of her clients.

It did make searching for Andrey's stolen shipment more difficult. Galina had searched the docks, and all of Sergei's known warehouses. And after Irina had found an old message about a shipment in Sergei's office, Galina had gone through their house and garage. She'd found nothing in his hiding places but cash.

She still needed to speak to Sergei's old crew, check the boat slips, and go over his car, but she was afraid those would come up empty too. Which meant he'd probably already handed off the product to his boss. And searching Alexei's place was going to be impossible.

Galina tried not to think about any of that as she walked Mr. Pleshenko to the door of Papa's house, warmly shaking his hand. She'd secured a bust from the Estruscan period to fill the gap in his collection. She'd made delivery arrangements through her gallery — she was a silent partner — and Pleshenko had just paid her for the piece. Half a million dollars in cash sat in a case on her father's desk. Papa had been very pleased with her work.

"Thank you again, Mr. Pleshenko," she said as she held the door open for him. "And if I happen across anything else you might be interested in seeing, I will be sure to let you know." Galina put a hand on his arm. "I hope I'll see you at the museum's donors' ball. I've arranged a private showing of several visiting pieces for those interested."

"Wouldn't miss it, my dear," he replied, patting her arm. He was pleased with the bust and the price he'd paid. The piece would be installed in his private gallery next week. Galina was going to oversee it herself. Just one more service she offered to her clients. "You have an exquisite eye."

"Thank you." She gestured to one of her father's guards on the porch to see Pleshenko to his car. When he was safely on his way down the drive, Galina shut the door, allowing herself a brief victory shimmy. Her first real deal was done!

Wandering into the front parlor, she poured herself a club soda. She heard voices from the hallway. Her father poked his head into the room, smiling broadly when he saw her standing in front of the windows.

"Galya!" he said, as if he was surprised to see her.

Her eyes narrowed. Papa had known of her meeting with Mr. Pleshenko, so why wouldn't he expect to see her here? Galina got her answer when Maksim Federov stepped into the room.

"I was just telling Maksim," her father continued, as if he hadn't planned to ambush her all along, "that we have excellent trails on the property if he was interested in going for a run. It can be hard for a wolf in the city, no?" Papa laughed, clapping Maksim on the shoulder with a heavy paw.

"I was hoping that Miss Sudenko would show me these trails," Maksim said, his gaze settling on her chest. "It has been a long time since I was able to run as I was meant to."

Setting her glass down, Galina crossed her arms over the objects of Maksim's attention. Usually she didn't mind being admired, but there was just something a touch creepy about his regard. He made her feel like she was nothing more than a body, only there to serve and entertain him.

Andrey never made her feel that way.

"Of course she will!" Papa answered for her. He took each of their elbows and led them to the front door. "Go, while it isn't raining."

Galina sighed. No way around it then, although she was glad to be able to shift in relative safety. She hadn't gotten much chance to run in wolf form; it was one of the drawbacks of living downtown. And now that she had the FBI watching her, Papa's house was the only really safe place to do it. Unfortunately there was a downside to Papa's house.

"If you see Alexei, tell him that I need to speak with him," her father called as they made their way across the lawn.

Galina waved to acknowledge she'd heard him, then led Maksim to the woods that bordered the house. Her father had carved out running trails for Irina years ago, but they all enjoyed using them in either form. "How often do you get to transform when you are at home?" she asked, just to have something to say.

Maksim looked at the trees, his generous mouth pulling down in distaste. "Whenever we want. We are not bound by the city or the government."

Galina gritted her teeth. She got it, she really did. Nothing compared to Mother Russia. Did he have to be such a twit about everything? Surely there was something to his liking in Seattle. "That must be nice," she answered.

As they approached the woods, she saw Alexei, Timur, and Vasily walking from the back side of the property. She cocked her head. There was nothing back there except the potting shed and the old guest house. What would they be doing out there? "Alexei!"

He ignored her. Opening her mouth to shout again, Maksim interrupted. "Alexei, your father wishes to speak with you!"

Turning to look at her escort, she saw that Maksim seemed eager to join her brother. When Alexei raised his hand in greeting, a huge smile split Maksim's face. He'd never looked that happy to see her before.

"We are going for a run," he yelled to her brother. "Come join us!"

Galina stared, at a loss for words. He liked Alexei? Maksim's head was thrown back and there was more of a swagger to his step. She wanted to smack him. Of course, he liked Alexei; her brother was every hotheaded young idiot's spirit animal. He was reckless, violent, and powerful. Maksim watched him with something close to adoration in his eyes.

"After I speak with my father," Alexei said, continuing on his way to the house.

Maksim's face fell, but he soldiered on gamely. Galina felt sorry for him for a moment, until he said, "You are lucky to have a brother like him."

She made a noncommittal noise. This would be a short run. She didn't want to be out here with Alexei and his two cronies. The less time she spent near him, the better it was for all concerned. And Maksim would appreciate her absence so he could further his bromance.

How on earth did Papa think this was the right man for her? Had he suffered a traumatic brain injury when she wasn't looking?

They entered the copse of trees that Papa had planted when he and Mama had first bought the property. It was a small space of calm beauty, all dappled light and pine scent. Her father had wanted a place where his pack could undress and shift in relatively privacy.

Galina quickly stripped, placing her clothes on one of the teak benches placed in a loose semicircle around the glade. When she turned back, Maksim was staring at her naked body, a flush rising in his cheeks. That wasn't the only thing that was rising, if the tent in his pants gave her something to go by. She triggered her change into a large white wolf, and then sat waiting for Maksim to pull himself together.

He undressed and transformed. He was umber colored in wolf form, with dark yellow eyes that glowed like amber. Maksim was smaller than she was, with less mass in his chest and haunches. He eyed her critically, as if the fact that she was larger offended him.

With a yip, she took off, pounding down the path that led deeper into the woods. Galina loved running. Wolves were built for it, able to cover many miles without needing to stop for rest. She heard Maksim scrambling to catch up to her. Slowing her pace to a lope, she turned her head to watch him run beside her.

He pulled ahead as soon as she slowed to wait for him. Galina caught up quickly, earning a snap and snarl from Maksim. She growled, hackles rising. Did he really expect her to run behind him? That was ridiculous! Putting on a burst of speed, Galina passed Maksim, swishing her tail as she passed him. She heard him snarl again, but then she was sprinting, enjoying the feel of wind rippling through her fur. Maksim could be mad at her later.

She left the trail proper, crashing through the underbrush to go deeper into the trees. The smell of wet earth and green growth filled her nose. Her paws thudded into the ground as she ran, knowing where she was even as she left the beaten path. She knew every inch of these woods. This was her second home.

A chorus of howls made her stop in her tracks. She'd recognized Alexei's wolf voice raised in a hunting call, along with those of his men. An answering howl rose from somewhere close by. Maksim.

Fear gripped Galina with icy hands. There was only one thing they could be hunting out here since Papa didn't have other animals roaming his property: her.

She heard bodies crashing through the trees as the other wolves caught her scent. Galina ran, planning on heading directly back to the house, but she realized that one of the other wolves was running parallel to her, blocking her flight.

Galina altered her course to go deeper into the woods where the trees were denser. It meant she couldn't move as quickly, but the same held true for her brother and his enforcers. She hoped to double back once they'd followed her trail.

Another howl, this one very close and to her left. From behind her came another. They were trying to box her in. Galina slammed a mental door shut on the fear that flooded her mind. Her brother might want to scare her, but he'd never do anything to cause her lasting harm. Papa would never allow that.

But what if she was wrong? Could he make her death out in the woods look like some kind of accident? Would Maksim back him up in his story? Remembering the adoring look in Federov's eyes, she was afraid the answer would be yes.

The howling grew louder, closing in on her from all sides. The attack in her garage popped into her head, and she remembered Timur's injuries from the next day. Could Alexei have already tried to get rid of her once?

Galina ignored the fear twisting inside of her. She stopped, sitting on her haunches, as if she didn't have a care in the world. If she didn't act like prey, didn't run like expected, maybe she could throw them off their game. Galina sat, waiting for them to appear.

Timur shouldered his way through the low lying brush first. Vasily circled behind her, nipping at her tail. She tossed a snarl at him over her shoulder. Alexei stalked over to her, Maksim behind him, tongue lolling out of his mouth happily. He thought this was all a joke.

Alexei growled, crowding into her space. Timur and Vasily began to circle. Galina watched them calmly, feeling the light wind ruffle her fur. The sharp musk of Alexei's scent assaulted her nose, drowning out the more pleasant scents of pine and water heavy in the air.

His teeth snapped close to her muzzle. Galina didn't flinch. Staring into his yellow eyes, she thought she saw a glimmer of enjoyment there. He wanted her afraid. He wanted her submissive. He hoped to show her where she belonged.

Timur went for her haunches, jaws open and slavering. Galina spun, an Alpha bark snarling up from her throat. He scrambled back, unable to resist the sound. She heard Alexei growl in warning, angry that she dared use her status in his presence. Maksim watched everything in confusion.

Galina snapped at Alexei's front legs, forcing him to back up a step. He bared his teeth, shoulders bunching beneath the heavy grey fur. He leapt at her, hoping to bowl her over, but Galina was ready for him. They rolled, jaws still snapping. Galina broke away from her brother, circling him, her teeth bared in warning. She didn't want to fight him, not here. Not without the proper witnesses.

She saw Timur and Vasily closing ranks behind her. Maksim stood to the side, pacing as if he wasn't sure what to do. He was the weak link. He would be easy to get past.

Galina didn't think. Her wolf instincts took over and her muscles bunched into a spring. Smashing into Maksim, she shoved him out of her way, and raced through the woods toward the safety of Papa's house.

She heard Alexei and his small pack give chase. They fell into step behind her, Timur and Vasily fanning out to the side in an effort to flank her. Galina ran, pushing her body for more speed, to run as fast as she could. She sprang away, a flash of white against the brown bark of the trees. Her claws dug into the earth, propelling her forward.

Galina didn't bother looking back. She could hear them, smashing through the undergrowth, losing all grace as they tried to catch her. But she was too fast, streaking around trees, her loping stride carrying her farther from her brother. The light changed as she approached the edge of the woods. She caught glimpses of green lawn through the breaks in the trees. She pounded over the running trails, bypassing them for a more direct route to the house.

She broke free of the tree line, skewing around to watch as Alexei, Maksim, and the rest emerged more slowly. Lungs heaving, Galina waited for them to pass before looking over to the windows of the house. She thought she saw her father staring down at her from the window, but then he pulled back, leaving nothing but a blank glass eye in the face of the house.

Shivering, Galina went to retrieve her clothes.

12

It's Like a Greek Tragedy but with More Fur

The waterfront in downtown Seattle glittered like jewels strung on a necklace as Galina walked in the morning sun. She ignored the white panel van that had become an almost constant companion in her daily outings, and enjoyed the sunshine. She'd jogged to the harbor, reveling in the pleasant weather.

Exercise wasn't the only reason for her visit to the harbor. Galina wanted to visit the boat slips, to check for the missing Bullet in the false panels and bottoms of the Organization boats docked there. She was running out of ideas. It was possible that Sergei—or Alexei—had already unloaded the drugs, getting them to the street or sending the Bullet out of the city. She doubted he'd have had the time to do so before his murder, but it was a possibility.

She started with the two boats her family had docked there. The false wall panels slid back when she hit a pressure switch, but revealed empty space. The other smuggling holes were also empty. Galina opened every cabinet and drawer, even checking the anchor line in case Sergei had hidden the drugs below the waterline. She found nothing.

It was the same with the Volkov boat, her search enabled by a bribe. Discouraged, Galina stepped onto the dock, shading her eyes from the light splintering off the water. She could see the top of the Great Wheel, the buildings of downtown behind it hugging the coast.

"Galina?"

She turned toward the sound Andrey's voice. His black hair was all wind-whipped snarls, blue eyes bright and cheeks red as he looked down at her. He wore casual clothes suited for sailing. "Good morning," she called. "Coming or going?"

Andrey smiled, a flash of white teeth more dazzling than the light off the water. "Just got back in. You?"

"Calling it a morning," she answered, feeling her spirits lift just from seeing him.

"Then I hope you will let me buy you breakfast." He offered her his arm.

Galina hooked her elbow into his. "I accept. I'm starving," she admitted with an embarrassed laugh.

"Do you usually run around here?" Andrey asked as he led her out of the harbor. He seemed to have a breakfast destination in mind, so Galina followed contentedly. "I haven't seen you."

"Trying a new route." She noticed the white van had pulled away from the curb to follow their path. "Just so you know, we have company." Galina jerked her head toward the street.

Andrey turned, frowning at the van. "Are they after anything in particular or is this a courtesy call?"

Shrugging, Galina pulled away from him to walk on her own. She would have loved to stroll the streets arm and arm with Andrey all day, but they were supposed to only know each other professionally. "They try every few years to dig up something on Papa." Her warning delivered, she changed the subject. "I didn't know you sailed."

He nodded, gesturing her inside Roxy's Diner. The scent of cooking meats and bread assaulted her nostrils, making her mouth water. They sat at a table near the back, out of view from the windows.

Once they were settled, Andrey said, "I like to go out on the water as much as I can. Unfortunately, I do not often get the opportunity."

"I'm surprised Konstantin isn't with you. Or any bodyguards, for that matter." Galina peered around, as if they were going to pop out of thin air.

"I prefer to go out by myself," he said, pausing to order for them when the waitress stopped by their table. "I like to wander, and it is easier to do without an escort." He shared a private smile with her. "I am Rom after all. We have a need to move. Itchy feet."

Galina nodded, doctoring her coffee. "It must be nice, to be able to do that."

"I don't see your guardians anywhere either," he pointed out.

She looked up from her mug, meeting his frank blue gaze. "I called them off. I don't trust them."

Before she thought about it, Galina told him what had happened on the trails at Papa's house. "I need to find a detail loyal to me, not Alexei. Right now, I'm not sure there are any."

Their food arrived: plates of bacon and sausage, scrambled eggs with chives and sour cream, roasted potatoes, pancakes, and piles of toasted brown bread. It looked like Andrey had ordered everything on the menu. Twice.

He waited until she'd begun to eat before answering. His eyes were dark, anger swirling in their silvery depths. "I want you to stop looking for the shipment. If Alexei finds out what you are doing, he will not stop as he did at your father's house."

Galina stopped with a forkful of pancakes halfway to her mouth. "I made a deal with you. I'm not going back on it." She continued eating. If she stopped doing things for fear of Alexei's reaction, she might as well buy herself a casket and plot.

Andrey captured her free hand in his. "Let me put my men on you."

Raising an eyebrow, Galina said, "There's a visual my father would love."

His throaty chuckle sent a thrill through her. The sound of it made her wish they weren't in so public a place so she could engage in some less than professional behavior with him. She contented herself with devouring her breakfast.

"You know what I meant." He took a bite of sausage and egg. "You need to have some protection, Galya."

Eyeing him curiously, she asked, "Won't your people be upset with you, putting security on a Russian?"

He took a sip of coffee before answering. "My people have any number of reasons to be upset with me." At her frown, he continued.

"I am thirty years old and have no wife. That is a sin to the Rom. I should have a handful of children by now. I am not doing my duty." He shoveled another forkful of eggs into his mouth. "What's one more offense?"

She bumped his leg under the table. "I'll think about it."

Later that day, Galina let herself into Irina's house, surprised when no one was there to greet her. Irina was still in seclusion, unable to go out on social calls for the length of her private morning period, so Galina stopped by whenever she could. Today, she came prepared with pastries from her favorite French bakery.

As she dropped off the box of goodies on the kitchen counter, she heard Alexei's angry yelling coming from upstairs. What was he doing here? Where was Viktor?

She raced up the stairs, following the shouting to Irina's bedroom. Viktor caught sight of her when she was almost to the top, gesturing for her to hurry. She heard Alexei say, "I would not do such a thing to you, Irina. I want you to paint the world with all of the colors of your soul."

Galina stopped in the doorway, taking in the scene before her. Her brother clutched Irina in a tight hug. Shredded clothes covered the floor. Irina's closet stood empty, all of her red dresses and skirts and blouses lying in ruins at Alexei's feet. Irina was trying to reach for a statuette sitting on a nearby table to presumably brain their brother with it, but it was just out of her reach.

"What in fucking fuck are you talking about?" Galina asked from the doorway. She leaned against the doorframe, arms casually crossed over her chest, glaring at Alexei. Blood stained the arms of Irina's shirt.

Galina stepped over the ruins of Irina's wardrobe, nudging the sleeve of a Calvin Klein dress with her toe. She kept her voice light, breezy. "What is going on in here? Irina, did you decided to do a makeover without me? I'm hurt. I make a much better fairy god-mother than Alexei here."

Alexei's eyes flashed at the word "fairy."

"This is none of your concern, Galina," Alexei snapped. "Get out of here."

"Oh, matters of fashion are always my business, brother dear." Galya smiled ever so sweetly as she wandered closer. She allowed her claws to extend, smaller and more oval-shaped than Alexei's, but twice as sharp. Her brother was too caught up in…whatever he was doing to notice. He was an idiot.

"You don't know what your business is," Alexei snarled.

"Oh, I think what is and isn't my business is about to be redefined, Alexei." She felt her smile fade from her face, turning her expression feral. The chase at her father's house came thundering back to her and she fought from growling at him.

Alexei roared with rage at the insult. Snarling, he tossed Irina aside like a ragdoll, sending her sailing. Viktor was already moving, interposing himself before Irina could collide with the bedroom wall. Galina watched him cradle her sister's body against his protectively as they fell.

Galina scowled, unable to believe her brother was so out of control. Alexei swung his massive hand toward her face, and Galina easily side-stepped the swipe. She stuck out her Louboutin-shod foot to catch Alexei's ankle, sending his over-extended frame toppling to the floor in a heap.

"Are you ever not going to fall for that one?" she asked him as he howled and beat his paws on the floor. He reminded her of a toddler who'd been told he couldn't have a sweet. She watched as Viktor hauled Irina out of the room, then turned her attention back to her brother.

"What the hell are you even doing here, Alexei?" Galina demanded, staring down at him. Her voice was poisonous with scorn. "You haven't bothered visiting Irina during her whole seclusion, but you swing by now to rough her up and play Edward Scissorhands with her work clothes? What the hell is wrong with you?"

"You have no right to question me!" Alexei exploded. He climbed to his feet, face red. "My relationship with Irina is none of your business!"

What the hell? What relationship was he talking about? "There are not enough Greek tragedy jokes in the world to cover what's going on with your brain, is there?" Galina said, shaking her head in mock dismay.

"Watch your mouth when you talk to me!" Alexei barked.

He began to unbuckle his belt, pulling it from the loops of his pants. Galina stared in shock. Alexei was going to try to whip her with a belt? The idea was utterly ridiculous. He had completely lost the plot.

"Really, a belt, Alexei?" Galina scoffed. "You're relying on an arsenal of accessories? What's next, you're going to come at me with your necktie?"

She hadn't thought it possible, but his face flushed even redder. "Mark my words, Galina, you will learn your place!"

She laughed outright at that. Alexei thought he was going to be the one to teach her? Unlikely. He and Maksim had so much in common, it was no wonder they were bonding.

"Yeah, yeah," Galina said, waving him away like he was an annoying mosquito. "Hey, instead of hitting you with my shoe, you don't mind if I shift into a state in which I have claws and fangs and twice your body mass, do you, *genius?*"

Galina smelled her father well before his booming voice shouted, "What do you think you are doing? Is this how my children behave when I am here?"

She crossed the room and kissed her Papa's cheek, as if this were no more than a simple friendly conversation about the weather. Galina brushed imaginary fuzz from her jacket.

"Papa, so good to see you. Alexei was just having a little temper tantrum. I think he needs a nap." Condescension practically dripped from her voice.

"I was not having a temper tantrum," Alexei snarled. "I was teaching your little princess how to speak with respect to her betters!"

"Tell you what, you bring me my betters, I'll be sure to speak to them respectfully," Galina retorted.

"You see?" Alexei snapped. "You see how she speaks to me, Papa?" His voice was almost a whine.

"Everybody will calm down now," Papa yelled. "Where is your sister? Have you forgotten that you are standing in her bedroom, screaming at each other like a couple of fishwives?"

Irina walked out of the bathroom in a clean white button-up shirt. Viktor followed a few seconds later. "I'm right here, Papa."

"Irina, what is this madness? Why are your clothes in ruins on the floor? Why are your brother and sister fighting? Tell Papa—" he demanded before stopping mid-sentence and inhaling deeply. He snarled. "Why do I smell your blood?"

"She fell," Alexei said quickly. "It was an accident."

"If by *fall*, you mean Alexei getting rough…" Galina began, but her father shot her a warning look. She subsided, incredulous that Alexei was trotting out that old saw again. It was his excuse when they were all kids, every time he "played" too rough and one of them got hurt. Papa couldn't actually believe that lie.

Papa turned to Irina. "Irina, how did you fall?"

"I tripped, Papa, and cut my arm. Viktor patched me up. I'll be fine," she said.

Galina stared. Irina was backing him up on his lie? She huffed out a frustrated breath. If Irina wouldn't tell Papa, then she would.

But then she saw the resignation on Irina's face. Her sister knew that Papa would buy whatever lie he had to in order to keep from admitting what a mess his oldest son was. No matter what Galina or her sister said, he would always back Alexei.

Ilya examined Viktor's face, which remained blank as a slate. "Well, Irina has always been a bit clumsy."

Galina huffed out a frustrated breath. Well, if he was going to be willfully blind, he could at least handle the expense of furnishing Irina with a new wardrobe. "By the way, Alexei destroyed all of Irina's clothes, Papa."

Ilya's gaze swung back to his oldest. "Alexei, why would you do such a thing?"

Alexei looked decidedly un-wolf-like as his mouth flapped open.

Galina grinned, giving her brother an evil look. "Yes, Alexei, what possessed you to shred all of Irina's clothes?"

Alexei snarled at her.

"Alexei, control yourself," Ilya warned him.

"It was a misunderstanding, Papa," Alexei protested. "Right, Irina?"

Irina's mouth dropped open. "Uh…"

Ilya surveyed the damaged clothes scattered across the floor. "Do you have anything left to wear, Irina?"

When Irina didn't answer, Papa took her silence for a "no," and began patting his jacket pocket for his wallet. "Well, Alexei, since you have left your sister without any proper clothes, I suppose she must go shopping for more. On your account. Clearly, you're not ready to have this back yet." Ilya pulled a shiny black credit card from his wallet and pressed it into Irina's hand. "Go now, *babochka*, buy yourself some pretty things. Enjoy yourself." He patted her cheek. "You deserve to have a little fun."

"Papa, I can't let you or Alexei pay for—" Irina began.

"What a generous gesture, Papa," Galina said, her voice saccharine sweet. She snatched the card from Papa's hand. She wasn't going to let her sister go all noble and let Alexei weasel out of replacing the wardrobe he'd ruined. She whispered, "Don't be an idiot, Rina. Grab your purse, I'm calling Franny."

"But Irina is still in seclusion!" Alexei yelled, his face flushing an unattractive shade of magenta against his black shirt. "It's not proper for her to be out until the full moon."

Ilya ignored his son's protests, making Galina smile. "Viktor, you will accompany the ladies anywhere they wish to go," Ilya commanded. "Be sure to keep Irina from 'falling' again."

Galina bustled her sister out the door before their father could change his mind.

13

How to Take a Really Expensive Nap

Alexei would not stop talking. The meeting could have ended a half hour ago, but Alexei kept jabbering on about God alone knew what. His pupil-blown gaze ricocheted around the room like a ping pong ball shot from a cannon and he had to mop at his sweaty brow every few moments. Galina was thoroughly disgusted.

Nik had tried to interrupt with more pressing business, but Alexei was like a dog with a pig's ear. Galina snuck a look at Andrey, who sat farther down the table. He looked amused, a small smile playing over his lips, as Alexei's talk grew more and more unhinged.

Papa looked in danger of apoplexy. His jaw was clenched so tightly that Galina was fairly certain they were going to have to call Franny to come and replace his back molars because they'd been ground into paste. He resisted doing anything to cause Alexei to lose face, showing him for the spoiled child he was, but Galina had no such problem.

Slowly she climbed to her feet. All eyes turned toward her, leaving Alexei to ramble on for a few moments before he realized that no one was paying him any attention. Ilya raised his brows, but said nothing.

"Gentlemen," she began, keeping her voice low, but firm. Let them lean in to hear her speak, let them get used to having to listen to her. "As fascinating as my brother's report has been, I regret that I have other appointments to attend." She gifted everyone at the table with a dazzling smile.

"Those shoes aren't going to buy themselves," Alexei snarked. A few of the older men snickered.

Galina's smile grew wider. Just the opening she'd been hoping for. "Actually, Alexei, I have a meeting with a buyer. I would hate to keep a man willing to pay a million dollars for fourteenth-century jewelry waiting. That would be rude and Papa taught us better than that."

Murmurings began to circulate around the table. Alexei looked murderous; Papa looked proud. Nik winked at her. If she'd wanted to show that her line of business was profitable, she couldn't have asked for a better opening. She should really send Alexei a fruit basket or something as a thank you.

Ilya stood as well. "I think we've all had enough talk for today," he said to those assembled. When it looked as though Alexei was going to protest, Papa put his hand on his shoulder, keeping him in his seat. Galina could see the fingers on her father's hand go white from the exertion it took to keep Alexei seated. "Thank you all for coming."

As the men around the table rose to depart, Papa said, "Andreyev, Galina, stay a moment, would you?"

Galina shared a glance with Andrey, arching a brow. What was her father up to? He couldn't possibly know about them. Andrey's eyes sparkled with mirth. He was enjoying this immensely. She felt a churning in her gut. She really didn't like surprises.

When the room was empty, Papa released Alexei and went over to the bar. He poured himself a generous glass of Stoli. "Would anyone care for one?"

Andrey shook his head. "No thank you."

Alexei got up and left the table as quickly as his legs would carry him, barely managing not to slam the door behind him. Nikolai rolled his eyes at Galina before following him. She covered her mouth to hide her smirk. Her oldest brother was like a giant, unstable baby that could turn into a ravening beast once a month.

"You know I have a box at the ballet," Papa began. Andrey nodded politely. Everyone knew Papa had box seats. He loved the ballet. "I would like it very much if you'd join me and my family for the opening performance of *Swan Lake*."

Galina's eyes narrowed. Just what the hell was going on? Then it hit her and she felt the blood drain from her face. No. He couldn't possibly…

His next words removed any doubt from her mind. "My daughter Irina will be there. I know she would like it very much if you would attend."

Galina had to fight back scornful laughter. Irina barely knew Andrey existed outside of a "condolences" flower arrangement. She was so entwined with Viktor it would take a nuclear bomb going off to pull her off of that man. She dug her fingernails into her palms in an effort not to react.

"It would be my pleasure," Andrey said, carefully not looking at Galina. "I can't imagine anything finer than spending the evening in the company of your lovely daughter."

Andrey was smooth. He hadn't said which daughter. Galina had to give him points for that. And it wasn't like he could actually refuse to go. It was a huge deal for Papa to invite him. It was just good business for him to say yes.

It didn't make Galina any happier to think of it that way though.

"Galina, I trust you don't have plans for that evening," Papa said, in a voice that told her that even if she did, she'd be canceling them so she could attend this latest farce.

"Of course not, Papa," she replied with icy clarity. "I wouldn't dream of missing it."

"Excellent. Maksim will be there as well."

Seething silently, Galina listened to Papa bend Andrey's ear about his abiding love for the ballet. Her father's attempts at matchmaking had to be stopped. Galina had had nothing to do with Maksim since that horrible chase through the woods. Even if he did have breeding and money and the right family, Galina couldn't imagine being with him for five minutes, let alone the rest of her life.

And Irina and Andrey? She felt the blood drain from her face as she realized that Papa must know about the stolen shipment. Why else would he be offering Irina? He couldn't offer up his legitimate daughter—she knew Papa wouldn't waste her lineage on a lowly Rom—but he could offer up Irina as reparation for her husband's mistake. He was handing off her sister like she was some kind of consolation prize. Just like he had with Sergei.

Galina wanted to be sick.

Andrey was good enough for Irina, but not good enough for Galina. So Irina was going to be married off to a man she didn't love—again—and Galina was being saved for a caviar magnate's idiot son who thought Alexei was a proper role model. She wanted to scream.

Galina excused herself quickly, unwilling to spend another minute in that room having to put a polite smile on her face. Her meeting with her client wasn't for another hour. She wanted to hit the gym, to take out some frustration on a heavy bag, but she didn't have enough time. She thought about stopping for a drink at the hotel bar, but thought better of it. She wasn't in the mood for company.

Andrey caught up to her before she'd even made it past the hotel lounge. He put his hand under her elbow and steered her away from the doors and into the VIP elevator. She allowed it, because jerking her arm away and storming off would cause a scene in the middle of the lobby. As much as she'd like to, she couldn't afford it.

"So you're dating my sister now?" she began as soon as the doors swished closed.

"Not to my knowledge." Andrey's eyes were a silvery grey as he stared down at her. "I'm not interested in Irina."

"My father appears to think otherwise." Galina took a step back, needing space between them. His nearness was doing strange things to her breathing. And she couldn't afford to think with her lady parts right now.

He followed her, hitting the button to stop the elevator between floors. "I don't care what your father thinks." Andrey leaned in close, sliding his mouth up the column of her neck. "Your father isn't here right now."

And thank God for that. What the hell was she doing with Andrey? He was supposed to be a bit of fun: some amazing sex, a few laughs, and a story to tell Irina when it was all over. She wasn't supposed to be feeling anything. Something bubbled in her gut that felt curiously like jealousy and possessiveness. She'd never felt that about a man—any man—before.

Andrey's lips hovered close to hers. His eyes had that smoky half-lidded look that he got just before he kissed her. His body was close to her, but not touching, and still her brain was short circuiting. "Tell my father you can't make it," she said before she could stop herself.

He pulled back, surprise on his face. "What?"

Galina pushed him away so she could hit the button to get the elevator moving again. "Make something up. An emergency, an act of God, a tragic boating accident. I don't care. Just don't come to the ballet."

His generous mouth turned down in a frown. "You know I can't do that."

Galina shook her head, her blond hair falling across her eyes. Of course he couldn't. And she wasn't sure if she could sit there and watch him play nice with Irina without wanting to scream. She hit the button for the next floor, needing to put some space between them. She didn't know what was happening to her.

"Galina," Andrey said, lightly touching her arm.

She shook him off. "Don't."

The doors opened and she was out of the elevator and down the hall toward the stairs before Andrey could say anything else.

Galina inspected herself in the mirror one last time before heading down to meet the hired car. Papa had ordered all of them to the ballet tonight. He always purchased a box at McCaw Hall for the season and tonight was the opening of the Pacific Northwest Ballet Company's performance of *Swan Lake*. Ordinarily, Galina would have been thrilled to get dressed up and watch a beautiful performance of just about anything, but tonight left a sour taste in her mouth.

Andrey was coming with them. As Irina's date.

And since the evening wasn't awkward enough, Papa had invited Maksim as well. Galina couldn't imagine a less fun way to spend an evening.

She applied a touch more mascara to her lashes. Her dress was a deep purple Eli Saab embellished with silver beads. It made her green eyes stand out like jade from the artfully applied shadow. Her nails were painted a dark burgundy purple called *F*ck You*. She frowned. She looked amazing. It was going to be totally and completely wasted.

Stepping into a pair of Gianvito Rossi peep toes, she grabbed her glittery clutch from the side of the vanity and headed down to the Maybach and driver she'd rented for the evening. The swirl of fabric against the flesh of her bare hips — she had foregone underwear as a way of passive-aggressively giving the finger to everyone in general and Andrey in particular — made her feel delightfully evil.

She spent the drive to the theater on the phone, contacting a wealthy buyer who collected ancient werewolf artifacts. She'd met him when she was working on her Masters, and it was he who had given her the idea of introducing high-end art smuggling as a line of the family business. There were plenty of wealthy collectors, both were and non-were, who would pay handsomely for art that couldn't be legally obtained.

This particular patron wanted a chalice from the early fifteenth century that had recently come to light on a dig site in Europe. She had a contact in place overseas to secure the item and get it here, but she needed to negotiate price. He'd hung up promising to call her with a desired delivery time frame and payment information.

When she stepped out of the car and made her way inside, Galina was feeling pretty confident that she would be able to handle whatever the evening held in store for her. She was making progress on establishing her line of the family business, she had a deal to occupy her mind, and she looked amazing. She could ignore Andrey playing the gallant knight errant with her sister and fawning all over her father. She could ignore Alexei being a chauvinistic jackwagon. If she ended up losing her patience, she could always hit the bar at intermission.

Nodding at the attendant who held the door for her, she crossed the marble floor of the atrium. She stopped just inside the door to take a moment and collect herself before heading up the massive double spiral staircase that would take her to the second floor and the private box where she'd spend the next several hours pretending that everything was peachy keen.

His scent hit her well before she heard him say, "May I take your wrap, Galina?"

Bracing herself against the sight of Andrey in a tuxedo, she slowly turned around. She almost turned back around to give herself more bracing time. Andrey looked like sin given flesh, so handsome that she almost didn't notice Konstantin standing a discreet distance behind him. Andrey's black hair was combed back from his forehead, highlighting the strong bones of his face. His pale eyes swept over her, taking in her face and dress. She felt a flutter in her stomach. Her eyes dipped down, tracing the breadth of shoulders in his black tuxedo jacket, the line of his strong thighs through the fabric of his pants.

Galina met his eyes, feeling it like a physical impact. This night was going to be harder than she thought. Still, she was going to try to make the best of it. "Thank you, Andreyev." She slid the wrap from her shoulders, revealing the deep V neckline of her dress. His nostrils flared and his pupils dilated as he took in the expanse of flesh being unveiled.

They walked to the coat check, the silence between them charged with anticipation. There was so much unsaid between them. Galina watched Andrey hand the wrap to the attendant and accepted the ticket, trying hard not to stare at him. She kept her eyes on his hands, but then she remembered how they felt sliding over her body when they were in the hotel room. She looked toward the doors to see Maksim arrive with Alexei. Irina followed with Ilya and Viktor.

He touched her bare arm, causing her flesh to prickle with sensation. "Galya," he began.

"Looks like your date's here," she murmured, inclining her head to the atrium and her incoming family. She saw his genial mask slide in place and excused herself to go to the powder room.

She waited in the lounge area for a good ten minutes, listening to the gossip and chatter of the women who came and went. Galina checked her phone for messages, hoping for something to distract her but there were no new calls. Finally, when she couldn't put it off any longer, she made her way to the base of the staircase and allowed Nik to escort her to the family's box.

"Galya!" her father called, giving her a hug and a peck on each cheek when he saw her. She greeted everyone, even Alexei who acted like he hadn't heard her, and then tried to disappear into the background, willing her phone to vibrate.

Maksim took her hand in his fingertips, kissing the air above her hand as if afraid to touch her more than he needed to. He was finally wearing something that fit him properly. His hair was slicked back and he was wearing a pinky ring. Galina glanced at Alexei, noting that he wore something similar.

"You look lovely," Maksim told her, before turning to her sister. "As do you, Mrs. Volkov." He sounded incredibly bored.

Irina nodded. "You are too kind." She was wearing a grey Grecian style dress matched with a set of sapphire hair combs that Galina coveted.

The lights began to dim. Papa occupied his usual seat on the end of the first row, with the best view of the stage. Alexei nearly shoved Nikolai over the railing into the seats below in his hurry to sit at Papa's right hand. Maksim moved to the chair next to Alexei. Nik sat, leaving only one seat left in the front row.

"Oh, you have to take this seat, Andrey," Irina said, gesturing to the seat like it was a prize on a game show. "Papa always says the end seats have the best view of the stage."

Papa looked at Alexei, raising his eyebrows but his oldest son ignored his unspoken signal. Maksim was speaking rapidly in her brother's ear, probably telling him how much better the ballet boxes were in Russia.

"I'll move," Nik said, quickly, hopping up from his seat. Galina shook her head at her brother's gallantry.

Andrey put a hand on her brother's shoulder and pushed him back down. "No, no, you're already seated," he said. "I'll sit in the second row."

"I don't mind sitting with Galina," Irina assured him.

"But your father was just telling me how much you love the ballet," Andrey protested, his gaze skipping to Galina. "I couldn't let you miss *Swan Lake*. Really, I insist." Oh good Lord, it was a gallant-off.

"But it would be rude to let a guest sit in the second row," Papa protested, flushing red now that he realized his error. He couldn't, in good manners, deny Andrey's request that Nik sit in the front row, and he couldn't ask a guest to move. As the host, it would look bad for him to sit anywhere but in the front row, near his guest. And they would need a backhoe to get Alexei out of that chair.

Irina shook her head. "I don't mind. I've already seen this company's performance of *Swan Lake*. And really, you see one evil wizard change a girl into a bird, you've seen them all."

"I don't mind, Papa," Irina insisted. "I promise. And I'll be sitting next to Galina, so it will be completely proper."

"Yes, yes," Galina urged, plopping into a seat in the second row. "We're all in agreement. Everybody sit down."

Irina slid into the seat on her right gracefully. "You okay?"

The curtain rose. Galina kept her eyes fixed on the stage, as she managed a not quite believable, "Fine."

"Okay then," Irina said, sounding irritated.

Galina felt bad for snapping at her sister, but it wasn't like she could tell her sister what was making her cranky. Still, it wasn't fair taking her temper out on Irina when her sister wanted to be at the ballet even less than Galina did. She vowed to keep her frustration in check.

Viktor and Konstantin stood sentinel—like living statues—at opposite sides of the box, each small movement pulling Galina's focus from the stage.

"Would you two sit, you're distracting me!" she said to the bodyguards. "It's like watching ballet with a couple of gargoyles lurking in the shadows."

They acquiesced. Konstantin sat on the end next to Galina, while Viktor took the chair beside Irina. Galina hoped that Viktor had the presence of mind to keep his blood pumping to his brain rather than his dick. She sat with her arms crossed across her chest and tried to pay attention to the dancers onstage.

"Oh, this is so much fun," Galina whispered to her sister. "I hope we can do this every Friday night."

Irina surreptitiously gave her the finger, keeping her eyes on the stage. Konstantin snickered beside her. With a sigh, Galina pulled out her phone to check for messages and saw the blinking light that indicated she had voice mail. She stood, gathering her skirts in one hand and slid past Konstantin. Andrey and Nik turned around in their seats to see what the commotion was.

"I need to take a call," she told them, excusing herself and leaving the box.

Galina found a quiet corner in the first floor atrium and returned Tol Aristov's phone call. In ten minutes she had verbal confirmation of the agreed upon price, the delivery date and location, and an appointment for a face-to-face meeting. When she hung up, she felt immeasurably better.

Putting her phone back into her purse, Galina turned and slammed into a wall of tuxedo clad man-chest. She staggered in her heels, clutching at the arms that steadied her. Andrey.

Galina looked into his face, eyes locking on his mouth. "Did you follow me?" Not the smartest question she'd ever asked, sure, but she was still on a high from the phone call.

"I told them I needed to get some air." He pulled her closer.

"Down boy." She slapped at his shoulder with her clutch. "They bought that?"

He loosened his hold on her, but didn't let her go. "Your father is really into the ballet."

"I'm going back up," she said, not wanting to get in the middle of anything else right now. She was barely tolerating this nightmare of an evening; she didn't want complications. Galina just wanted to revel in her good news for a few more minutes.

"Come with me," Andrey said, tucking her arm into his.

Galina looked around, seeing that there were a number of patrons milling around. Normally she wouldn't have cared about causing a scene, but her father was here, as was Alexei. She needed to stay above reproach for the time being. So she strolled along with Andrey through the atrium as if they were simply a couple out for a special evening.

"I'm surprised Konstantin isn't with you," Galina observed, just to have something to say. "Doesn't he follow you everywhere?"

"He wanted to stay in the box," Andrey answered. "He likes being close to Nik."

Galina felt like her eyes bug out of her head, then reminded herself that frog eyes weren't a good look for her and blinked. Andrey used her shock to usher her into the room where the coats were checked. Did he know about Nik? And, more importantly, was he okay with it?

"Wait, wait, wait," she said finally, pulling her arm from his. "You know Konstantin is gay?" Then she stared up at him in horror. "You know *Nik* is gay?"

"Konstantin is my best friend. Of course, I know he's gay." Andrey stalked over to her, backing her up against the wall. Galina put her hand against his chest, pushing back. "I don't want to talk about Konstantin or your brother anymore."

He lowered his head slowly to hers. Galina stared at him, shocked into stillness, feeling her nerves sing at his nearness. Andrey's lips brushed hers lightly, a whisper of a kiss. She felt it sizzle through her, liquid heat pooling in her belly.

Galina pushed him back with both hands. It was a lot like trying to move a wall. "And what about my sister? Do you want to talk about why you're here with her?"

Andrey stared down at her, his pale eyes dark with lust. She felt a pulse slide through her, feeling wetness between her thighs. That look in his eyes was for her and her alone, but that wasn't an answer.

"I'm not with your sister right now." Andrey leaned forward, sliding his hands down her waist to her hips, yanking her close to him. "I'm here with you."

"You are." They stared at each other, the tension between the two of them building until it had a kind of presence, filling up the confines of the room. Galina closed her eyes for a moment, trying to get her body under control. Everything inside of her ached for him. She wanted his kiss, his touch, his cock. Even if it was only for tonight. There was a hunger inside her that only he could sate.

"Oh, fuck it," she said, opening her eyes. She locked her arms around his neck and pulled his mouth to hers.

Fire blazed through her at the feel of his lips on hers. Her mouth opened, and she pushed her tongue into his, sliding it over his teeth, licking at the roof of his mouth. Her pussy spasmed, a greedy throb that drove her to the edge of wanting, pushing her into the realm of need.

Andrey's mouth was everywhere: trailing along her throat, moving over the exposed flesh of her chest, nipping at her earlobes. She gasped, rubbing against the bulge in his pants. His hands scrabbled at the fabric of her skirt, pulling it up so his fingers could slip inside of her. Galina gasped as first one, then two fingers plunged inside of her, spreading her wetness over her folds. His thumb brushed her clit, the callous catching against the sensitive flesh and she bucked against him.

"You didn't wear underwear," he observed, a pleased grin on his face.

Her fingers dipped to his fly, unzipping his pants and reaching inside to wrap her hand around his cock. It throbbed against her palm as she began to move her hand along his shaft, running her thumb along the head of him. His breathing sped up, matching her panting breaths as his fingers stroked inside of her. Galina thought she might erupt like a volcano as she chased her orgasm, moving on his hand.

Andrey broke their kiss. "Lie down," he ordered, ripping some furs down from the hangers around them. "On these."

Galina moved to obey, dropping down on the coats that Andrey had spread on the floor. When she didn't move fast enough, Andrey positioned her himself. He bent her knees, yanking the skirt of her dress up and pushing it around her waist. He looked like a man who'd just been offered a banquet.

She wanted to say something, anything, but then Andrey's mouth was on her, lapping at her clit. Galina moaned softly, lifting her hips upward, wanting more. Andrey obliged, applying more pressure as his tongue licked over her sensitive flesh and sliding his fingers back inside her. She locked her hands in his hair, writhing against the furs as his fingers and tongue pushed her closer to the brink.

"You have the most perfect pussy," Andrey murmured, lifting his head to watch her come undone. His fingers pumped into her, driving her mad with need. She cried out softly, a low keen rising in the back of her throat.

He lowered his head to her once more, sucking her clit into his mouth. Galina arched up, feeling like he'd just sent an electric current from her sex straight up the center of her spine and into her brain. All thought stopped as every muscle in her body clenched in delicious pleasure. She knew she was making noise, but she couldn't help herself, didn't want him to stop making her feel this way. And Andrey's tongue was still stroking at her clit, not allowing her a chance to recover, to breathe. Shudders moved through her as his fingers sped up their rhythm, and Galina's hips moved in time with his thrusts.

A horrified squeak pulled Galina from her pleasure. She levered herself up to look over Andrey's back. Irina stared at them, a look of shock and surprise plastered all over her face. Galina waved at her, wearing what she was sure was a stupid grin. Andrey lifted his head and turned it toward the door, his fingers still deep inside of her. She made an outraged noise at him for stopping, then looked again at her sister still standing in the doorway.

Irina could pull up a chair and watch or get the hell out and let Andrey finish what he started. But she couldn't just stand there with the door wide open, gaping like a landed fish. "Would you shut the fucking door already?" Galina growled.

"You two are—oh, my god, there are just some things I will never be able to un-see!" Irina slammed the door closed.

Galina couldn't help but laugh at the outraged look on her sister's face. Andrey's deep chuckle joined hers and his steely eyes snapped with amusement.

Then Viktor stuck his head into the cloakroom. He muttered, "Oh, come on, Lupesco!" Galina and Andrey both snarled at him. He shut the door.

She tapped Andrey on the head, and said, "You've got a job to finish, mister."

"Yes, ma'am." And he lowered his mouth to her once more.

Galina arrived back at the box first, having stopped off in the powder room to check her hair and makeup and spray on some of the wolfsbane perfume she always carried. It would dull a werewolf's keen sense of smell, helping to mask the scent of sex-and-Andrey that fairly enveloped her. She reapplied her lipstick, fluffed her hair, and rejoined her family.

Irina leaned over to hiss in her ear as soon as she sat down. "I am going to *murder* you."

Galina ignored her sister's threat and turned her attention to the dancers on the stage. She felt much more relaxed now that she'd had an orgasm or five. She heard the door to the box open, forcing herself not to react when Andrey ran warm fingers down her shoulder. Konstantin returned to his seat behind her a few minutes later. She wasn't quite sure where Nik had gone.

Alexei and Papa were asleep in their seats. It figured. Papa spent a ridiculous amount of money on the box seats and then slept through most of the performance. Why Alexei even bothered to come, she'd never know. Maksim had disappeared. She wondered if he had hightailed it to the bar when the snoring started.

The curtain lowered and Galina stood smoothly, clapping for the ballet she hadn't bothered to pay attention to. Papa and Alexei awoke from their expensive nap at the applause and rose to their feet. Papa shouted, "Brava, brava!" as if he'd been awake for the whole show. Galina stifled a chuckle behind her clutch. Alexei blinked sleepily and stumbled out of the box as Papa clapped Andrey on the shoulder and interrogated him on his favorite parts of the ballet. Galina caught Andrey's wink at her sister and had to smother her grin behind her purse. She waited while he and Papa left, taking the time to fluff her blond hair and reapply her lipstick.

"You—" Irina pointed at her, a dire look on her face. "We're going to have a talk."

Galina gave her a placid look. "About what, dearest sister?"

"You know, you have a little carpet fuzz on your dress," Viktor told her, waving his hand at her skirt.

Galina stuck out her tongue at Viktor, then took Irina's wrist and led her out of the box, speaking low so only Irina could hear. "Consider it payback for finding you in the funeral home after you rode Viktor's hand to happy land." She grinned when her sister looked offended.

"That is hardly the same situation at all!" Irina exclaimed as they carefully navigated the sweeping staircase.

Andrey helped Irina on with her wrap, to Alexei's obvious dismay, while Konstantin did the same for Galina. Papa returned with Maksim and Petyr in tow. The two had become friends at the bar as they waited out the second act together, drinking vodka and swapping tales of their beloved Russia. Maksim was swaying a little on his feet. Galina felt a bit sorry for him. No one but Papa could keep up with Uncle Petyr.

Papa suggested an outing to a gentleman's club, intending to spend some quality time with a bottle of Stoli, insisting that Maksim, Andrey and Alexei join him. Alexei agreed immediately, followed quickly by Maksim. Andrey begged off, pleading morning meetings.

"I'll get Mrs. Volkov home safely," Viktor told Papa. Galina kept her face conveniently blank.

Papa beamed at Viktor and patted him shoulder. Alexei's face went red as he realized that he'd missed the opportunity to take Irina home himself and tried to hedge his way out of late-night drinks at the club. "Well, maybe I should take Irina home. I don't know if I trust Viktor to keep her safe."

Galina practically snorted in amusement. After the incident with him shredding Irina's clothes, he was delusion if he thought he was fooling anyone. He was so transparent that he made glass look opaque.

"Viktor has my complete trust," Papa announced, making even Andrey's eyebrows rise. Irina clutched at Galina's hand, her eyes wide. Galina watched her father thoughtfully. This was the first time she could remember Papa contradicting Alexei in public since they were children. Could this mean that their father's "eldest is the only option" mind-set was finally changing? Could her continuous questioning be undermining Papa's stubborn confidence in Alexei's ability to lead? She certainly hoped so.

Maksim pulled Alexei aside, already talking about his plans for expanding the import business. Alexei had no choice but to drop his argument.

Viktor inclined his head and fell in step behind Irina. "Thank you, sir."

"Then Konstantin should go with Nik, and Andrey can escort Galina since Viktor will be coming with me," Irina offered, a knowing look in her eyes.

Galina frowned, certain she was missing something, especially when Nik wouldn't look at her. Had something happened while she and Andrey had been busy in the cloak room? Irina looked positively giddy. She was definitely going to need to speak to her sister tomorrow.

Andrey's lips twitched as he said, "That's fine. I can see Miss Sudenko home."

"I can see my own self home, thank you very much," she said tartly. "I did make my way here all by myself, after all." She batted her eyelashes at everyone.

"Of course," Irina said, just as sweetly, shooting her an evil smile. "But I would feel more comfortable if you had an escort."

Galina wanted to reach out and shake her sister until her teeth rattled. What the hell was she playing at with this? She felt Andrey move closer. She wished she wasn't so attuned to his presence. He was getting to be a constant distraction. A pleasant distraction certainly, but a distraction nonetheless.

She shot her sister a pointed glare. "Fine."

"Fine, fine," Papa said dismissively, and cuffed their brother on the shoulder. "Come, Alexei, Maksim, join the men at the club. We have many things to talk about."

Papa dragged a reluctant Alexei toward the door. Alexei kept shooting poisonous looks at Viktor. Galina couldn't help but grin. "I wish I could have recorded that and posted it on YouTube," she said, laughing when Alexei was out of sight. "Alexei knows he got tricked but he's not sure how. The gears in his head are smoking."

"Well, I can't look at any of you right now, so we're going to go," Irina said, taking Viktor's arm. "Galina, if you're not at my house at nine a.m. sharp, I will bring a tranq gun and a net to yours."

Galina sighed. "You are so dramatic sometimes." She laughed as Irina dragged Viktor off.

"You could have sounded a bit more pleased with the outcome," Andrey whispered, his breath fanning the hair at her neck. "I don't bite."

"Maybe that's the problem," Galina murmured without thinking. When she realized what she'd just implied, she felt a flush creep across her face. Had she just really insinuated the mating bite? Really? Was she an idiot? She had no interest in tying herself to Andrey permanently; he was just a great bit of fun. Especially since it looked like Papa was serious about pairing him with Irina. To want more than that was ridiculous.

She felt his hand at the small of her back. "I've got an early morning, so I'm going to call it a night." She was ready to be out of the eyes of her family and back in her apartment where she could berate herself in private. She said her good-byes to Nik and Konstantin and walked to where the Maybach waited, not bothering to see if Andrey followed.

His hand slipped under her elbow when she was halfway across the wide expanse of stone tiles that separated the theater from the line of cars in the front of the building. He said nothing as they walked, both of them mindful of the eyes of her family that watched from the glass walls of the theater's atrium. Galina nodded to her driver who held the door open for her and Andrey. She slid inside, moving to the far side of the bench seat.

"How did you find out about Nik?" was the first thing she asked him once the driver closed the door on them.

Andrey ran a hand through his dark hair, disturbing it from its neat coif. It fell across his forehead and into his eyes, making him look younger. His steel blue eyes locked with hers and Galina felt those damn flutters begin in her belly. How could he do this to her with just a look?

"Konstantin suspected and mentioned it to me about a year ago." He rubbed a hand over his jaw. Galina's sensitive ears picked up the sound of stubble prickling across his hand. "I just accepted it as truth. I trust Konstantin in these things."

She turned her body to face him. "You've known for a *year?*"

He nodded, hair falling back into his eyes. "More or less."

"And you haven't told anyone?" Galina's head spun. All she could think about was protecting Nikolai. She knew the organization's feelings on same sex pairings. Nikolai could be killed if he were outed. It was part of why Papa wasn't willing to promote him to family head, even though Alexei was clearly unsuited for the position. Papa loved Nikolai and shielded him as much as he could, but there was only so much he could do. If anyone found out, Nik would be sacrificed to maintain the appearance of machismo within the family.

Andrey put a finger under her chin. His lips were very close to hers. "Why would I tell anyone about Nikolai? I like him. He's a good man. And Konstantin likes him."

Galina blinked, feeling tears of relief spring to the back of her eyes. She would *not* cry, damn it. But the thought of Andrey knowing and not saying anything about her brother's sexual orientation, even when it could have improved his position in the organization undid her. "Thank you," she whispered, placing a gentle hand on his knee.

"Galina, I would never hurt Nikolai. Or you."

She blinked, surprised by his admission. She lowered her gaze to her hand on his leg, lashes sweeping low to hide her eyes. This was more intimate than she got with anyone. She wondered how close to her apartment they were.

"How long have you known about Konstantin?" she asked, just to have something to say.

He laughed softly, a low, mellow sound. "Since we were in high school," he admitted easily, taking her hand in his and bringing it to his lips. He lightly kissed each of her fingertips. "We were best friends, as I've said. I was the only one he trusted enough to tell. It was a great honor." He licked at the pad of her index finger.

She inhaled sharply at the heat of his tongue on her hand. "You're a good man," she whispered, her insides twisting. She was out of her depth here.

He took her face in his hands, forcing her to look up at him. She stared into his face, searching the strong planes and angles of it for what she didn't know. He looked tired. She reached a hand to his cheek and he nuzzled his head against her palm, eyelids dropping closed. Her fingers stretched out to stroke at his temple, brushing the hair back. "You *are* a good man," she repeated.

His eyes snapped open and his head jerked out of her palm, putting them nose to nose. He smiled darkly, his eyes looking more grey than blue as he stared at her. His mouth thinned, the smile turning cruel. "But I'm not a good man, Galina." He pulled back suddenly. "In that you are very, very mistaken."

She caught his face in her hands, stopping his escape so he had to look at her. Carefully she moved to sit in his lap, her dress pooling around them. Her naked sex was pressed against the rough fabric covering his crotch and it took all of her self-control to not move herself up and down over him. "I think you're mistaken." She leaned forward, running her tongue over the hard line of his lips. She caught the look of surprise in his eyes. "And I'm the only one who matters."

Galina claimed his mouth, showing him without words what she thought of him. For Nikolai alone, she would always be grateful. But it was more than that. She liked Andrey, and not just for the sex. He surprised her. Not many people did that anymore. His lips opened, softening beneath her kisses. She kept the pace slow, taking her time to learn the shape of his lips, the taste of his mouth, the feel of his teeth. Her hands held his head in place as she kissed him deeply, not allowing him to pull away from her.

His hands grasped at her waist spasmodically. Galina took her time, sliding her tongue around his, sucking on it until he moaned against her mouth. She felt his cock stiffen and push against the fabric of his pants, pressing against her wet pussy with every flex of her thighs as she held herself just above his lap.

She released his mouth to press her lips to the pulsing beat at his neck. She licked over it, then closed her mouth over it to tease it with her teeth. He surged up, wrapping his arms around her tightly. "Fuck!" he shouted hoarsely, shaking his head. His cock spasmed against her, and Galina smiled against his neck.

Her hands worked to free him. He shuddered, dropping his head against her shoulder when her hand wrapped around his shaft. His breath gusted out of him, like he'd just run a sprint. She pressed her thumb into the slit at the head of him and he cried out. His head fell back against the backseat, eyes almost rolling back in his head. His hips pumped his cock into her hand, and Galina flexed her wrist, keeping her strokes long and even. She used her hand to spread the pre-come over his shaft, twisting her thumb over the head.

Andrey lifted his head once more, his eyes hungry and desperate. She increased her speed, feeling his hips thrusting as she drew him closer and closer to the edge of his release. His mouth opened and closed, but no words came out. Keeping the rhythm of her strokes even, she lined up the head of him, stopping and holding the base of his cock as she lowered herself onto him.

Galina watched Andrey's face as she slowly sheathed him within her walls. She kept a tight grip on the base of his cock to keep him from spending himself too soon. He groaned, pushing up into her blindly. She brushed hair away from his face and kissed him again as she began to move, setting the pace.

His hands clutched at her back, grabbing and pulling at her hair. Galina smiled, enjoying the cries she wrung from Andrey as she rolled her hips against him and tightened her hand around him. He growled, snapping his hips hard against her, trying to drive the rhythm to what he wanted. Galina pulled back, keeping only the head of his cock inside her, giving him a warning squeeze. This was her show to run. She wanted to do this for him, to him.

"Сладкая," he whispered, his head dropping to her shoulder once more. He sucked gently at the space where her neck joined her shoulder. He'd just called her sweet in Russian.

"Mine," she whispered back, sheathing him once again.

"Yours," he agreed, moaning as her pace quickened. His eyes met hers, desire and something else burning in his gaze. He kissed her, his mouth a burning brand against her own.

She released him, raising her hand to his shoulder. He shouted into her mouth, his whole body driving forward as he plunged into her. Galina writhed against him as his cock pulsed deep inside her, his climax ripping through him suddenly. He sagged against her, and she reached back to hold the top of the headrest to keep them both upright.

"God," he murmured, pressing his forehead to hers. His voice was shaking.

She smiled, carding her fingers through his hair with one hand. "That's a proper fucking," she whispered, nibbling at his earlobe. She felt good all over, slow and lazy like a big cat after a feed. "Although I despair for the state of your tuxedo pants."

"I really don't give a fuck about my pants right now." Andrey pulled her closer and she felt him slip out of her. Her dress was probably ruined but she couldn't bring herself to care.

Andrey held her against his chest, her head tucked on his shoulder, stroking her hair and back. His head was thrown back against the head-rest, eyes closed. Galina thought he'd fallen asleep, so she lifted a hand to lightly trace his lips. His hand came up and grabbed hers, holding it loosely so she could pull away if she wanted to.

She didn't want to.

His blue eyes cracked open. "Mmmmmm," he hummed, sounding exhausted and pleased. "I should go to the ballet more often."

Galina laughed softly and snuggled against him.

14

When in Doubt, Send Pastries

Galina looked up from the catalog she was perusing at the sound of a knock at her door. A delivery man stood holding a clipboard and pen.

"There's a delivery you need to sign for." He held them out to her.

"Art shipments are usually signed for at the loading dock," she told him, getting to her feet.

"It's not an art delivery," he said. "It's personal. For Galina Sudenko."

Galina cocked her head, as if she didn't comprehend what he'd just said. Who would send her something here? While she was signing for the delivery, he lifted a huge urn of two dozen roses so dark red they were nearly black. Interspersed among the stems was aconite and wormwood. She peeked among the leaves for a card, finally finding it tucked into a particularly dense knot of aconite. When she opened it, she broke into a smile. Written on the card was one word: *Yours.*

Staggering a little under the weight of the arrangement, Galina she set the urn atop a bank of filing cabinets that lined one wall and picked up her phone to call Andrey.

"You got the flowers then?" His deep voice sent a shiver through her. She remembered how his voice sounded in the car last night: broken, wanting.

"I did. They're beautiful. And the aconite and wormwood are nice touches." She couldn't keep the smile from her voice.

"I'm glad you like them." She heard voices on the other end of the line. Andrey said something she didn't catch to someone with him, then said, "I have to go. I will see you later."

"I'm counting on it," Galina answered. "And thank you for the flowers. You didn't have to do that."

"Yes, I did." He hung up.

Galina spent the rest of the day arranging exchanges of collections from other museums, trying to track down a painting that had been on loan for over a year, and gathering information about several pieces likely to be up for private auction in a few months. But every time she looked up and saw the flowers from Andrey, she smiled to herself.

She locked her office behind her and made her way to her car, only to find Alexei leaning against it. Galina looked around for her security detail, but her brother must have sent them away. She narrowed her eyes, stopping some distance from Alexei. He pushed himself up from the hood of her car and folded his arms across his chest.

"I know what you're up to," he began without preamble.

Galina kept her face neutral, but her mind went into overdrive. Did he suspect she was looking for the stolen shipment? There's no way Irina would have told him about what she'd discovered in Sergei's office. Had he heard of her discrete inquiries? When it came to Alexei, she had no illusions the depths he would stoop to in order to get what he wanted. That's why Nikolai was so busy all the time; he was the one responsible for cleaning up Alexei's messes.

"And what would that be, besides leaving work to go see our sister?" She kept her voice level, spearing him with her gaze.

He moved closer to her, a stalk rather than a walk. Alexei was powerfully built and she had no doubt if angered he would do something stupid. Having witnesses had never bothered him before. Papa would be furious with Alexei if he really hurt her. Then she recalled the snarl on his face when he'd chased her through the woods. Perhaps Papa's anger was no longer a deterrent to Alexei.

"Your little 'business.' That's cute, by the way." He circled her, and Galina turned to keep him in her sights. "I know you're trying to replace me as father's choice for head of the family."

She didn't try to deny it, but she wasn't going to openly antagonize Alexei when she wasn't in a position of power. "I just asked Papa to let me start a new line of the business. That's it. Don't go getting all paranoid about it." She took another step toward her car.

Alexei blocked her, his bulky body and barrel chest intruding into her personal space. She didn't appreciate being crowded. "You asked for a seat at the table," he growled, eyes narrowing as he leaned in even further. "Women don't get a seat at the table."

In heels she was taller than Alexei, a fact which she was certain he didn't like. She raised herself up to her full height on the stilts she liked to wear and said, "I'm not just a woman." She was a purebred Alpha female and a prized commodity.

"You're a bitch whose only purpose is to breed pups," he snapped, lips pulling back from his teeth in a human version of a wolf's snarl.

Galina jerked her head back as if he'd slapped her. He did *not* just say that to her. "Wow, Alexei," she began, keeping the bone-shaking rage out of her voice, "with that kind of sweet talking it astounds me that you don't have a bevy of women vying to be your wife."

His hand lifted as if he were actually going to backhand her across the face. Galina raised her head high, her eyes daring him to touch her. "Go ahead then. Do it."

They glared at each other, neither willing to back down. After several minutes of silence, Galina smiled coldly. "By the way, what was all that stuff you told Irina about her painting the world with all the colors of her soul? That doesn't sound like the kind of thing a brother would say to his *sister*."

Alexei snarled again, turned on his heel, and loped off to where his car waited. Galina watched him go, surprised to feel her knees shaking. She waited until his car pulled out of the lot and disappeared down the long, winding drive that led from the museum. "Dickhead," she muttered before getting in her own car to go see Irina.

When Galina rang the doorbell, Irina answered it so quickly that she wondered if her sister had been waiting in ambush for her. She was dragged inside unceremoniously, only managing to get out a, "Nice to see you too," before Irina shoved her down on the couch.

"Explain." Irina sat down and stared at her.

"Okay, so there are clearly some developments we need to talk about," Galina said reasonably.

"Explain," Irina said again.

Galina smiled. "I can draw diagrams if you need visual aids," she offered. When Irina gave her a dirty look, she put up her hands. "Okay, okay. What do you want to know?"

"How about you start when you met Andrey and end when you climaxed in the coatroom?"

Galina's lips quirked at her sister's choice of words. Galina had always been a fan of alliteration. "I'm going to assume you mean meeting Andrey this year and not when we were kids."

Irina shook her head. "You met him when you were younger? Where was I?"

"Training to be a cosmonaut. I don't know!" At Irina's frown, she got to the point. "I saw him the night Sergei was shot—he was at Katya's party. We kind of hooked up in the kitchen."

"Galina!"

"Oh, don't act so scandalized, Miss Funeral Fingerbang. We didn't get too far because Sergei getting shot sort of killed the mood."

Irina scowled. "Do you actually hear the words coming out of your mouth?"

Galina shrugged. "Sorry." She leaned back against the couch cushions, sinking into it like it was made of marshmallow. "We've kind of been seeing each other on and off."

"So when you say you're seeing each other, what you really mean is seeing each other naked, right?"

Galina deadpanned, "Yes, Irina. We fuck. I'm sure you've heard of it. It's what we do."

Irina rolled her eyes. "Well, that might be a little hard to *continue* to do since Papa wants me to marry your boink-buddy. Hence the family outing from hell."

"I highly doubt Andrey's going to let that happen." Galina smiled, remembering the car ride from the previous night.

"I wish I could be free of it all," Irina sighed. "Franny has asked me, over and over, why I don't just walk away, making a life away from Alexei and Papa and…everything. I'm not pack, not subject to Alpha influence. I'm an adult. I have a degree, skill and reputation enough to get a job anywhere I want. Franny doesn't understand that no matter where I go, no matter how many layers of false identification I put up as protection, Papa would send his goons after me and drag me back. There's no escape, nowhere to run."

Galina allowed Irina to have her moment of misery. She figured her sister deserved a bit of wallowing, but there were limits. "I noticed that you didn't include 'abandoning your fabulous baby sister to a pack full of misogynist idiots' on your list of reasons not to leave."

Irina snickered, letting Galina nudge her with her shoulder. "Oh, you would be fine without me and you know it. You've always been the strong one, Galya."

"I think you're going to surprise yourself someday, Rina."

Quirking her lips, Irina said, "I suppose there has to be some mettle in me, if I survived walking in on both Sudenko siblings mid-coitus."

"Wait, who else did you walk in on besides me and Andrey?" Galina thought for a second. "Oh god, did you walk in on Alexei with one of his cocktail skanks?"

"No, it was Nik."

Galina furrowed her brow. "Who did Nik—*Konstantin!* Holy crap, he got it on with Konstantin!"

"I know, it's huge. Nik could be starting a real relationship instead of geographically convenient hook-ups," Irina said, smiling. "I'm so proud of him, even though it's a huge risk and it could go badly at any moment, but really…good for him. I feel like we should get him a cake or something to celebrate this momentous occasion. What kind of baked goods do you get for someone to say 'congratulations on getting a blow job from a person you're going to see regularly'?" She thought for a moment. "Italian cream?"

Galina shook her head. "Cannolis."

Irina frowned. "I gave you this idea. I had that coming."

The sibling dessert war escalated quickly. Nik's return salvo was a gift bag filled with English fruit puddings for each of them, and message telling them to "Eat a bag of spotted dicks. Love, your brother."

Galina returned serve to Nik with a box of éclairs and a note that read, "Cream filled, just the way you like them. Love, Galina."

He sent her a frangipane tart, and his message was, "Since you are one. Love, Nik."

She and Andrey shared it over coffee at his condo. "I do not understand you and your siblings," he said around a huge mouthful of it.

"I forget, you didn't grow up with brothers and sisters." She smiled at him over the rim of her coffee cup.

Andrey shook his dark head, shoveling another piece of tart into his mouth. "No, but I have many cousins."

"That can be kind of the same thing." She wiped her mouth on a napkin. "What's to understand anyway? We like giving each other a hard time, that's all."

"You do not treat Alexei like this."

Galina frowned, tossing her napkin onto the table in disgust. "Alexei doesn't *want* to be treated like this. He's never had much of a sense of humor, even when we were kids." She paused to look up at Andrey. "Well, you remember what he was like."

He nodded thoughtfully. "He has gotten worse as he has gotten older."

"He wants to be an Alpha so bad," Galina agreed, tapping her fingernails on the table. "Thankfully for the family he'll never be one." She shuddered. "Can you imagine what he would do if he was one?"

Andrey reached across the small table and took her hand in his. "Your father is still backing him, Alpha or not." He tilted his head, giving her a curious look. "You and Nik are both Alphas. It's odd that it skipped Alexei."

Galina shrugged. Her oldest sister, Elena, hadn't been an Alpha either, but she didn't want to bring her up in conversation. Elena had married someone Papa didn't approve of and it hadn't ended well for either of them. She swallowed around the sudden lump in her throat.

"Let's just be thankful it did." She sighed when Andrey lifted her hand to his lips and pressed kisses to each of her fingertips.

"I have to go to work," she warned even as heat began to curl in her pelvis.

"The museum can wait," he said, eyes turning a silvery blue with lust. He nipped at her knuckles.

She pulled her hand free. Galina would love nothing more than to drag Andrey across the table and have ridiculously mind blowing sex with him. But she couldn't today. "But million dollar smuggling deals won't."

Andrey frowned. Galina got up and crossed the space between them. She leaned forward and kissed him. Her lips softly touched his, coaxing his mouth open to taste the sugar on his tongue. His mouth was all wet heat, a heady sensation that made Galina press herself against him. Her hands framed his face, fingertips scratching lightly at the hair at his temples as she kissed him breathless.

"I'll see you tonight," she promised, pulling away reluctantly.

Andrey grabbed her waist, pulling her roughly down into his lap. His mouth devoured her, his tongue sliding against hers. Wetness blossomed between her legs as Andrey sucked on her bottom lip, catching it in his teeth. His strong hands spanned her back, pressing her close. His lips moved over hers, a study in the contrasts of hard and soft. She wanted nothing more than to lose herself in him.

Just as suddenly as he dragged her down, Andrey let her go, setting her back on her feet. "Count on it."

15

Put a Ring on It

Galina had been closing a deal over dinner when she got the announcement of Irina and Andrey's engagement. Uncle Petyr had been busy spreading the good news all over town, despite the fact that Irina was still supposed to be in mourning for several more months.

When Mama Anya heard about this, she was going to have a litter.

She finished her negotiations, but didn't linger over a congratulatory drink. Her phone had been buzzing at her continuously as call after call came in and went to her voice mail. While she waited for the valet to bring her car around, she scrolled through her missed call list.

Nik, Irina, Andrey, Papa, Andrey again, Irina, Andrey, Sveta, Nik, Andrey, Andrey, Irina, Papa.

She wanted to ignore them all. Galina knew she couldn't, but she wanted to just the same. She hadn't expected to feel so hurt by the news. She knew what Papa had planned. Why had it come as such a shock then?

Because Andrey had agreed to it. And that stung the worst of all.

As if thinking about him conjured him, her phone rang again, caller ID confirming him. Galina weighed her options: she could let it go to voice mail again or she could woman up and deal with it.

The sooner she spoke to him, the sooner she could begin to purge him from her mind.

"Galina Sudenko," she said into the phone, all frosty professionalism.

"Galya, it's Andrey," he said, as if she didn't know.

"Yes, Mr. Lupesco?"

"I would like to talk to you." Andrey's voice was dark and throaty, like he was holding something back.

Galina didn't particularly care. "Is it about business?"

"You know damn well what it's about!" he shouted.

"I'm sorry, but unless this is about an artifact you're interested in procuring, I'm afraid we have nothing I am interested in discussing."

"Your father found out about the missing shipment shortly after Sergei was put down. I don't know how he found out—I certainly wasn't going around telling anyone—but he knows that Sergei stole from me."

Galina closed her eyes, feeling exhaustion settle over her like a coat. She didn't want to hear this right now. She didn't want to deal with this whole stupid Bullet business anymore. For the first time, she wished she'd been born into a normal family.

"And?"

"Your father suggested the engagement to your sister," Andrey explained. "I suppose it is his way of making amends."

Of course. Papa had sealed the deal with the Volkovs with Irina's wedding to Sergei. He thought he could accomplish the same thing with Andrey.

"Is that all?" she asked, voice dull and clipped.

His growl of frustration reverberated in her ears. "Galina, don't..."

"Good night, Mr. Lupesco."

Galina seethed. She didn't remember a time she'd been so angry. She'd been stewing for days, since Papa mentioned the stupid, god-damn engagement party for Andrey and Irina. She stayed in her apartment for the past few days, working from home, and ignoring Andrey's calls. But there was no way she could *not* go to the party. So she'd put on her best to-die-for little black dress, her spikiest pair of heels and headed to her father's house to put on a happy face for her sister and her…whatever Andrey was.

A waiter passed by with a tray of champagne flutes. Galina snapped her fingers at him and snagged two, downing one in a swallow, and polishing off the second on her way to join her father where he stood with Andrey. Ilya wore a beatific expression — the content look of a man who had solved a particularly knotty problem. Galina ground her teeth together. If she'd just been able to find that stupid shipment, Papa wouldn't be trading Irina off like she was a prize mare. Galina refused to look at Andrey.

Maksim arrived in another ill-fitting suit, immediately going to her father and Andrey to offer handshakes and congratulations. Papa pointed him in her direction, and the Caviar Prince joined her in the corner. She snagged another glass of champagne from a passing tray, exchanging it for her empty.

He frowned in disapproval. "I should think you've had enough," he sniffed, his voice reproachful.

"That's where you would be wrong," she snapped back, too keyed up to pretend he didn't annoy the living crap out of her.

"It's unseemly for a woman to drink to excess." His dark eyes were alight with his displeasure.

Galina turned her snarl into a tight-lipped smile, stopping the hasty words that leapt to her tongue. "It's a party." She handed him her champagne flute and escaped into the press of people mingling in the formal living room.

Viktor stood off to the side, looking like someone had just killed his favorite puppy. She grabbed two more flutes from a passing waiter and shoved one into his hand.

"You're going to need this," she told him.

"I'm working," he practically snarled at her.

"And there are like eight hundred bodyguards here also working. Drink the damn champagne." She finished her third glass, placing the empty on a nearby table.

Viktor glared at her but emptied the flute. Galina nodded, then approached her father.

"Ah, Galya, there you are!" He saw that she wasn't carrying a glass. "You must have a drink to toast the new member of the family." He beckoned another waiter over.

"Don't mind if I do," she said, taking two more flutes. Knocking back one for courage, she raised the other to Andrey. "Congratulations!" She finished the other, stepping in to give Ilya a kiss on the cheek.

Galina had no intention of saying anything else to Andrey, but her father intervened before she could disappear back into the crowd. "Come Galya, Andrey will be part of the family soon!" She looked at her father in a kind of fascinated horror. His cheeks and nose were flushed; it was obvious he'd been hitting the vodka pretty heavily in celebration of his future son-in-law.

She extended her hand to Andrey, who at least had the grace to look uncomfortable. They shook hands, she murmured, "Congratulations," once again, and she would have been content to leave it at that. But Papa decided to be helpful one more time.

"Family doesn't shake hands!" Papa shoved the two of them together.

"What does he expect me to do?" she snapped at her soon to be brother-in-law. "Give you a lap dance to say welcome to the family?"

Andrey sputtered out a laugh that transformed his face from dour to startlingly handsome in an eye blink. Galina pulled away after the briefest embrace to excuse herself so she could get some stronger booze.

As she mingled, Galina heard the whispered threads of conversation as she passed the knots of partygoers. Most everyone appeared to be having a good time, but she caught a few angry comments about Irina and Andrey's pairing. One man Papa's age went so far as to say that at least Ilya hadn't wasted a real Sudenko on Andrey. Galina winced in sympathy for her sister.

The few Rom that Andrey had invited stood in a cluster close to the bar. They were unusually quiet, their faces somber. Edging closer, Galina heard one of them say that they'd prefer Andrey not marry at all rather than wed a Sudenko. The muttering stopped as she moved past them.

On her way to the kitchen, she passed Alexei. If possible, he looked even less happy than Andrey, Irina, and Viktor combined. "You should be up there with Papa," she noted as she passed him.

"This is a fucking joke," he fumed. "I can't believe he's marrying Irina to that fucking Rom. It's like marrying a queen to a dog. The old man is senile!"

"Papa wouldn't have had to marry off Irina if Sergei hadn't stolen that 'fucking Rom's' drugs," Galina retorted, keeping her voice low. "Didn't Sergei's team work under you?"

"If the Rom had been able to protect his product, he wouldn't have lost it in the first place!" Alexei's voice shook with rage.

Galina moved on, shaking her head. It was crazy person logic. She couldn't argue with that. Instead, she pulled out a bottle of bourbon, poured it into a Tervis tumbler and went back out to the party.

The evening wore on slowly. Irina was upstairs, still getting ready. The caterer's waiters began circulating with trays of hors d'oeuvres. Galina snagged a tray and sat down on the front porch with her bourbon.

Damn it, she could have found out where the drugs were. If Papa hadn't gotten wind of Sergei's massive fuck-up, he wouldn't have offered Irina up to Andrey like some kind of consolation prize. Galina couldn't be mad at her sister—this wasn't her fault. But there was no reason for her to be around the happy couple either, at least not until she'd gotten her anger under control.

She dumped the empty tray on the seat next to her and polished off the bourbon. The alcohol hadn't hit her yet, but she was hoping it would soon. Then she'd be able to go back inside and pretend a happiness she did not feel.

As she sat on the front steps, feeling sorry for herself, she noticed Vasily walking from the free-standing garage to the back of the house. Galina perked up. There was nothing back there except an old potting shed and the guesthouse. Why would Vasily be heading there in the middle of a party where all of the Sudenko bodyguards were supposed to be on watch? She followed.

Vasily loped along the garden path, hands tucked in his pockets. Galina kept him in sight, grateful for the light mist that kept everyone out of the garden for the evening. She ducked behind a wall of fragrant night-blooming jasmine until he passed beyond the garden's borders.

She moved quickly, keeping as close to cover as possible without completely losing sight of Alexei's guard. As she rounded a tall hedge, she stopped, ducking down. Timur stood in front of the shed, watching Vasily approach.

"About damn time," Timur rumbled, cracking his neck.

"Any trouble?" Vasily asked, eyes scanning the nearby surroundings. Galina hunched down even lower, making herself as small as possible. She was glad she'd worn her wolfsbane perfume.

"Nah. Who the hell's going to bother me out here with that party going on?"

Vasily nodded. "That's what the Boss said." He held out a cigarette to Timur. "You can come inside."

Timur lit the cigarette, drawing in a lungful of smoke. He released it slowly, a stream of grey that dissipated in the moist air. "You sure?"

Vasily nodded, lighting up his own cigarette. "Boss was pretty confident."

The two began their return to Papa's house, smoke billowing around them like a tattered cape. Galina waited, scenting the air to make sure they were gone. Then she got up and went over to the shed.

It was a small white clapboard structure, set near the stone wall at the back of the property. The paint was peeling and it needed a new roof, but it was perfect for what held: garden tools, seeds, and fertilizer. But there was a shiny new lock on the door. Since when did they lock up the gardener's shed?

One good thing: the lock might be new but the wood the metal plate was attached to was old. If Alexei had men out here, that must mean there was something worth guarding. And she had a good idea of what that might be. Lifting her foot, Galina kicked against the wood with all of her strength. She heard a snapping sound, but the door remained shut. She kicked it two more times and the wood splintered, the door finally swinging open.

The interior smelled of decaying plants and the sharp tangy mix of mulch and fertilizer. Her gaze wandered around the shed, cataloguing the clay pots, the trowels, the seed bins and small stacks of spare paving stones for the paths that wound through the garden. She stepped inside carefully, intending to search behind the tarps and rakes, when her heel sank into a partially rotten floorboard.

Slipping her foot out of the shoe, she knelt down to try to pull it out. At first, the shoe didn't budge, but when she really put her strength into it, the shoe—still spearing the plank—came loose from the floor.

Galina stared dumbly at her shoe and the impaled piece of wood that she held in one hand. Dropping her gaze, she froze. Blocks of grey powder wrapped in plastic sat stacked in the hole. "You are fucking kidding me," she said to no one in particular as she knelt down to inspect her find.

Stacks of bricks were shoved into the hidey hole. Galina would lay odds that the number of bricks under the floor matched up with the number of bricks in Andrey's missing shipment. This is why she couldn't find the Bullet in any of Sergei's usual hidey-holes. He'd already passed it off to Alexei.

Galina ripped her shoe from the board, sliding her foot back into it, and pulled down one of the tarps from the wall. Spreading it out, she began to stack the Bullet on it. There was no way she could leave it here, not with the evidence of her snooping there for Alexei to see. She'd move the product somewhere safe and then let Andrey know she'd found it.

When all the Bullet was sitting on the tarp, she replaced the board over the gaping hole. Then she pulled the sides of the tarp together, gathering it in her hands like a bundle. She swung the package over her shoulder, staggering a bit beneath its weight. As quickly as she could, she made her way back to the garage where she'd parked her car, keeping as hidden as she could.

By the time she entered the garage, she was sweaty and winded. Popping the trunk, Galina dumped the tarp and its contents into her car. She leaned against the side of the Mercedes, feeling her body shake with exertion and adrenaline. Galina placed her hands against the cool metal, taking comfort from the solid mass, letting it ground her.

When she felt less shaky, Galina leaned forward to check her reflection in the side mirror. She pushed her hair back in place, brushing bits of grass and twigs from her dress. She cleaned her shoes with a rag she found on a rolling toolbox in the corner of the garage. Feeling better, she squared her shoulders and made her way back to the party.

Papa grabbed her elbow as soon as she came through the front door of the house. "Have you seen your sister? She should have been down by now." There was a dull note of panic in his voice.

She grasped her father's hand, trying to soothe him. She understood his concern; the last engagement party they'd thrown hadn't ended well. Papa was wary if he didn't have eyes on Irina at all times.

"I bet she's just preparing herself to be the center of attention in front of all of these people. She's still supposed to be in mourning, Papa. I'll go check upstairs for her."

He patted her hand, leaning in to give her a kiss on the forehead. Galina waited until he toddled back into the main party before she climbed the stairs. She stopped in front of the door to her old bedroom. If Irina had her door locked, Galina would need the key she kept in her jewelry box.

She turned the handle to her bedroom, but it was locked.

Galina felt like her stomach fell through the floor. Who was in her room?

She didn't bother to knock. Long ago, she'd learned how to unlock her door—she used to lock it every day before leaving for school so her family couldn't snoop while she was gone. She'd had to figure out a way to get back in without climbing in and out of the second story window.

Pulling a bobby pin from her hair, she stuck it in the hole in the knob and popped the lock. She opened the door and stepped inside. Her room hadn't changed in all the years since she left. It was a testament to her growing up and teenage taste. Except for her brother Nikolai and Konstantin locked in a very intimate clinch in the middle of her bed.

"Jesus!" she yelped, slamming the door shut behind her.

"Shit!" Konstantin shouted, pulling away from Nik.

Galina clapped a hand over her eyes. "Have you lost your fucking mind? There's a room full of people down there who will happily kill the both of you if they knew what you were doing up here."

She heard Nik laugh. She wanted to argue more, but she turned to give them a moment. Ignoring the boy band posters on the walls, she pulled out the top drawer of her nightstand and snagged the key she had to Irina's bedroom.

"I am going to try to find where Irina's gone off to. When I get back, I expect you two idiots to be fully clothed and someplace else!"

"She was asking for you," Nik said, still laughing as he disengaged himself from Konstantin who didn't look embarrassed in the slightest. "I think she's in her room."

Slipping out of her bedroom, she continued down the hall. When she tried the door to Irina's room, Galina wasn't surprised to find it locked. She used the key to unlock the door, pushing the door open and immediately wished she hadn't. Viktor and Irina were locked together, clearly celebrating her engagement to another man in a very interesting way.

"Oh, come *on*," she said, pocketing the key and shutting the door behind her. She turned the lock again to make sure they weren't interrupted. "What is *wrong* with you people? People who should not be having sex in Papa's house should stop having sex in Papa's house. Do you guys have *no* sense of self-preservation?"

She saw Irina's shoulders shaking and realized her sister was laughing. Had she lost her mind completely? Viktor moaned and dropped his head to Irina's neck. If Papa or Andrey or Alexei came upstairs they were all going to be epically fucked.

Galina crossed her arms in front of her chest and glared at the two of them. This was not happening to her. This just couldn't be happening to her. "Could you at least pull out of my sister, so we can discuss how we're going to get out of this colossal shit storm you have created?"

"We can't," Irina said, looking helplessly over her shoulder at her. She looked like she was going to laugh again.

"What do you mean, you can't?" Galina demanded.

"Viktor knotted me," Irina told her calmly. "I'm locked on. He can't pull out."

Galina wanted to slap herself. This could not be happening. Not today. Knotting was part of the wolf side of mating. The male's member swelled — knotted — so that it was impossible for him to pull out until he'd finished ejaculating. And that could take a very long time. "Holy shit. How long ago?"

"Just a few minutes," Irina said. "So we could be stuck like this for —"

"Hours!" Galina hissed, feeling the rage she'd been holding back all day bubble to the surface. "You could be stuck like this *for hours*. You asshole!" She picked up the nearest thing to hand — a Kleenex box — and chucked it at Viktor's back. "A whole house full of very hostile guests and you pull this? I thought you guys were able to control it! This is some crazy higher level mating shit!"

"Your voice is helping," Viktor groaned. "Keep talking."

"You bet your ass I'm going to keep talking." Galina began to pace, needing to do something with her pent up energy. "Are you mentally deficient in some way? You are balls deep in my sister at her engagement party! This is a whole new level of stupidity!" She fixed Viktor with an angry glare. "I can't believe we trust you with our lives! Seriously, we'd be better off with an idiot five-year-old for a fucking bodyguard."

"Hey!" Irina protested, obviously offended on behalf of her paramour.

"No, no, this is good," Viktor interrupted, pulling away from Irina a bit. "It's working."

"Papa is having a damn litter downstairs in the front parlor, worried that you might be pulling an Elena. I can only imagine what he would do if he came up here and found you two like this." Galina threw up her hands in utter exasperation. "I just can't even anymore! It's like I'm babysitting a couple of hormonal fifteen-year-olds who don't have the sense that God gave a duck!"

"You're the one who didn't think Papa would go through with this engagement!" Irina whisper-shouted.

"I didn't think *Andrey* would go through with it!" Galina growled before she could stop herself.

Everyone in the room went quiet. Irina wore a stricken expression. "Oh, Galya," she said, opening her arms as if she wanted to give Galina a hug.

Galina looked at her in horror. "I am not hugging you while you're still…*attached* to him. That would just be weird and there isn't enough therapy on earth that could fix it." She waved away Irina's sympathy. "I'm fine. It's just not what I expected."

Viktor pulled free of Irina. Galina turned around, not needing or wanting to see any more of him than she had already. "Clean yourselves up and then get your asses downstairs. I'll cover for you with Papa. And lock the door behind me. Morons."

When she was back in the hallway, Galina pressed her forehead against the wall, striving for a calm she did not feel. Everything had turned out wrong. Irina was tied to a man she didn't love. Alexei was probably going to take over the family and run it into the ground. She would be married off to some inbred dimwit that Papa deemed worthy for her. It was enough to make her want to scream.

She was never attending another engagement party as long as she lived.

Galina ducked into a bathroom and washed her hands to give herself a bit of space to collect herself. Checking her make up in the mirror, she put on her iciest expression. She could do this. She could watch Andrey suck up to her father and watch her sister be trapped in another loveless marriage. She could raise a glass and toast their misery.

Gripping the edge of the marble vanity with shaking hands, Galina lowered her gaze from her reflection. She just had to get through the next few hours and then she could fix everything. She hoped.

When she found Papa and informed him that Irina would be down in a few minutes, he looked relieved. He collected Andrey and the two men went to wait for Irina at the bottom of the stairs. Her duty done, Galina tucked herself into a corner close to the door so she could make a quick escape should she be unable to keep her fake smile plastered on her face.

Her sister appeared at the top of the staircase, utterly breathtaking in her green dress and emerald necklace. Unfortunately, Irina wore an expression that said she'd rather lose her arm in a garbage disposal accident than be tied to Andrey. But she eventually managed to hide her feelings behind a blank mask as she descended the stairs to meet her betrothed.

Galina watched as Papa placed Irina's hand into Andrey's and realized she couldn't stay at the party another moment. She'd done her daughterly duty: she'd made sure everyone saw her face, she'd congratulated Andrey publicly, she'd stood by her father, and she'd gotten Irina downstairs. There was nothing left for her to do except watch her sister and Andrey mingle.

And that she just couldn't bring herself to do.

She slipped out the front door and into the night.

16

Engagement Doesn't Mean What You Think It Means

Galina sagged into her couch with a sigh. Even the bath hadn't relaxed her after that heinousness that called itself an engagement party. She'd managed to drive off the property and make it a few miles before she had to pull off to the side and beat the ever-loving shit out of her steering wheel.

Now she just wished she could get the image of Andrey lowering his lips to Irina's out of her head. Galina stretched out and snagged a blanket from the back of the couch. She was wearing her comfort pajamas: a black tank top and her fleecy Stewie pajama pants, washed so many times that they felt like silk on her. She only busted them out in times of dire need. The present moment certainly counted.

If only she could fall asleep. But her mind skipped from the party to Nik and Konstantin, then back to the bricks of Bullet, only to circle back around to Viktor and Irina in their mating clinch. That was something she was never going to be able to unsee. Why didn't someone make bleach for the brain?

Galina picked up her battered copy of *The Three Musketeers*—her go-to book when things were just too complicated in real life. She loved the swordplay and the intrigue and the fact that Athos was all tortured and had made some really bad decisions in his love life. She could totally relate. He'd been her first book crush when she'd read the novel for the first time over a decade ago. She needed some quality escapism right now.

She'd just reached the part where the Musketeers were dropping off one by one in their quest to get to Buckingham, when her doorbell buzzed. She padded to the front door, expecting a neighbor on her floor looking to borrow something.

Galina was not expecting to see Andrey Lupesco, still in his sharp engagement party suit, standing at the threshold. It was obscene how good he looked. She swung the door shut in his face, but he caught it with an outstretched hand.

"Galya," he began, but she cut him off, already walking away.

"You don't get to call me that anymore," she snapped. "And how the hell did you get past my doorman?"

He stepped inside her apartment, closing and locking the door behind him. "He remembered me. Also I gave him an absolutely ridiculous amount of money so he wouldn't spoil the surprise I had for you." His black hair hung in his eyes.

"I am so getting him fired." She put her hands on her hips.

"Sweet, please," he began, taking a step toward her.

Galina held up a hand to stop him. "And don't call me that either. I am not your sweet, I am going to be your *sister-in-law*." She gave a short, broken laugh, the events of the day hitting her all at once. She felt unhinged, like she could fly off the handle at any moment. She put her back to him as she tried to get herself back under control.

His hand touched the middle of her back and she shrugged him off. He did not get to touch her. Without turning around, she said, "I found your shipment, by the way. Alexei had it, but it's sitting in the trunk of my car. So, you know, *woohoo*." Galina waved her hands in the air, imitating excitement.

"Galina." Andrey's voice was quiet but compelling. "Look at me."

Galina felt her lip tremble. She was furious with him. But she wasn't entirely sure she could face him without falling apart and she did not want him to see her like that. He had no right to it. "What?"

"*Look* at me."

Galina blew a stray hair out of her face and spun around. Rage flared inside of her as she looked at him, standing there with his eyes and his mouth and his stupid hair and those hands, and she couldn't hold anything in any longer. "What the hell do you want from me, Andrey?" she shouted, spreading her arms wide. "I thought you were going to give me time to find your damn drugs—I thought you were just dating Irina to keep Papa happy!"

"I was," Andrey snapped. "And then your father—well ahead of the mourning schedule, I might add—suggested I marry Irina as repayment for my missing shipment. I don't know how he found out about it. None of my people would have told him. So tell me, how the hell am I supposed to say no to him without giving offense? I'm not engaged, I'm ambitious, and I sure as hell couldn't tell him that I'm already fucking his youngest daughter!"

Galina didn't want to hear his logic right then. She was angry. "You knew Irina had feelings for Viktor—they've knotted for chrissake—and yet you went along with it anyway!"

"Wait, back up a second. They knotted? When?" Andrey's eyebrows shot up in surprise.

Galina mimed checking her watch. "Oh, maybe about five hours ago. You know, at your *engagement party*. I got to walk in on it, which was so awesome for me. And that was after I interrupted Nik and Konstantin engaging in the love that dare not speak its name in my old bedroom!" She was shouting at him now, stepping forward for emphasis with every point.

She threw her hands up in the air in surrender. "I just don't care anymore! Alexei was busy doing his best Charles Manson impression watching you and Irina next to Papa, Nik's determined to get himself outed by hooking up with the help of a rival family right under Papa's nose, and Irina and Viktor, well, I just don't even know when it comes to them. It's like all of them want to get killed!"

Galina stopped her rant, panting with rage. It boiled beneath her skin. How could they all be so stupid? Didn't they see what they were risking?

"And what about me, Galina?" Andrey's gaze roved over her, so powerful she felt like he was actually touching her.

"You?" She met his eyes. "I want to slap the shit out of you."

He took a step closer to her so they were almost touching. "Go ahead. Hit me."

Galina clenched her hands into fists. "I'm not going to hit you." She wouldn't look at him.

He lightly touched her cheek. She held herself stiff. His fingers were gentle against her skin, stroking lightly. "You can if you want," he whispered, putting his head close to hers. "I probably deserve it."

She shoved him away. "Damn it, what's wrong with you?" Galina raked her hair back. "I don't want to hit you!"

Andrey moved forward, crowding her. "What do you want?" His voice was a deep rumble that Galina felt all the way in her bones.

She inhaled sharply. Slowly she met his eyes, every nerve ending alive at his nearness. "You," she said simply. "I want you."

Andrey's eyes lit up, seeming to glow silver. His hands came up to cup her face, his thumbs brushing against her cheekbones. He held her gently, as if she was made of the most delicate porcelain. "I've wanted you since the moment I saw you watching me beat Sergei."

He lowered his held to hers, kissing her gently. Galina closed her eyes, reveling in the sweetness of his lips on hers. Andrey took his time, drugging her with long, slow kisses. He coaxed her mouth open, sliding his tongue inside her mouth to twist and lick along hers. She sighed into his mouth, slowly relaxing into him. His hands wrapped around her waist, drawing her closer and closer still, until her body was pressed up against his.

Galina clutched at his arms, unwilling to let him go. His tongue traced the confines of her mouth, licking along the edges of her teeth, flicking against the underside of her tongue. His hands slid up her back, his fingers tracing the line of her spine up to her neck. He found the knot of her hair at her nape and pulled it loose, letting her blond hair tumble about her shoulders.

Andrey broke their kiss to stare at her with hooded eyes. "Galina." He whispered her name like a man at prayer, with a sort of reverence that made her breath catch in her throat. "I'm sorry."

Galina blinked, her eyes feeling suddenly full of tears. She shook her head, unsure what he was apologizing for. They didn't have any kind of commitment. Aside from great sex and an innate compatibility, they had no ties to one another. She had no real reason to be angry with him about his engagement to Irina. She knew this logically. It was the rest of her that had the problem.

Smiling, Andrey traced her lower lip with his thumb. Galina nipped at it playfully. He stopped, tilting her head up further with his hand under her chin. "I'm sorry that I made you think there could ever be any other woman for me. It's you. It's *been* you—probably since that day at your father's house when you shoved your brother off me and cleaned me up." He lightly kissed each corner of her mouth. "You're the only one I could ever want."

Galina wrapped her arms around Andrey's neck, a tear falling down her cheek. He wiped it off with a gentle finger, then put it in his mouth, tasting the salt of her tear. "Are you sure?" she asked, a quaver in her voice. "I'm kind of a lot to take."

Andrey smiled, his white teeth sharp and perfect. He bumped his forehead against hers. "I can handle it." He began to kiss her cheeks, her eyelids, the tip of her nose. "I want everything. Your mind." His hand slid down to cup one ass cheek. "Your passion." His other dipped down to the waistband of her pajama pants. "Your humor." He slowly pulled down one side of her pants. "Your laughter." He lowered his head to kiss her bared hip. "Your love." He nuzzled up the hem of her tank top. "Your rage." His hand moved from her ass to slide up her side, pushing the shirt up as he went. "Your body." His breath ghosted over her flesh, turning her to liquid fire. "Everything you want to give me, I'll take."

He pulled her tank top over her head, laying her breasts bare to his eyes. Andrey lifted his head to hers so he could see her face. "I was yours the night of the ballet."

Galina stared at him for a long moment, searching his face. She wanted him more than any man she'd ever had, but it was more than that. Somehow, amidst all of the stupid shit with Sergei and her family, she'd fallen in love with him. And she didn't regret it.

"Then you've got me," she whispered, holding on tightly to his shoulders. "All of me."

Andrey's grin spread his face like light across water. He claimed her mouth, licking inside it as he lifted her into his arms and carried her to the bedroom. He put her on the bed, following her down to the mattress, his mouth never leaving hers. Galina felt like she was going to combust from the heat of his mouth on hers, and from the delicious way his rough hands felt as they moved over her smooth skin.

She buried her hands in his hair, digging her fingers into his scalp as he made her wet with wanting. Gasping against his mouth, she raised her hips to rub along the length of him resting on top of her. He broke their kiss, groaning, "You feel so good."

"Undress," she said. "I want to feel your skin on mine."

He grinned, skimming a hand over her breast. She arched up into his hand, feeling her pussy clench in anticipation. Andrey's dark head lowered to her breast as he cupped it in his hand, pushing her peak up to his lips. Galina cried out, feeling spasms across all her nerves. His mouth lit a fire in her chest that spread to her clit. She throbbed, spreading her thighs so she could rub against his leg.

His tongue teased her nipple, laving the stiff flesh. He closed his mouth around it, capturing it in his teeth to worry at it lightly. Galina hissed, bucking against him, fingers grabbing fistfuls of his thick dark hair. Her fast breaths forced more of her breast against his mouth and he greedily devoured it with tongue and teeth.

Galina moaned, writhing against Andrey, wanting more, wanting everything he could give her. "Please, Andrey," she begged, voice shaking. "Let me feel you."

He pushed away from her so he could undress. He stripped quickly, and Galina watched greedily as more and more of his flesh was exposed to her wide eyes and desperate hands. He put a knee on the bed and Galina surged up from the bed to grasp his cock in her hand. She licked the sensitive head, then wrapped her mouth around him and sucked hard. His hips bucked against her as she took more of him into her mouth, her tongue pressing firmly against the underside of his sensitive shaft.

Galina shifted so she had unfettered access to him, and swallowed, feeling him go deeper. She opened her mouth wider, her lips stretching around him as his hardness scraped against the back of her throat. His length made it hard to breathe, but she was committed to this; she wanted to feel him at the back of her throat—to feel the ache and burn the next day. She'd heal quickly.

Andrey dragged in great lungsful of air as Galina sucked, her head bobbing up and down. She felt his hands on her head, guiding her but not holding her. She moved, her tongue tasting the salty taste of him as he swelled inside her. She couldn't really use her tongue with this much of him down her throat but she did the best she could with her mouth.

He pulled out of her suddenly with a groan. Galina let loose, surprised, and wiped at her streaming eyes. "I want to come inside you," Andrey murmured, pulling her up to sit on the bed.

Galina nodded enthusiastically. "Yes."

"First, these need to go," he ordered, pulling off her pants and underwear in one swoop and throwing them to the floor.

He pulled Galina to him, pressing her back against his chest. His hands splayed over her breasts, pinching and teasing as he licked at the back of her neck. She groaned as her sex swelled, feeling full and wanting. As one hand played with her nipple, the other crept down her stomach, fingers searching for her cleft. Galina spread her legs wider, crying out as his fingers rubbed over her clit, teasing the throbbing nub. "Andrey!" she gasped, moving against his hand, desperate for more friction, more sensation.

One finger plunged into her, burying itself in her folds. Galina ground down on his hand, already so wet and ready she ached. "Oh God," she gasped, feeling her climax approach as Andrey's finger pressed into her spot. Her knees trembled and she leaned against his strong chest. She wasn't sure how much longer she could hold herself upright.

Andrey growled against her neck and pushed a second finger inside of her. "Please," she keened, unable to do more than plead for release. In response, Andrey bent her down until she braced her hands on the blanket. He grabbed her hips, roughly lining himself up with her entrance and pushing inside her with one stroke.

Galina gave a strangled scream, thrusting her hips back against his to take him deeper as her walls spasmed around him. She shuddered out her release, jerking and gasping as Andrey pumped his hips against hers. His busy fingers kept teasing her clit, giving her no relief after her orgasm. She felt as if she'd been blown apart and put back together with the pieces in the wrong place.

"Jesus," he whispered as he fell against her back, cock spearing her with his hard thrusts. "You feel fucking amazing." He rolled his hips against hers, now holding her hips with both hands as he pistoned into her.

Galina turned her head so she could watch him, a wicked expression on her face as she watched him come undone. He buried himself in the heat of her, and she met his thrusts, their bodies moving in a primal rhythm.

She felt him swelling inside of her, his cock bulging against her walls as his flesh knotted. Galina's eyes widened as she felt it happen.

Andrey was knotting her. She shivered, feeling full like she never had before as his cock continued to grow inside of her.

He growled, a low rumble against her ear as he leaned forward, the mating drive taking hold of him. His fingers dug into the flesh at her hips as he yanked her even closer, until there was no space between them. One hand slid between her thighs, finding her clit and tweaking it, rubbing slow circles, then stroking it firmly with his thumb.

Galina bucked against his hand, against his cock, a low wail escaping from her lips as the tension once again built inside her. She was close to the edge, ready to spiral over it.

Andrey threw back his head and pounded into her one last time. Galina felt the heat of his come as it bathed her insides. He howled, hips still pulsing against her as another jet of come filled her. She felt it begin to run down her legs, and then Andrey ground his palm against her clit and she cried out as the force of another climax blew through her like a hurricane.

Her vision went gray and it took her a minute to come back to herself. She felt Andrey's release still pulsing inside of her. He held her against him, one hand on her hip, the other braced against her stomach. Galina lolled her head back to rest against his shoulder, completely exhausted from the force of her orgasms and the events of the day. Andrey pressed kisses to the side of her neck, his body still shuddering through his climax. The sheets beneath them were soaked and would likely become more so before he was done.

He laughed softly, his hot breath brushing over her cheek. Their mingled juices ran down her thighs and still he pulsed inside her. Andrey nuzzled her neck. "You are the most perfect woman ever created," he whispered. "Сладкая."

She sighed. He'd called her his sweet again. She could get used to him saying that. "That's a very nice thing to say, but it's not entirely accurate." She rubbed her cheek against his stubble, relishing the feel of him. "I'm a lousy housekeeper. And I may snore. You'll have to tell me in the morning."

Andrey chuckled, biting lightly at her shoulder. "So that means I get to spend the night?"

Galina wrapped her fingers around his hand, holding him tightly. "Well, since I'm tired and there's no telling when we'll unknot, I guess I can put up with you."

"It's a burden to bear, I'm sure," he murmured, his mouth still on her neck.

She laughed. "I do make really good pancakes though."

He squeezed her tightly and Galina sank into him, a part of her wishing they could stay like this, in this moment forever. Without her father, or Alexei, or Irina, or all of the family drama that came with being a Sudenko. Maybe with a little less come, but this was one of those times she wished would never end.

Andrey turned his head, eyes lighting on her clothes. "Nice pants, by the way," he said, nodding to her Stewie pajamas.

"Oh shut up."

Galina woke, groaning at the sunbeam that hit her face. "Ungh." She burrowed into her pillow, only cracking an eye open when she heard a deep chuckle next to her. "What's so funny?" she asked, her voice hoarse from the carnal activities of the previous evening.

Andrey pressed a kiss to the top of her head. "Are you always so articulate in the morning?"

She yanked the covers up over her head. "I'm sleepy and I have sex hair. Don't be mean."

Andrey's loud laugh boomed out over her head. She tried to elbow him, but being wrapped in the blankets made it difficult to cause him any lasting pain. "Why are you waking me up?"

He ducked his head under the blankets, nuzzling her cheek with his nose. His fingers traced a warm line down her spine. He stopped at the small of her back and pressed his hand to the hollow there. Galina made a pleased sigh, arching into a stretch. His hand urged her to roll onto her side, and she did so, curling around Andrey.

"I believe you mentioned pancakes?" He took her earlobe in his mouth and sucked it gently.

"You woke me up because you're hungry?" She draped a thigh over his and felt his erection press against her belly.

"Among other reasons." Andrey's voice was husky, his eyes a smoky blue.

She grinned, still sleepy. "I can think of one good reason and it's poking at my stomach."

His big hands came up and cupped her breasts, pushing them up into his mouth. Galina dropped her head back, inhaling sharply at the heat of his mouth on her quivering flesh. A coil of heat wrapped around her pelvis, making her move restlessly against him.

"What are you doing?" she asked softly.

"Saying good morning." He lowered his head to her nipples, sucking one and then the other into his mouth.

Galina's breath stuttered out in sharp gasps. Andrey's tongue rasped across her sensitive flesh. He pulled his mouth off and then blew over the erect peaks, smiling as the skin dimpled and pebbled. "I'm fairly certain you have the most perfect breasts."

She watched him from half-closed lids. "And I'm fairly certain that most men think any breast is perfect."

Andrey smiled before biting at her nipple. He worried it in his teeth, making her arch and gasp. She felt her pussy spasm, leaving a trail of wetness on his leg as she moved up and down on him. "I've engaged in an exhaustive study of the female breast."

"Do you have pie charts?" Galina asked, gasping on the last word as he sucked on the underside of her breast.

He nodded, his head moving heavily against her. His silvery eyes met hers. "And line graphs. I believe in being thorough."

"I can tell," she managed, before she lost the power of speech when he pushed the head of his cock inside of her.

He moved slowly, filling her inch by inch. When Galina tried to quicken the pace, he held her still. She lay on her back, legs wrapped around his waist, gasping as he speared her. She shook her head on the pillow, straining against his hands. "Andrey, please."

He bottomed out, then pulled out just as slowly. He mouthed her breasts, his lips and tongue driving her closer and closer to the edge as his cock teased her lower lips. "What do you want?" There was a dark joy in his voice as he watched her flushed face.

"You," Galina choked out. "All of you."

"Your wish is my command." His hips snapped forward, sheathing himself deep inside her in one stroke.

Galina shouted, her hips rolling against his as she tightened her legs around his waist. He pinched her nipples before he captured her mouth, swallowing her cries as the burn inside of her turned into a white hot conflagration. He broke off the kiss and placed his fingers into her mouth, urging her to suck.

He removed them. Andrey's hand swept around her hips, lifting her up to get a better angle. Her eyes popped open when he slid a finger inside the puckered ring of her ass. She felt herself tighten around him and he urged her to relax. Galina dropped her head back. Andrey licked up the line of her neck, his stubble rubbing her over-sensitized skin.

"Andrey," she managed to get out in a garbled voice, every fiber of her being so stimulated she thought she might die.

"Hmm?" He sounded inordinately pleased with himself. She would have smacked him if she had any muscle control left in her body.

"I…" She stopped as he changed angles and his cock bumped against her g-spot. She lost the capacity for words, having to resort to gasps and inarticulate mumblings as her body clenched, bowing her back as her walls tightened unbearably.

"Fuck!" Andrey cried out as her pussy gripped him, squeezing his cock through her orgasm. He picked up speed, chasing his own climax as his hips snapped into hers. Galina stared up at him blindly, almost insensate from the mind bending sex of the last twelve hours. He crashed into her, shouting her name, as he finally came.

Slowly Galina came back to herself. She felt like she was floating. Aftershocks rolled through her body, making her twitch and jerk. Andrey was a heavy weight on top of her, but she didn't mind. He could lie on top of her all day long if it meant she could have sex like that again.

It was like he knew every cell of her body, like he'd gotten a Masters in the study of giving her orgasms. She threaded her fingers through the damp hair at his temples, content to just feel his breath against her, his chest rising and falling in time with hers. She wasn't worried about how they'd get around his engagement to Irina, she wasn't worried about Alexei or Papa or any of the other million things that were going wrong within the family.

Andrey was here. He was hers. And that was all that mattered.

"You're smiling."

She opened her eyes to find him propped on one elbow, watching her.

He looked delectable. His eyes were sleepy, the blue gleaming beneath heavy lids. His black hair hung in his eyes, tousled and messy.

The lower half of his face was covered in dark stubble. His mouth was red from kissing her.

"I'm happy," she told him.

A shadow passed across his face, taking the joy from his eyes. "We're going to need to talk about your father. I can't marry Irina."

She felt a little leap in her chest at his words. Galina hadn't expected him to go through with the wedding, especially after last night, but it still thrilled her to hear him say it. That made it more real somehow. She ran a hand across the stubble on his jaw. "I haven't figured out how to get you out of that yet."

"I'll just tell him I don't want to marry her." He kissed her palm. "Now that I have the Bullet back, there's nothing to repay."

Galina shook her head. "You've already accepted. If you back out now, you'd insult him and cause a rift between the families." She sat up against the headboard, wrapping her arms around his waist when he followed her up.

"Well, I can't just pretend I'm interested in your sister." He rubbed at her neck with one hand. "And we can't let this drag out indefinitely. Ilya is already asking for a wedding date."

She ran her finger through his hair as she ordered her thoughts. "Something else is going on for Papa to push your engagement so fast. I think he's worried about Rina. Let me make arrangements to get her out of town before you break it off."

"That still leaves Alexei. He's the one who ordered the theft of my product in the first place." Andrey's voice had darkened, the threat implicit. "I don't want to kill your brother, but he needs to pay for his actions."

"I know. I'm not suggesting you not get retribution." She shook her head. "I know how these things work." She paused, thinking. "Let me talk to Papa. Maybe we can figure out a way so all parties are happy and nobody looks like a fool." She sighed, stretching. "I should probably call Rina and see how the rest of her night went. And I need to have a serious talk with Viktor."

"Why's that?" Andrey ran a hand through her hair, curling a lock of it around his fingers.

Galina sighed. "He's endangering Rina—all of us really—but most especially her. You know we had an older sister, right?"

"I remember hearing something about it, but I was much younger." He took her hand in his.

"It's a long and sordid story, and Papa really doesn't come out great in it. Let's just say that she met and fell in love with the wrong man and Papa ended it for her." Galina kept her voice light, but inside her stomach churned. She hadn't known Elena very well, being a decade younger than her, but still she felt the loss of her.

"Where's Elena now?" Andrey's eyes narrowed. "I've never met her."

"She's dead." When Andrey kissed her shoulder, she squeezed his hand tightly. "Now you see why I need to talk to Viktor."

"I do." He nuzzled her cheek with his nose. "And I am sorry."

Galina blinked, feeling her sister's loss more than she had in years. But there wasn't time to wallow. "Thank you," she murmured. Then, shaking off her mood, she pushed herself out of his arms. "We should get a move on."

Andrey pulled the blankets off of them. "I suppose I have to let you out of bed at some point." He offered her a hand up. "But you at least owe me pancakes."

17

Let's Dredge Up the Past, Shall We?

Galina pulled Viktor aside as soon as she was able. "Let's go for a walk," she said, hand clamping down on his arm in a nonverbal cue that refusal was not an option. He looked at her, surprise registering on his elegant features before nodding.

They strolled around Irina's large backyard. Galina hoped that their casual attitude would persuade Irina they were just having a business discussion, not the info-dump of family backstory she was going to drop on him for his own — and Irina's — safety. Reaching the far end of the walled yard, she pulled Viktor down on a bench.

"There's something you should know about Irina." Galina shook her head. "Or really, about our sister Elena."

"I know about Elena," he told her, blue eyes betraying nothing of what he felt. He was staring at her like someone who worked for her father should: dangerous, deadly, with the eyes of someone who could, and had, killed a man.

"You've heard what everyone's heard, not the real story." She tucked her legs underneath her on the bench. "So shut up and listen because I'm not saying this again."

She took a deep breath. "Our sister, Elena, was a few years older than Rina. She was beautiful, but very headstrong. Where Irina was

Daddy's good little girl, Elena was the rebel. She fought tooth and nail for more freedom. My father always asked why she couldn't be more like Rina. But Elena always got what she wanted, even when she was being punished."

Galina shrugged. "At least that's what it seemed like to me. I was still pretty young when all of this went down. Anyway, when she turned eighteen, Papa started arrangements for Elena's marriage. He chose a nice, established man from a good family back in Russia. A doctor, someone respectable. He thought it was a great match and that Elena should have been happy."

Galina watched as Viktor shifted uncomfortably. "You can imagine how well that went over. Elena had been seeing a boy from her college classes, Brian McKenzie. She'd been keeping it on the down low, but when she found out about the arranged marriage, she went to Papa and told him that she was in love.

"You can imagine how he reacted." She paused, remembering the fight between Papa and Elena. It was the loudest she'd ever heard her father get. "I'd like to think my mother, had she still been alive, could have intervened. But since she died giving birth to me we'll never know."

Galina slanted a look at Viktor. She had his full attention. "Anyway, Papa told her she was too young to know what love was and that she would get over Brian. I think he even said that she and this doctor would grow to love each other in time.

"But on the night of her engagement party, Papa found a note in her room telling him that she and Brian had eloped. You could hear my father screaming over the sound of two hundred guests."

"Wow." Viktor's face paled, as if he finally realized just how close he and Irina had come to repeating a family disaster.

Galina nodded. "Yeah, Elena always did have a flair for the dramatic. Papa completely lost his mind. He had every available contact out looking for her; he called in every favor. It only took them three days to track Elena down." Galina tilted her head, thinking about how careless her older sister had been. If it had been her, she would have had a plan in place, some way to truly disappear. "She wasn't particularly smart about the way she ran. Maybe part of her wanted to be caught, like she thought that Papa would be so frightened by her running away that he'd forgive her. Maybe she hoped he'd realize she'd never be his good little girl and he'd let her marry her Irish boyfriend in a big church wedding."

Viktor scowled. "Clearly, she didn't know your father very well."

Galina frowned. "When Papa and his men found them, they shot Brian in the face in front of Elena and left his body to rot in the desert. Papa wanted to teach her an important lesson. He wanted her to see the cost of her disobedience. And then he had his men drive her home."

Galina looked down at her hands. "But Papa didn't really know Elena either. She'd always been so stubborn, but she'd always kind of had a short attention span. You know, kind of flighty and shallow. He expected her to forget about Brian. He thought she'd stay in her room and cry for a few days, but that she'd get over it. Move on to the next shiny thing. He thought he'd scared her so badly that she would just fall in line with his plans for her. He didn't even think to take the razors out of her bathroom."

Galina grimaced, remembering the scene. "She looked like something James Waterhouse painted. Like his *Ophelia* or *Lady of Shallot*. She was laid out on her bed in a white dress, her hair spread out on the pillow. She'd sliced herself open from wrist to elbow. There was blood everywhere." She swallowed, feeling the hurt well up inside her chest. She shrugged it off. "Dramatics."

She stared at Viktor, willing him to understand. "Papa didn't handle it well. Irina and I were put in lockdown. Irina was barely allowed to leave the house to attend her classes. I had a detail that followed me around. In elementary school. I don't know how the hell Irina convinced Papa to let her go to college after what Elena did. It was easier for me, because Papa had mellowed some by that point, but it was still a fight to go out of state. My scholarship helped."

Galina met Viktor's eyes, seeing the horror there. Good. He needed to be aware of what the stakes were if he wanted to keep seeing Irina. She would not have her only remaining sister end up like Elena. Or worse.

"What about you and Andrey?" Viktor's voice was low, as if he were afraid someone would overhear them.

"We're careful." When she saw him open his mouth to contradict her, she amended, "Mostly." She smiled. She had no illusions about the risk she was running with Andrey. "But I'm not the one Papa is trying to marry off. I'm trying to figure a way out of this for Irina, but you're going to have to give me a little time."

"I don't think time is something we have a lot of," he said, firm mouth turning down in a frown.

"Agreed." Galina stood. She wanted to get back inside. "Just remember what I told you, okay?" It was the closest she could come to pleading with him for the sake of her sister.

Viktor nodded. "Tell Rina I'll be back inside in a bit."

Galina nodded, squeezing his shoulder. Then she left him to his thoughts.

18

Car Trouble

Galina was in the research library of the museum looking into the provenance of a donated painting, when her phone rang. Nik. She stepped out into the back hallway so she wouldn't disturb the other patrons.

"What's up?" she asked.

"Galya! Can you get to a television?" Nik's voice was as close to frantic as she'd ever heard it.

"I…I'm not sure," she said, walking as quickly as she could to the employee break room. She rarely used it, but perhaps there was a TV in there. "Why, what's wrong?"

"Papa," Nik managed to get out before a burst of voices on his end drowned him out. "Meet me at Irina's as soon as you can. I have to tell her." He hung up.

"Nikolai!" She looked at her phone in astonishment, a cold feeling of dread pooling through her extremities. "Damn it!"

She was nearly at a run now, not caring who saw her. She had to get to a television. There was something wrong and it had to do with Papa. Galina barreled into the break room, mercifully empty at this hour, and turned on the television. As she waited for it to warm up, she pulled up the Internet on her phone to see what was going on. There didn't appear to be anything, but even in e-reporting there was a delay.

The local channel had halted regular programming for breaking news. A helicopter team was filming at the scene of an accident that had all lanes of the freeway blocked. Galina watched in stunned silence as the camera zoomed in on the wreckage of a car, getting close enough to get a shot of the hood, engulfed in flames. A wolf's head hood ornament shimmered in the fiery haze.

She felt her face grow cold and then burning hot. Galina dropped into a chair, knees giving way in shock. Papa. Papa's car—with Papa presumably in it—was on fire. More than that, his car was in pieces *and* on fire. She watched numbly as the reporters relayed information about the scene, but it was like her ears had stopped working. She heard nothing.

Her phone buzzed in her hand. Galina stared at it stupidly, as if she suddenly didn't understand how the thing worked. Blinking, she answered.

"Are you okay?" Andrey's deep voice held a faint edge of fear as he almost yelled his question at her.

"I am. But Papa…" She trailed off because she couldn't wrap her brain around it. Papa was forever. He was an old lion, but she never thought he'd die. Not like this.

Andrey's voice was soft. "I know. I saw the news. Where are you?"

"At work." How could she be answering him so calmly?

"I'm coming to pick you up."

The small, fully functioning part of her brain kicked into overdrive. "No, don't do that. You should be comforting Irina, not me." If Andrey were seen with her it might cause problems. They still needed to maintain the ruse that he was interested in Irina. "I'll be fine."

She could swear she heard the sound of teeth grinding. It made her want to laugh in an entirely inappropriate way. Is that what shock felt like? She'd never experienced it, so she didn't really know what it was like. "I'm sending Konstantin to get you and take you to your sister's house. I will meet you there. You are not driving yourself, not in this state."

It was a measure of how stunned she was that Galina didn't even bother to object to the order. "That will be nice for Nik," was all she said, thinking that he brother needed someone to offer comfort to him.

"He's on his way." Andrey told her. "Galya, be careful. I'll see you soon."

"Okay." She waited until he disconnected before she got up on shaking legs and went to find her supervisor.

Konstantin walked with her into her sister's house, his hand beneath her elbow. He'd told her that Andrey would be along as soon as he could get away from the chaos that the car bomb had caused. The bodyguard hadn't said much on the ride over to Irina's, his mouth set in a grim line. Galina had stared out the window, her thoughts scattered and unfocused. She was glad he didn't say anything other than to ask if Nik was okay. Galina hadn't known what to tell him. She wasn't sure any of them were okay.

She opened the door to the house and went straight to the living room, where the television was blasting all the news of the crash. She watched dully as they showed another close-up of the burning wreckage. The emergency vehicles were finally getting through the massive traffic jam.

Irina ran to her, hugging her tightly. Galina wrapped her arms around her sister, feeling Irina's body-wrenching sobs. She buried her head in her sister's neck and stayed there for a long moment, just happy to have someone to share the pain and shock of it. Then Galina realized that Papa always had a driver. And Viktor wasn't at the house.

No. Oh, no.

Nik came up behind Irina and enclosed both of them in his arms. The three of them stood there, holding on to each other, none of them wanting to be the first one to let go. Finally Nik pulled away, eyes red.

Galina glanced at the television, then looked away quickly. She didn't want to see any more. She didn't want to think of Papa in there. Of Viktor…She grabbed Irina's hand and squeezed it tightly.

"Has anyone heard from Alexei?" she asked.

"I've called and left messages with him," Nik said. "I know he was out of town last night. He should be on his way back by now. I'm still waiting to hear from him."

The door alarm beeped as Andrey ran into the house. He crossed the space separating them and wrapped her in his arms. Galina allowed herself to lean against him, if only for a moment, before breaking away. "We're not alone," she warned.

"That's bothering you now?" His voice held a note of fondness. "Who's going to say anything? Nik and Konstantin? Irina?"

Galina had to admit Andrey had a point. Nik and Konstantin had a bigger secret to keep than they did, and Irina was mourning two people. "I guess not." She made a mental note to reapply the Eau d' Wolfsbane she carried with her to help mask Andrey's scent. While it did make sense that she might smell of him if he came by to visit Irina, there would be no way to explain how his scent had gotten all over her.

"This is the kind of day where I wish I'd never gotten out of bed." Galina felt numb, like the news of her father's death still hadn't sunk in yet. She knew she hadn't processed it yet, even if she'd seen the flaming wreckage on television.

Andrey said nothing, simply pressing a kiss to the top of her head. "Thank you for being here," she whispered, her voice perilously close to tears. She gritted her teeth. She would not cry. Not here.

"There's nowhere else I would be," he answered, pulling her down on the couch so she was in seated in his lap.

They sat in silence for a few minutes. Then Galina said, "I don't know what to do about the Bullet now that Papa's…" She couldn't finish the rest.

"I'm going to have to deal with your brother." Andrey lifted her head so he could look into her eyes. "At some point anyway."

"It's not like he doesn't have it coming," she agreed. Swallowing, Galina wondered what was wrong with her. She should be more worried for her elder brother, but Alexei had long since squandered whatever good will he may have stockpiled.

"Where's Irina?" She hadn't seen her sister since Andrey arrived.

"I think she went to lie down upstairs." Andrey's hands kneaded into painfully tense shoulders. "You should rest."

"I think it's going to be a while before any of us can do that," she told him, resting her head against his shoulder.

The doorbell broke Galina out of her stupor. She'd been sitting on the couch, leaning against Andrey, doing her best not to think about anything. She looked at Nikolai who blinked as if surfacing from a dream, unsure of whether he wanted to wake up. Andrey moved to answer the door, but Galina put a hand on his knee. It was probably just one of the other families coming by to pay their respects to Irina.

Instead of a Demidov or Oniayev, a man with dark hair cut in the Captain America special stood at her door. He was in his mid-thirties, generically good looking, and had that apple pie appearance common to federal agents. He wore a dark blue windbreaker over a white polo shirt and a pair of khaki slacks. Galina looked behind him and saw a blue panel van, similar to the white one that had been following her, parked across the street. A black SUV was parked behind Andrey's Audi.

The man flashed his credentials. Standing before her was Assistant Special Agent in Charge John Gregory of the FBI. How lucky for her.

"Special Agent Gregory. I was wondering if you had time to answer a few questions, Mrs. Volkov?"

"Sudenko. Galina Sudenko. Mrs. Volkov is my sister and she's sleeping upstairs." Frowning, she opened the door wider to let him pass. *Assistant* Special Agent Gregory knew damn well she wasn't Irina.

"Ms. Sudenko, I am sorry for your loss."

He came close to sounding like he meant it. "Thank you," she murmured, leading him into the kitchen. "Would you care for a cup of coffee?"

"No, thank you," he said, sitting down in a chair at the kitchen table.

Galina poked her head into the living room. "Nik, I need you."

Her brother joined her in the kitchen. "Nikolai, this is Assistant Special Agent Gregory," she said, emphasizing the Assistant. "Agent Gregory, this is my brother, Nikolai Sudenko." She went to the coffeepot and poured out two cups. "Nik, Agent Gregory said he'd like to ask us some questions."

"I was hoping to speak to Mrs. Volkov," he began.

Nikolai cut him off. "My sister is indisposed. Losing her father so soon after her husband has been quite a blow." He leaned forward, a pleasant smile on his face. It didn't reach his eyes. "I'm sure you can understand."

"Of course," Gregory answered. He folded his hands on the table.

Galina carried the mugs of coffee to the table and sat next to Nik. "You'll forgive me for being blunt, Agent Gregory, but our father just died. What do you want?"

Gregory looked from her to Nik and then back to her. His eyes assessed them, determining which tactic he should use to get what he wanted. She could almost see him discard one plan for another. Wrapping her hands around her mug so she didn't wrap them around his throat, she waited.

"Do you know of anyone who would want your father dead?"

He'd gone with the direct approach. She appreciated that. She didn't have the patience left to pussyfoot around; she was very close to curling up into a ball and pulling a blanket over her head, hoping to wake up and find this was all just a nightmare.

Taking a breath, she shook her head. "No, not that I can think of."

Nik agreed. "Same here."

Agent Gregory's jaw jumped beneath his skin. He was gritting his teeth. He knew they were lying, but there wasn't much he could do about it. "Are you sure about that? Your father had no enemies?"

Galina took Nik's hand in hers as if she needed his support. "People loved my father," she said.

"How did you find out about your father's death?" A small smile played around his lips.

Nik squeezed her hand tightly. He wanted to jump across the table and rip out the agent's throat; she knew that because she wanted to do the same thing. "I was filing some papers at the courthouse. Our housekeeper called me—she saw it on the news."

Agent Gregory's gaze met hers. His eyes were a dark blue, cold and flat. She could see her face reflected in them, two small Galinas trapped in his gaze. "Nikolai called and told me to turn on the television."

"And where were you?"

Now it was her turn to study him. She put everything she had, everything she was feeling—the rage, the pain, the loss—into her stare. "I was at work. The Seattle Museum of Art. I'm an assistant curator there. Which you already know because you've had two agents in a white van following me around for weeks. So exactly what are you hoping to unearth with this little fact-finding interview?"

Nik's hand tightened on hers, reminding her that he was there. She leaned back in her chair. She hadn't realized she'd pushed herself forward so that she was lunging halfway across the table at the agent.

"My apologies, Ms. Sudenko." Agent Gregory didn't look sorry at all.

Nik let go of her hand and stood. "Special Agent Gregory, we are more than happy to cooperate with the FBI, but perhaps we could do this some other time." He pulled a small case out from his jacket pocket and handed the other man his business card. "*After* we've buried our father."

"Of course, Mr. Sudenko." But Agent Gregory didn't take his gaze off of Galina.

Konstantin emerged from the living room to escort the FBI agent to the door. Nik followed them.

Galina sat in her chair, staring into her coffee cup. The image of her father's car engulfed in flames would not leave her. Her hands gripped the white ceramic, her knuckles going pale with the force of her grip. If she just held on long enough, maybe her hands would stop shaking.

Andrey wrapped his arms around her shoulders, his spicy scent filling her nostrils. His hands slid down her arms until they came to rest over hers, urging her to release the coffee mug. "Galya," he whispered, his mouth against her ear. "What can I do?"

Standing up, Galina pulled Andrey out of the kitchen and down the hall until she came to the powder room. Yanking him inside, she closed the door behind them, turning the lock. There wasn't a lot of room to maneuver between the pedestal sink and the commode, but she didn't care.

"Gal—" he said, but her lips stopped his words.

She kissed him, her mouth ravaging his. She didn't want words, she didn't want logic. She wanted sensation, physical relief. Andrey's hands stroked her neck, his thumbs resting against her jaw. Her tongue slid inside his mouth, licking at his teeth, the roof of his mouth, the inside of his cheek. She could feel the fabric of her panties clinging to the warm wetness between her thighs.

Yanking his belt open, Galina unbuttoned his trousers, plunging her hand down the front of his boxer briefs. Andrey was half hard, and as she stroked him, Galina felt him stir to life. She worked him with the palm of her hand, her thumb twisting over the head of his cock. His hands grabbed her waist, turning her to face the mirror.

His gaze locked with hers in the flat glass. "Tell me what you want." His voice filled the small room, intimate yet almost overpowering.

"Make me hurt. Make me feel." Something, anything. Galina could feel the yawning emptiness spreading inside of her, the fear and the loss. Papa may not have always understood her, but he had done his best for her, even if they quarreled over what that best was. She needed to know she wasn't alone in the dark.

Andrey lifted her skirt, bunching it around her waist. His eyes stayed locked on her reflection, gauging her response in the mirror. Pushing her ass against him, she braced her hands on the sink.

He ripped off her panties, the lace tearing with a snarl. Andrey bent her over the sink, one hand in her hair to keep her head up so he could watch her expression in the mirror. With a quick pump of his hips, his cock filled her. She inhaled at the stretch, at the sweet ache that came with him inside of walls.

Andrey didn't give her time to adjust. His free hand dug into her hip, fingernails biting into her flesh so hard he drew blood. She bit her lip to keep from moaning with how good it felt, how much she wanted the pain to go along with the pleasure of him pounding into her. She canted her hips, eyes sliding closed.

He yanked at her hair, jerking her head even farther back. Galina's eyes flew open. "Look at me," Andrey commanded her. "I want you to see what you look like when I make you come."

When she nodded, he let go of her hair. Her eyes never wavered from his reflection. Andrey's hand slid between her thighs, finding her throbbing clit and stroking it slowly with his finger as his pace increased.

Galina's mouth opened on a soundless cry as Andrey ruthlessly worked her body, his fingers and thumb roughly bringing her to the edge of release before backing off again. He leaned into her, forcing her even farther forward as his cock speared her over and over again. Every time her eyelids dipped closed, Andrey thrust into her, reminding her of his command. She panted, aching for a release he denied her over and over again, until her muscles burned with the tension of her frustration.

He refused to let her set the pace, to dictate anything about their coupling. Galina could only grasp the black porcelain sink and wait until he'd decided she'd had enough, watching his blue eyes sparkle with hellish glee in the mirror. Her nipples were diamond-hard as they moved against the lace fabric of her bra, sending jolts of pleasure to her clit. She wanted to scream with how good he made her feel, how alive in this instant, but kept silent, eyes on his face.

Increasing his rhythm, Andrey teased her, his thumb rubbing almost painfully against her wet flesh. Her orgasm built within her, a hunger that wanted to consume everything it touched. Andrey's fingers moved faster, in time with his thrusts and she came with a force that made her forget to breathe. Her walls contracted around his cock, urging Andrey deeper.

Her climax spiked, but still Andrey worked her clit, refusing to grant her relief. His every touch brought her closer to frenzy. With his eyes boring into hers in the mirror, she writhed in his grasp. His fingers dug into her hip so hard she'd have bruises.

Tears spilled down her cheeks. It was too much, all of it. Her father's death, her sister's loss, her feelings for Andrey. She gasped around the pain in her chest, not knowing how to make it all fit together inside of her, how to make sense of both the sweetness and the sorrow.

Wrapping his arms around her waist, Andrey gave one last thrust. Galina felt his cock pumping his seed deep inside of her. She grabbed his arms, knuckles going white, and wept for everything she had lost.

Pulling her close, Andrey nuzzled her neck, holding her as gently as if she were made of spun sugar. "Was this what you needed?" he whispered, pressing a kiss to her cheek.

She nodded, taking a shuddering breath that sounded close to a sob. She closed her lips over the sound.

"I've got you, Galina," he said softly, something that was meant to be heard only by the two of them. "And I will never let you go."

Closing her eyes, she turned in his embrace, putting her face against Andrey's chest and letting her grief roll through her like the tide.

19

That's One Way
to End an Engagement

Galina sat at her desk at work and rubbed her eyes. The last week had been a whirlwind of preparations, meetings, and family obligations. Being at work, even late at night as she so often was of late, was a reprieve of a sort.

Papa's funeral had gone off without a hitch, primarily because Alexei hadn't bothered to even show up. She and Nik had done the heavy lifting, since Irina was lost in the ozone and Alexei was MIA—although Galina suspected if she checked with the local hookers she'd find her brother coked up and balls deep in some unfortunate woman.

She massaged her temples, a headache threatening. The memorial for her father had been tasteful and beautiful, Galina had made sure of that. All of the heads of the other families had shown up and offered condolences. Nik and Galina formed a united front, assuring everyone that the businesses would still be taken care of and that there would be no interruptions in the day to day workings of the organization.

Andrey had backed her wherever he could without being obtrusive. As Alexei's absence from meetings was noticed and commented on, Galina's handling of the family business was impressing the men running the show. Nik was beside her the entire time, but Galina knew that all eyes were focused on her. She had to succeed.

"Alexei's been seen out and about these past few days." Andrey's voice was low, disapproving.

"And we were having such a nice conversation," Galina said with a sigh.

Andrey wrapped his arms around her. "He hit all the major bars and clubs two nights ago, acting like a big man and throwing money around. He wants everyone to know he's the one running the Sudenkos. He's making a giant ass of himself."

"I just have to hope it's enough," she told him, leaning her head against his shoulder.

Galina slid into the chair on the left side of Alexei, ignoring his warning glare. Nikolai took the seat on his right. They'd decided to show a united front to the other families in the wake of Papa's death. She didn't like it, but she understood the need for it, at least for right now. The Sudenko family was vulnerable during this shift of power. There could be no public display of dissension in the ranks.

She felt Andrey's presence as soon as he crossed the threshold and was grateful for the millionth time for her wolfsbane perfume. He took a seat at the end of the table, directly opposite Alexei. Galina had to bite back a smile. The significance of Andrey's position was not lost on her.

Nor was it lost on Alexei. He practically snarled when he saw Andrey. Nik put his hand on Alexei's arm and leaned over to whisper something in his ear. Galina simply nodded at Andrey, as she would any other head of a family. He looked delicious in his navy suit and silver tie. She wanted to order everyone out and have her way with him on the conference table.

That would definitely be an interesting meeting.

As the other family heads filed in and took their places around the large round table, Galina tried to gauge the mood of those assembled. The men seemed stunned, as if surprised to see Alexei seated in Papa's place. Perhaps they hadn't believed the news reports, or they were unsure of what the future would bring with a new leader. Regardless, there was a sense of shock surrounding everyone in the room.

Alexei stood, welcoming the other leaders. He introduced Nikolai, but ignored Galina, not bothering to mention her presence at the table. She gritted her teeth and nodded calmly to the others, all the while imagining what her brother's blood would look like on her claws. It helped soothe her.

"As you know, I will be taking over as head of the Sudenko family after the unexpected death of my father," her brother began. "Let me just say that business will continue as usual. I'm not interested in making sweeping changes to my father's organization." The murmurings of the other men in the room interrupted him.

Alexei smiled, his lips stretching in a horrifying approximation of a grin. "However, there is one thing I do need to address." His gaze swept the assembled group. "I am afraid that the engagement between my sister, Irina, and Andreyev Lupesco can no longer continue."

Galina stared into space, shocked at her brother's announcement. He certainly hadn't run it by her, and from the look on Nik's face, he was as much in the dark as she was. Indrawn breaths and mutters filled the room. Galina risked a glance at Andrey, seated across the table, and wished she hadn't.

His face was thunderous. His eyes gleamed gray, like the barrel of a gun. His lips were pressed in a thin line, his jaw clenched in rage, frightening in his utter stillness. His gaze never left Alexei's face, and there was a leashed energy gathering around him. Galina looked at Alexei nervously. Her brother sat back in his chair with a small smirk on his face.

Was he trying to provoke Andrey? To what purpose? What was this nonsense about canceling the engagement? Galina wasn't going to complain; it certainly saved her trying to figure out the problem of extricating her sister from marrying her boyfriend. But this was an insult that Andrey couldn't possibly let stand.

Andrey slowly rose to his feet, planting his fists on the table. Galina found herself wanting to back away from the table as quickly as she could at the dangerous look in his eyes, but she kept still by telling herself that at least the look wasn't directed at her. She swallowed, suddenly nervous, her gaze skipping to Nik and then to Alexei.

Black hair fell into Andrey's eyes as he let out a low growl. The sound made the hair on her arms stand on end. It was a challenge and a warning, an Alpha letting the other members of the pack know that he was angry. The points of his jaw jumped as he clenched his teeth even tighter. His brows were pulled down low over his eyes, hiding the silver in shadow.

"You would do this?" Andrey snarled, his voice soft but threatening.

Please just shut up, Alexei, Galina thought, trying to will her brother to silence. Andrey had never looked more dangerous. She was fairly certain that if he wanted to rip out her brother's throat at the table, no one would stop him.

"You made an agreement with my father," Alexei said, as if that explained everything. A few more whispers went around the table. It was bad form to not honor the agreements made by the previous head of the family.

"I made an agreement with the Sudenko family!" Andrey snapped.

"I *am* the Sudenko family!" Alexei shouted back, jumping to his feet.

Oh, he did *not*. Galina would have dropped her head into her hands at this display of stupidity from her brother, but she didn't want to appear disrespectful at the negotiation table. Nik put his hand on Alexei's arm and had it shaken off. The other heads of the families of the Organization had pushed back from the table.

"Then I challenge *you*." Andrey leaned forward to punctuate his words. "Now. Here."

To his credit, Alexei didn't blanch at Andrey's words. That just proved how dumb he actually was, at least to Galina's mind. She had no doubt Andrey could take her brother in a fight, in either human or wolf form.

"Irina needs to be here," Galina whispered to Nikolai.

"Do it."

Galina excused herself from the table, not that anyone was listening to her. She trusted Nik to keep anything from erupting in the conference room and to let Alexei and Andrey know that Irina was on her way. She was the one they were basically fighting over; she had to be present by the rule of law.

Irina picked up on the second ring. "Galya? Is the meeting over?"

"Nope. You need to grab Konstantin and get your butt over to Papa's house right away. Alexei's called off your engagement. Andrey's just challenged him."

"As in 'outdoor werewolf gladiator' challenged? Wait, don't we want the engagement canceled?" The sound of Irina slamming drawers closed carried over the line.

"Yes, but not like this. Alexei basically whipped it out and wanted to measure. Andrey can't just walk away from that. So you need to hustle since you're the bone of contention—so to speak."

"Gee, thanks." Irina's voice was so icy, Galina could have chilled vodka with it.

"Sorry, sis. Now get a move on."

Nik was waiting for her when she finished her call. "They're prepping the yard now."

She nodded. "Irina and Konstantin are on their way." She noticed the faint rush of color to her brother's face. "When all of this ridiculousness is over, you and I are going to have a nice, long talk." Galina began to walk. Nik kept pace with her. "What the hell is Alexei thinking? He can't afford this right now."

Her brother shook his head. "Wish I knew. He said nothing about breaking Irina's engagement before. I mean, I know he wasn't in favor of it—he made that *very* clear when he was arguing with Pop about it—but I can't believe he'd go against Andrey directly like this."

Galina didn't say anything; there was nothing to say. "He's up to something."

Nik didn't look so sure. "I don't know, Galya. Alexei hasn't been what you'd call a model of restraint. And he *hates* Andrey."

"And he's a little too focused on Irina," Galina muttered, pulling Nik closer to her.

"What are you talking about?"

She raised an eyebrow at him in disbelief. "Come on, Nik. You can't tell me you haven't noticed how twitchy he is around her. He threw away all of her clothes and told her to paint the world with all the colors of her soul! He watches her all the time. I think if he could have, he would have spent the two months of mourning at her house for as often as he came by to check on her."

Nik gave her a dubious look. "Aren't you exaggerating a little?"

"You'd think so, wouldn't you?" Galina pushed the door open that led out to the back of the property. The whole place was fenced and incredibly private, which came in handy when there was a challenge in the offing. As they crossed the yard, she said, "But if you don't believe me, ask Irina. Or just watch Alexei when the two of them are together. And then tell me there isn't something wrong with him."

Alexei was already at the circle, removing his cufflinks and rings. Galina looked around for Andrey, but she didn't see him or his retinue. She hurried over to Petyr to try to get an idea of what the others thought of the challenge.

She didn't have to wait long. "Ilya isn't even in the ground and his son dishonors his orders," he was saying to the older man beside him. When he saw Galina, he waved her close. "My dear, you should not be here."

"Hello, Uncle Petyr." She gave Papa's oldest friend a hug and nodded at the man on the other side of him.

"Ah, your father, he would not stand for this," Petyr continued. He put a hand up to Galina's cheek. "This is shameful, the way your brother is behaving."

"No arguments there, Uncle." She shook her head, as if in regret, but inside she felt hopeful. If Alexei kept on in this vein, he would quickly demonstrate why he shouldn't be in charge of anything more complex than a tea party. As much as she hated that Irina had been dragged into this mess, she was glad that Alexei was doing his best to prove why Galina would be a better choice for the next head of the family. "Papa would not be pleased."

"Where is Lupesco?" Alexei shouted to no one in particular. It was machismo, one step removed from beating on his chest like Tarzan. Galina sighed. Her brother was looking for a fight and he was anxious to get it over and done.

She carefully stepped over to Alexei. "Irina is on her way," she told him, knowing that Nik would have already passed along that information. "You can't get started without her."

He greeted her reminder with a snarl. She raised her hands and shrugged, not wanting to antagonize him further. The delay was brief before Nik and Konstantin were escorting her sister toward the assembled group. Irina looked pale and tired, a woman in the midst of grieving. Galina was sorry for having to call her here. Irina should have been able to stay home and grieve for Papa and Viktor for as long as she needed, not come here and be paraded around in her sadness.

Before she could greet her sister, Alexei had rushed past to enfold Irina in a gentle hug. His hands lingered on Rina's back, stroking up and down in a very non-brotherly sort of way. Galina caught Nik's gaze and raised her eyebrows. There was no way he could ignore or explain that away; Alexei's behavior toward Irina was not the way a brother treated a sister.

"I'm going to end this farce of an engagement," Alexei was murmuring into Irina's ear, his arms tightening around her as she tried to pull away. "You deserve better than a thieving mongrel."

Nik interrupted this heartfelt talk smoothly, gently extricating Rina from Alexei's hold, a worried look on his face. Galina wanted nothing more than to smack her oldest brother, hoping to knock some sense into him, but knew it would be useless. Alexei always did what he wanted to do and left other people to clean up his messes, whether it was grand theft, assault, or dead girlfriends.

Galina blinked, wondering why she hadn't put it together before. All of Alexei's past girlfriends and conquests had all been similar in coloring and height to Rina.

No, that couldn't be right. She eyed her brother carefully, wondering if she was just jumping to a conclusion or if Alexei was really that twisted. It didn't matter that Rina was adopted and not actually related by blood to them; she'd been raised as their sister and Galina couldn't think of her as anything else.

But could Alexei?

Before she could think on this further, the heavy scent of wolf hit her. The crowd's low rumble of conversation stilled and Galina turned around. Andrey had come into the circle, already in wolf-form, and stood in the center, awaiting Alexei. Galina's breath caught in her throat at the sight of him. He was majestic: an enormous black wolf with silvery blue eyes. His fur was thick and glossy, the muscles beneath sleek and powerful. The elegant head swung in her direction. Galina saw the Andrey-wolf inhale, picking out her scent from all of the others. His tongue lolled out in a wolf's grin, causing her to glare at him. So much for majestic. Idiot.

Alexei stripped down, ready to change. He had no problem dropping into wolf form in front of people. Galina liked a bit of privacy for her own transformations, preferring to do it out of the sight of others. Irina took her hand and squeezed as their brother dropped to all fours, now a massive gray wolf with startlingly yellow eyes. Galina squeezed back.

"What's going to happen?" Irina asked softly.

Irina had never been to a challenge before. There was never a need, and since she wasn't a werewolf, Papa had kept her away from the furrier side of things. Galina explained in a voice just as soft, "Alexei and Andrey will fight to disable, not to kill. Andrey's the offended party here since Alexei broke the agreement Papa made with him. If he wins, the engagement stands. If Alexei wins, Andrey loses power and face and you don't have to marry him anymore."

"Do you think Alexei will win?"

Galina couldn't tell if that was hope or dread in Rina's voice. Her eyes hadn't left the two wolves circling each other. As she watched, the black wolf snarled and attacked, bowling the grey wolf over with his greater mass. The two wolves locked together, a blur of black and grey. "We just have to watch and see."

Galina had never seen Andrey fight in wolf form before. She'd seen his strength against Sergei, felt it when they were together. She should have expected that he'd be adept at fighting as a wolf. Where Alexei used brute force and cruelty, Andrey countered with controlled strength and ferocity. He wasn't divorced from his human mind while in wolf form, at least to Galina's assessment. She could almost see him calculating where his next bite should go, the placement of paws and jaws, the counter to Alexei's next move.

The two wolves broke apart to circle once again. Galina could hear bets beginning to be made on the outcome of the challenge. The odds were favoring Andrey at present. She thought about putting her own money down but that would be disloyal. She wasn't actually going to bet against her brother, as much as she might want to.

Irina gripped her hand so tight Galina thought she might lose it from lack of blood flow. Alexei had gone on the offensive, jaws snapping at Andrey's throat, backing him up. Galina grimaced. It looked like Rina was on Team Andrey then. She put her free hand on her sister's arm, reassuring her. Galina trusted that Andrey had a plan.

The black wolf surged upward, jaws snapping closed around the grey wolf's throat. A high whine carried across the open lawn, to be cut off as Andrey ratcheted down on Alexei's throat. The grey wolf struggled, but couldn't risk breaking away without tearing out his own throat. His feet scrabbled wildly, ripping up huge chunks of earth as they bicycled uselessly. Andrey's hold did not falter.

The grey wolf's struggles began to subside, growing looser and less coordinated. Still the black wolf held fast. Finally Nikolai stepped forward to end the challenge. "Lupesco. You won. Let him go." The mutterings of those men gathered agreed.

Irina let loose the death grip on Galina's hand with a sigh. "Looks like you're still engaged," Galina whispered to her with a smile.

"Not funny, Galya."

Andrey changed back, surprising her. He stood in front of the assembled families, wearing his nakedness like an emperor's cloak. Galina blinked, feeling a kind of possessive pride in him. He was beautiful and he was hers. His torso was scratched and bloodied from Alexei's claws and teeth, but he exuded strength and confidence.

Irina clapped her hands over her eyes. "I should not be seeing this." Galina grinned.

When Andrey spoke, his voice still held the growl of a wolf. "As the victor," he began and Galina felt Irina flinch beside her. She put her arm around her sister, as Andrey continued. "I am altering the terms of the contract, as is my right." His voice carried to everyone assembled, even Alexei who had changed back into human form and lay at Andrey's feet, chest heaving.

"There's nothing homoerotic about this *at all*," Galina whispered to her sister, trying to tease a smile from her. Irina managed a weak snicker. Nik shot them both a warning glance.

Andrey's next words stole the smile from her face. "I hereby dissolve my engagement to Irina Sudenko and choose instead Ilya Sudenko's other daughter, Galina, as my future wife."

"You have got to be fucking kidding me," she gasped, as Andrey's gaze locked on hers.

"No. If he were kidding, he would yell, 'Haha!'" Irina said, shaking her head. "There is a distinct lack of 'Haha!' in this situation."

20

Raise Your Hand if...Ewwww

Galina took off. She didn't know where she was going; all she knew was that standing with the rest of the family representatives was no longer an option, not with all of them staring at her like they were checking out the breeding stock. She had a feeling this was close to how Irina felt. And she absolutely hated every fucking minute of it.

When Andrey had looked down at Alexei, still panting on the ground, her brother had nodded. She could have killed him then, but she couldn't bear the staring another moment. Galina turned on her heel and walked away before Andrey had finished pulling on his pants. Her heels sank into the damp ground, making it harder for her to storm away properly. She yanked her shoes off and ran to the farthest point on the property.

There was a small guesthouse at the back of the property. Papa had kept it for important guests who required privacy—mostly his girlfriends, back when her mother was alive. It had been unused for most of the past decade as far as she knew. Papa had chosen to have his dalliances in the main house or elsewhere once she was gone. Galina kicked her way through the flimsy door lock, shoving the door open with her shoulder, and slammed it behind her to give vent to her anger in the only way available to her.

Flipping the switch, she looked around and stopped, stunned. Papering the walls of the small living room were photos of Irina. Alexei's scent was all over the place. Galina took a step inside and saw that the furniture was lying in pieces around the room. She wiped her feet on the carpet, then tucked them back into her shoes before walking inside to take a closer look at the pictures.

Some were of Irina in high school, photographs taken from family albums that now hung on the wall. They seemed to be sequenced from youngest to oldest. There was Irina's graduation from high school, then long distance photos of her on her college campus — had Alexei had her followed? Then photos of her wedding to Sergei, followed by more long-lens shots of her at her job at the jewelry shop. The most recent was her arriving at Sergei's funeral in that hated red dress.

"This isn't creepy *at all*," Galina murmured to herself, astounded at the level of obsession on display against the walls.

She wanted to pull every photograph down and set the house on fire, but she knew that wouldn't solve the problem. What she'd found here certainly explained Alexei's swiftness in breaking up Irina's engagement. How long had he been following Rina, or paying someone to follow her?

Fear ran cold fingers down her spine. Did he still have someone following Irina? If so, had he managed to capture any images of Irina with Viktor? She began to look through the stacks of photos lying around the room, scattering them on the floor as she searched for anything that might answer the questions she had. If Alexei had seen anything that led him to suspect Irina and Viktor had a relationship, would he have eliminated Viktor, no matter who else might have gotten in the way?

Even their father?

Galina had to admit that if that were the case, then Alexei was more efficient than she thought. He'd wanted Papa out of the way, he hated Andrey and the idea of Irina marrying him, and he would have wanted Viktor dead for touching Irina. As she flipped through stacks and stacks of photographs, she found nothing to link Viktor and Irina together outside of his being her bodyguard.

When she was finished searching, she stood in the middle of the room, surrounded by still images of her sister. Nothing here indicated that Alexei knew anything about Irina and Viktor. Galina felt a small sense of relief, followed by an even greater sense of unease.

What the hell was wrong with her brother? And how long had he been hiding this?

She spun when she heard the door open and close again, eyes darting for a way out. She did not want to be trapped in here with Alexei. There was a window to her left, and she edged her way over to it.

Andrey filled the doorway of the room and Galina was alternately relieved and irritated. Remembering the looks of the men in the circle, she settled on irritated. The top two or three buttons of his shirt were undone, his black hair was in disarray, and his pants were creased. "You left."

She smiled her sweetest smile, so sweet she was fairly certain she'd have two cavities by the time she was done. "I'd heard quite enough, thank you. I didn't think it was necessary for me to witness the fawning and congratulations."

Andrey raised one black comma of an eyebrow. "Am I to understand that you are displeased with the outcome?"

"Whyever would you say that?" Yep, she could feel her teeth rotting as she kept the smile plastered on her face.

"Galina, you just used the word *whyever* in a sentence. Everything is *not* okay." He crossed his arms over his chest and waited.

She looked around and shuddered. Galina crossed into the small kitchenette and waited for Andrey to join her. This room was clean and tidy, unused. And there were no pictures of Irina anywhere in sight.

"Galina?" Andrey said her name in same way a principal might say it after she'd been called to his office. It inflamed her already raw nerves. The unspoken *I'm waiting* in his tone crawled right up her back, making her want to gnash her teeth.

"Did you expect I would be pleased with that display?" she asked archly, leaning one hip against the counter.

Anger flashed silver in his eyes. "I told you I would have to deal with Alexei at some point. You're surprised that it was now?" His voice held irritation and disbelief. "I would expect you'd be happy with the outcome!"

She slapped a hand flat on the counter, the sound a sharp punctuation to her next words. "Oh yes, I love being treated like an object in front of men I'm trying to get to accept my leadership! And I absolutely adore having my sister humiliated in front of a houseful of those same men!"

Andrey's temper snapped and he crowded her into the corner of the kitchenette. Galina looked up at him, seeing the sharp tension in the line of his jaw, hearing the growl at the back of his throat. They shouldn't be arguing, not this soon after a change. But Galina had never been good at not doing things she shouldn't.

"I released your sister from an engagement she didn't want!" Andrey pressed his body against hers. "I won the right to wed you, so we don't have to sneak around any longer! Irina's free to do what she wants."

Galina laughed mockingly. Did he really think that was a valid argument? "First of all, Irina's not free. Viktor's dead and Alexei now gets to determine who she'll marry, which—given the state of the next room—is likely to be him!"

She tried to push past Andrey, but he didn't move. He just stared down at her with angry silver eyes. "And second, did you really just say 'you won the right to wed me'?" She shook her head. "You've won the right to exactly nothing, you jackass. *I* decide who I'm going to marry, not the results of some outdated, dick swinging cage match!" Andrey blinked. "You could have just asked me," she snapped.

Andrey's mouth dropped to hers in a bruising kiss, stopping what she wanted to say next. Galina tried to push him away, still angry with him, but he wrapped his arms around her waist, pulling her into his body so she could feel his erection pressing insistently against her belly. His mouth mauled hers, his tongue sliding inside. She bit at it warningly and Andrey growled.

He wanted to rut. And she was *not* in the mood. This was the problem with challenges.

Since trying to move him was out of the question, Galina slid her hands down the front of his pants, cupping his hardness through the material. Andrey whined low in his throat, a hungry, needy sound. She unbuttoned his pants, unzipping his fly so his cock popped free into her hand. His trousers pooled at his feet.

She used her other hand to cup the heaviness of his balls, as she began to slide her palm up his length. She twisted her thumb over the head of him, feeling the droplets of pre-come slide against his flesh. She kept her strokes steady and slow, trying to ground Andrey back in his body.

He tried to turn her, but Galina tightened her hold on his balls the slightest bit and he went still, a rumble of a growl erupting from him. He stopped kissing her, pulling his head back so he stared at her, a confused look on his face. She rewarded him by increasing the speed of her hand, her thumb spreading more of his juices over his length as he continued to leak. His eyes slid closed in pleasure.

Andrey's hips began to move in time with her strokes, thrusting into her hand. His head dropped against hers, their foreheads touching. They were locked together, bodies close but not touching as her hand worked on him. Galina tightened her fist around him, squeezing at the base of him and he cried out, hips jerking against her hold. "Shhhh," she whispered, smiling. She picked the rhythm back up once more, fondling his balls as she pumped him faster.

Throwing back his head, Andrey cried out, his hips working mindlessly. Galina felt him swelling, could tell he was close to release by the noises that spilled from the back of his throat. "Come for me, Andrey," she whispered, watching his face as his release blasted through him.

He pitched forward as he came, eyes unseeing, hips still pumping. His release painted her hands in strips of warm wetness. Galina gripped him through his tremors, then let go, bringing her hand up to her mouth to savor the taste of him with delicate licks. He leaned against her, heavy and still, his breathing hitching like he'd just run a race. She could hear the staccato beating of his heart as it pounded in his chest.

He raised his head, looking dazed and relaxed, all signs of the tension from the challenge now gone. It was difficult not to kill your opponent, and Andrey had clearly held back. He'd needed some kind of release. "Thank you," he breathed, his eyes back to their normal steely blue color. He dropped his forehead to hers, nuzzling at her temple. "Very much."

She grabbed a hand towel from the counter, cleaning the rest of him off of her, then proceeded to wipe him clean with gentle hands. "My pleasure."

His lips quirked into a brief smile. "I highly doubt that." He looked around at where they were, as if it were a hovel.

Galina stopped her ministrations to wind her arms around his neck. "Then you don't know me as well as you think you do." She kissed him sweetly, gently. If he thought she needed romance and hotel rooms and wooing, well, he was way off base. All she needed was him.

She wasn't about to tell him that very often, of course. A girl had to have some secrets.

He broke the kiss, tracing his index finger down the side of her neck. "What was that you said about Alexei marrying Irina?"

Galina grinned wickedly. "Pull up your pants and I'll show you."

He grimaced, reaching down to yank up his trousers and fasten them. When he was moderately put together again, she led him into the living room. Andrey surveyed the walls with an angry look on his face, eyes dark. "We should speak with Nikolai."

"My thoughts exactly."

Galina arrived home in advance of the rest of the group, grateful for the break to get her thoughts in order. Alexei's stalker pad had thrown her; it was why she had suggested they all meet at her place. If her brother was so far gone that he was paying someone to watch Irina at her own husband's funeral, then she didn't want to take the chance that he hadn't bugged her house or have cameras wired in it. She knew her place was secure.

Andrey was coming with Konstantin, Nikolai with Irina. Galina pulled out some snacks and chilled a bottle of vodka. She'd already sent someone to fetch some clothes for Irina. As far as she was concerned, her sister wasn't going to be left alone until Alexei was ousted. She didn't trust her brother to make good decisions anymore.

She changed out of her business suit and pulled on a pair of fleece yoga pants and a cashmere sweater. Galina had just pulled her hair into a simple ponytail when the doorbell rang. Nikolai had his arm around Irina, but she looked miserable. Galina gave her a hug, ushering them both inside. As they settled in her living room, she got her sister a glass of vodka.

"Sip this," Galina ordered, handing Irina the rocks glass. "You're going to need it." She returned to the kitchen to fetch glasses for the rest. The doorbell rang. "Nik, can you get that? It'll be your boyfriend."

"He's not my boyfriend," Nik snapped.

"Okay, it'll be your *lover*." Galina stuck her head out of the kitchen and gave him her best lascivious grin. "That better?"

"You're impossible!"

A few moments later, Andrey wrapped his arms around her, pressing her back against him. "I missed you."

Galina smiled, her hands busy with the tray she was holding. "Grab that bottle, please."

Andrey released her and did as he was bid, following her into the living room. Nikolai sat in the wingback chair, Konstantin standing guard behind him. Irina sat on the couch, glass clutched in her hands, knuckles going white. She looked lost and alone. Galina's heart went out to her. She set the tray on her coffee table and sat next to Irina, taking one hand in both of hers.

"Everyone help yourselves." She leaned in close to her sister. "How are you doing?"

"Besides being humiliated and confused, and mourning the one man I've ever loved? Motherfucking peachy, darling, thanks." Irina gave her a bitter smile.

"Drink up, Rina," Galina warned, giving her hand a squeeze. "The evening is just getting started."

"There's more?" Irina asked. "You know, you don't have to sugar-coat things for me, Galina. I can handle it. Just tell me. You didn't find a dead hooker in Alexei's Dumpster or anything, did you?"

"Actually, this is the one instance where a dead hooker might have been preferable," she said. Galina waited until everyone who wanted a drink had one, then began. "It's worse than we thought." She gave Nikolai a pointed look. "We've always known that Alexei is…unhealthily interested in Irina."

"We did not always know this," Irina said, shaking her head.

"Those of us who are not Irina have always known this," Galina amended. "But now, his obsession is to the point that he's turned the guest house at the back of Papa's property into stalker central."

"What are you talking about?" Irina looked at Galina, trying to understand.

"Alexei has a wall of you, Rina. Pictures—some old, some as recent as Sergei's funeral—all over the place. And he's got quite the little, ah, collection." Galina met Nik's gaze, holding it with her own. "He had Irina's old teddy bear—the one that Papa won her at the carnival. You know, the one you slept with until you left for college. And the garter you wore on your wedding day."

"Oh God," Irina gasped, going white. She tipped the glass back and drained it.

"You're going to want another." Galina gestured for Nik to refill her sister's glass, then continued. "Andrey saw it too."

Andrey nodded. "I think it's safe to say that Alexei is not just a passenger on the crazy train, he's the conductor."

Galina grinned at him. "So we have to figure out what to do next. While I'm sure we all appreciate the fact that Irina is once again a free agent, it does present us with the problem of what to do about Alexei."

"It's only a matter of time before he makes a move on Irina," Andrey said, dropping a hand to Galina's shoulder. "Had I known that he was this obsessed, I would not have called off the engagement."

"I don't think any of us knew he was this bad," Irina said, polishing off another glass. "A lot of what he said in my house that day he destroyed all of my clothes makes sense now." She waved the empty at Nik. "Another."

"I think you've had enough," Nik said, looking at Galina.

"Nope, I still have functioning brain cells, so I haven't had nearly enough." Irina waved the glass at him again.

Galina snorted indelicately. "Go ahead. She's staying with me tonight anyway. She can get as drunk as she likes."

"Yay for me." Irina looked at Kon.

"What's the next move?" Konstantin asked, taking the bottle and refilling both Nik and Irina's glasses. "After we have a lengthy discussion of Irina's interview with the FBI this morning, while you morons were 'too busy' to answer your phones."

"Oh, you…козел ебарь," Irina snapped at him.

"Did she just call you a 'goat fucker'?" Andrey asked Kon, a huge grin on his face.

Kon scratched the back of his head, looking offended. "Yes, she did."

"I am starting to like her more and more," Andrey told Galina.

Smacking Andrey's chest, she rounded on her sister. "We are talking about this, in detail. We need to know what was asked, what was said, and how much you cried."

"Fine." Irina grunted. "And for the record, I didn't cry. Jerk."

"Now that that's settled, we get Irina as far away from Alexei as we can, at least for the moment." Nik nodded a thank you to Konstantin for refilling his glass. "Give us time to plan, time to look for some evidence that he was involved in the bombing."

"Wait, what?" Irina sat up, nearly dropping her glass. "You think Alexei had Papa and Viktor killed?"

Nik threaded his fingers through hers. "Think about it, Irina. Papa doesn't have any active feuds going. He was on the cusp of making a strong connection with Andrey's operation, which would make him someone to do business with, not murder. Who had the most to gain from getting Papa out of the way? Alexei. He's been itching to take over the family for years and it was pretty clear how he felt about Papa's plans to marry you to Andrey. I think he got tired of waiting."

"So, you're sending me away?"

"We need to get Irina as far away from Alexei as we can, at least for the moment." Nik nodded a thank you to Konstantin. "And in that, I think I can help. I've got a cabin a few hours from here. Irina and I can go there for a little while—I can say we're taking some time to grieve away from the constant reminders of Pop. No one will think to question that, not even Alexei."

Galina nodded slowly, already thinking. "That will give me time to figure out a way to counter him." She sighed. "I may as well tell you this, Nik," she said, staring at her brother. "I want more than just a seat at the table."

"Let me guess, you want to *be* the table." Nick gave her a tired smile.

Andrey let out a wild laugh. "Close!"

"I want to run the table." Galina gave her brother a small smile. "But I need to prove that I'd be better at it than Alexei."

"That shouldn't be too difficult," Konstantin offered, coming to sit on the arm of Nikolai's chair. Unconsciously, Nik leaned into him.

Galina smiled over at Andrey, feeling a thrill run through her. It was wonderful to see Nik happy and truly himself. She felt it was a gift she was being given, a special glimpse into her brother that she rarely got to see. She wished he could be this comfortable and open everywhere he went.

Konstantin continued, wrapping an arm absently around Nik's shoulders. "I listened to the others at the challenge. The old guard wasn't impressed with Alexei's decision to break the engagement. And they were less impressed with his performance in the challenge itself. They may not be ready for a woman at the head of the table, but they're unlikely to support Alexei for much longer."

Irina raised her glass and said, "Then we need to make them ready because nothing is going to stop Galina." She drained the vodka in one swallow. "She's like the unholy child of ambition and a steamroller."

"That I can drink to," Andrey said, also raising his glass to Galina.

"It's not my line," Irina said, shaking her head. "Vitya said it once."

Galina felt like she'd been punched in the gut. The desolation in her sister's eyes made her want to howl in sympathy. When the tears started the slow slide down Irina's face, Galina had to swallow against a choking lump in her own throat.

Nik plucked the glass from Irina's hand. "And you, my dear Rina, are officially cut off."

Irina glared at him, making a wild grab for the glass. "Konstantin, how do you stand this utter stick in the mud?"

"He's got a big dick."

Nik spit out his vodka.

Irina shook her head. "I'm suddenly so glad I wasn't drinking just now."

"Waste of good vodka," Andrey noted with a smirk.

Galina had never seen her brother turn quite that shade of red before.

21

Spying Is Such a Dirty Word

Irina had been gone for a few days and Konstantin along with her. Galina had been fine with that arrangement until she realized that Andrey had not assigned himself another bodyguard and was wandering around relatively unprotected with her psycho brother still at large and probably nursing a massive vendetta. She was a firm believer in what was good for the goose most definitely being good for the gander; if he was going to preach at her about the importance of personal safety, then he had no right to object to her doing the same.

Which was how she found herself watching Andrey pull his car into the parking lot of the run-down motel that advertised rates by the hour, the night, or the week. She felt like she had contracted chlamydia just by setting eyes on the place. What the hell was Andrey doing here? And why had he stopped for food?

He'd been disappearing quite a bit over the last week and a half. Galina knew he liked to ditch his security detail, so she had assigned herself as Andrey's own personal protection detail. Just because Alexei was a coward and unlikely to attack Andrey openly, didn't mean that he was safe. She'd dismissed her own detail since she knew it would be made up of men loyal to her brother.

The man in question stepped out of the car, a bag of fast food in his hand. He stopped at the door of 121 and knocked twice, paused, and then knocked twice again. A few moments later, the door swung open and Andrey disappeared inside.

Galina pulled her car into a spot half the parking lot away from Andrey's and pulled out her phone. She might as well be useful while she waited. She dialed Irina's cell number.

"How's my favorite sister?" Galina asked brightly when her sister answered.

"Fine, I guess. Other than feeling utterly and completely useless." Irina sighed. "I think I need to come back, Galina. I shouldn't be up here hiding—I should be there helping you."

"Rina, I understand you're frustrated. I get it. But short of finding a handily written confession that Alexei decided to blow up his father because it was a day that ended in Y, I don't think there's much you can do here. If Alexei knows you're back in town, he's going to try to see you. And we've seen how well that ends."

"I take it your search efforts have not been successful?" Irina asked.

"No," Galina bit out. She was getting tired of spinning her wheels searching for anything that might make it possible to move on her brother. "He's moved into Papa's house, along with his whole operation—computers, goons, any records that he keeps. It's like the Waco compound now. I bribed his building's maintenance guy to let me into his condo, but I got nothing. He took everything with him to Papa's."

"What about Nik? Can he get anywhere with him?"

"No. He barely lets Nik onto the property. I can't get near him unless I do some serious Black Ops shit." Galina had been sorely tempted to do just that but decided against it.

"He would let me in," Irina said.

"No, absolutely not!" Galina's voice dropped to Alpha command level, the gravelly tone she used to compel a Beta to do her bidding.

"Do not pull your Alpha crap on me, missy. You know that doesn't work on me."

"Then stop suggesting highly dangerous things!" Galina snarled. "We'll get him, Irina. I just need a little more time."

"Meanwhile, you're in danger and Kon and Nik are stuck babysitting me."

"And you're healing, which is what you need to be doing right now," Galina told her. "Just relax, Irina. Let us take care of it."

She thought she saw movement against the curtain. "Look, Rina, I need to go. I've got something I need to take care of. We'll talk again soon, okay?" She didn't wait to hear her sister's response; she just hung up and scooted out of the car. She walked to the door.

And she waited.

It was perhaps ten minutes later when she heard the rattle of the doorknob. In that time, Galina had concocted and discarded about fifty reasons why Andrey would be at this hotel with cheap, greasy food. *Closet fast food addict* was quickly thrown out as a possibility, as was *kept woman with a penchant for curly fries*. She knew that certain deals required less than ideal spots but that spot was usually not a no-tell motel. Nor did those negotiations involve Chubby Burger.

The door opened. Andrey's tall frame filled the entrance. He turned back and said, "Soon, I promise."

A voice Galina never expected to hear again said, "Check on Rina for me."

She wasn't very often left without words, but this was just such a time. "Viktor?" she whispered, trying to see around Andrey's back.

"Galya?" Andrey spun around, a horrified look on his face.

She shoved past him into the grotty motel room.

Viktor climbed to his feet.

Viktor.

Was.

Alive.

She looked from her sister's love to her own and then back again.

Her first thought was that she was going to kill him.

Galina lunged farther into the room, fury boiling up inside her. She swung her arm backward, intending to slap the taste right out of Viktor's mouth, but Andrey stopped her. She had to satisfy herself with shouting, "What the fucking fuck is going on?"

Andrey released her arm, then turned and locked the door. "Galina, if you will just calm down…"

"Are you kidding me?" Galina didn't take her eyes off of Viktor. He was dressed in his usual white button down shirt and black slacks. He looked tired, but otherwise unharmed. How had he escaped the explosion? And why hadn't he let Irina know he'd survived. "You asshole!" she seethed, advancing on him. "My sister's weeping for you. Weeping!"

Viktor had the grace to look saddened by that. "I'm sorry. I never wanted to make her cry."

"She's not crying, you imbecile. Did I say crying? No, I did not!"

Andrey looked confused. "There's a difference?"

Galina threw him an exasperated glance. "Weeping is tragic. It's all about heartbreak and shit. Crying is something you do after watching long distance telephone commercials." She rounded on her fiancé. "How long have you known he's alive?"

"I asked him not to tell anyone," Viktor broke in.

Galina ignored him. It was safer for everyone. "How long?"

Andrey's face was a cool mask. "Perhaps a few days after the explosion."

On the verge of transforming and letting her inner wolf destroy the world's grossest motel room, Galina stood very still, letting the anger flow through her. She imagined herself a tree, her legs like a trunk, her feet rooting her to the ground. The rage flowed down her body and into her feet before dissipating out of her. It helped her to calm; she kept up the visualization for a few moments more, then opened her eyes.

She now felt much more equipped to deal with a werewolf back from the dead. "I would greatly appreciate it if you would explain the events of the past few weeks to me, specifically detailing how he is not a charcoal briquette." Galina was proud that she managed to sound reasonable and logical and not like she wanted to wear Viktor's ribcage as a jaunty chapeau.

Unfortunately, Andrey still eyed her like she was a dirty bomb in danger of detonating and taking out half of the Pacific Northwest. Damn. She gave him a pleasant smile. His concerned look deepened until it looked like a plow had furrowed lines in his forehead.

Galina walked to the room's lone chair and perched on it, crossing her legs with a prim flourish. She gestured for one of them to start.

"I'm waiting. And this had better be good."

"He wasn't in the car, sweet," Andrey began, but Viktor shook his head.

"Is Rina okay?" His bullet-blue eyes bored into hers.

Resisting the urge to smack him, she rolled her eyes. "Did you not hear what I just said, Viktor? She loves you and she thinks you're dead. Pretty sure she's not dancing in the streets with a martini in her hand!"

He hung his head, wiping his hand across his face.

Galina gave him a moment, then asked, "So you weren't in the car with Papa? Where were you?"

Viktor looked up, his face dark. "I was worried about Irina. She'd been attacked in front of the jewelry store. I wanted to check things out, make sure she was safe."

"Irina told me about it. Did you find out anything?"

He shook his head. "It was just a random attack. I put in some cameras watching the parking lot just in case though." He paused. "When I was finished, I heard about your father and I decided to lay low."

"Why didn't you get in touch with one of us immediately?"

Viktor's blue eyes met hers. "Ilya's car was gone over with a fine tooth comb every couple of weeks. The family has its own mechanic that worked on it. It had just been inspected a few days before."

Galina knew all of this. She waved at him to go on.

He glanced over at Andrey, who spoke. "Think about it, Galya. How would a bomb have gotten in the car? Especially when it was parked at your father's house. In his garage."

"Someone close to the family had to put it there." Her eyes narrowed. Nikolai had his own place, but Alexei would occasionally spend nights in the house with Papa. And then he'd gone on a business trip so he had an alibi.

Viktor nodded sadly. Galina looked from him to Andrey.

"So let's say Alexei planted it." She frowned. "How was he able to trigger it or set the bomb to go off when he was out of town?"

"Your father always went to play chess with Petyr at the same time every week. That's where Ilya was going when the car blew up."

Galina leaned back in her chair. She closed her eyes briefly. "Do you have proof?"

Andrey answered. "That's what we're working to find. Alexei has covered his tracks remarkably well."

She sighed. It figured. The one thing Alexei turned out to be good at was covering up patricide. Turning to Viktor once more, she asked, "When did you get in touch with Andrey? And why didn't you contact me or Nikolai?"

"A few days after the funeral." Viktor stood and began to stalk around the room, covering the distance in a few quick strides. "I needed eyes on Alexei and I couldn't risk being seen. Andrey seemed the likeliest candidate. Everyone knows he and Alexei can't stand each other."

Galina quirked her brow at him. He frowned at her. "I couldn't risk getting in touch with you or Nikolai or Irina. Not if I wanted Alexei to keep thinking I was dead."

She nodded. This she understood. If Irina had known he was alive, she wouldn't have been able to contain her joy. She might be a good actress, but no one was *that* good—not with Alexei obsessively watching her.

"So you helped him," Galina said to Andrey. "You falsified his dental records for identification."

He nodded. "I didn't tell you. Viktor was correct in keeping things quiet."

Galina wanted to be angry, but she knew that Andrey and Viktor were right. She wouldn't have been able to keep this news from Irina, not if she could have eased her suffering. Still, she was still displeased to have been left out of the search for her father's killer, even if it led to her brother.

Andrey's phone beeped. While he stepped out to take the call, Galina tried both Nik and Irina's cell phones. Both went directly to voice mail. She shook her head at Viktor, who looked like he wanted to punch his fist through the cheaply hung drywall of the motel room. She left a quick message for Nik to call her back, and then hung up. Viktor being alive was news she wanted to deliver herself.

"Did Andrey tell you he called off the engagement to Irina?"

Viktor nodded. His mouth was pressed in a grim line. "He may have said something."

Galina rolled her eyes. "Then I hope you've picked out a ring because if you don't propose to my sister, you are a deeply, deeply stupid mammal."

Viktor looked like she'd hit over the head with a piano. "Wh-What?"

"You are planning to marry Irina, right?" She stared at him, waiting for an acceptable answer.

"I...I didn't, I mean, I hadn't expected I'd be allowed to." He didn't drop his gaze from hers, even though a flush crept up his handsome face.

"Buy the ring."

Andrey returned before Viktor could say anything else. "I need to go. Sit tight. I'll be back later. And you, my dear stalker, need to get back to work." He held the door open for her.

Galina gave Viktor a wry smile before following Andrey out to their cars.

22

Is That a Knife in Your Pocket or Are You Just Happy to See Me?

Galina knocked on the door to Maksim's room at the Hotel Andra. He had the penthouse suite in one of the poshest hotels in Seattle. She hadn't seen him since Papa's funeral. Between the FBI inquiry into her father's death, Alexei's absence, and the need to keep the business running, she hadn't gotten a chance to speak with Maksim to iron out the final details of the caviar import deal.

He ushered her inside, placing his hand on the small of her back. She could feel the dampness of his palm through the thin fabric of her blouse. Galina moved away from him, walking over to the window that looked out over downtown.

"Thank you for coming," Maksim began. "I wanted to speak with you before I leave."

"You're going back to Russia?"

"Eventually." He joined her at the picture window, standing easily beside her. "First a trip to New York, and then home."

"I'm sure you'll be happy to get back." She turned her back on the view. "So what can I do for you?"

Maksim's slap came out of nowhere, stunning Galina. He backhanded her, the force snapping her head to the side. Galina gasped, staggering. Maksim grabbed her hair, yanking her head back. She slammed her palms against his chest, shoving him away, taking a lock of her hair with him.

"What the fuck do you think you're doing?" she shouted, anger and fear sparking along her nerves.

"блудница!" he yelled back, grabbing for her again.

He'd called her a whore. She dodged, feeling the ache in her cheek. She wanted to work her way back to the door of the suite, but he blocked her way.

"You and that Rom, spreading your legs to him," Maksim spat, eyes glowing with fury. "You think you can embarrass me? I am Federov!"

Galina jerked to the side, hoping to make it past him, but he grabbed her upper arm. "You will not make a fool of me," he hissed, spittle landing on her face. "I will show you your place."

"Like hell," she snarled, ripping free from his grip. She was too angry to be afraid.

He snatched at her again, dragging her against his chest. Galina brought her knee up to catch him in the groin, but he twisted away. "Alexei told me you would need to be broken in," he whispered against her cheek. "That you need a firm hand." His hand slid down to her ass.

Galina snarled, lifting her foot and slamming her heel down on his instep. Maksim howled in pain. She broke away from him, running for the door.

She'd only made it a few steps when he tackled her from behind, throwing them both to the floor. "чертовски сука!" he yelled. His hands tore at her clothes, his claws ripping her blouse.

"Get off me!" she screamed, unable to trigger her change with him on top of her.

"Bitch!" Maksim lifted her head in his hands and slammed it into the floor.

Fireworks went off behind her eyes. An icy spike of fear speared through her. She needed to get out of this room, away from Maksim. He was crazy, his eyes wild and unfocused.

He bent over her. Galina reared up, smashing her forehead into the bridge of his nose. She saw stars, but it was worth it when she heard the satisfying crack of Maksim's nose breaking. She shoved him off of her and managed to get to her feet as he screamed behind her.

She was out the door, her phone from her pocket now in her hand. She hit Andrey's speed dial number as she raced to the elevator. She slapped the down button as Andrey answered.

"Galy—"

She cut him off, panting heavily. "I'm at the Hotel Andra. Maksim…"

Something sharp and fiery plunged into her back. Galina screamed as pain flowed through her, hot and wet and burning like a brand. The elevator dinged, and she stumbled through the open doors. Galina spun, dropping the phone to the elevator floor so she could use both hands to fight to fight off Maksim.

Blood covered his face from where she'd broken his nose. He swung at her again, dagger clutched in his fist. The blade slashed across her forearm and Galina felt like she was igniting from the inside out. Another stab to her upper arms, then a swipe that missed. She saw the red blood turn black as it poured out of her.

Silver! Maksim was stabbing her and he was doing it with a silver blade. It was weakening her rapidly. Galina snarled, lashing at him with her claws. She caught him across the face, raking down his forehead and across his nose. The knife went flying as he threw up his arms for protection.

Galina shoved him away weakly, but it was enough. Her muscles were getting harder to control as the silver scorched through her system. Maksim stumbled backward, out of the elevator. The doors closed in his face.

"Son of a b…" she managed to get out before she felt bile rise in the back of her throat. Galina leaned over and threw up, feeling the silver working into her bloodstream, poisoning her system.

Hitting the button for the lobby, Galina slumped against the wall. The world was spinning too fast, just one big mass of light and color. She heard Andrey's voice shouting at her from somewhere very far away.

Then everything seemed to telescope inward, turning her upside down and she tumbled into darkness.

She heard a frantic voice, shouting her name. Galina wanted to open her eyes, but it seemed to take a thousand years and all of her energy. It took her a few moments to recognize the voice, and to realize there were hands on her, gently cupping her face.

She managed to crack open one eye. "Andrey?" she croaked, barely able to see his stern face. He looked so worried. It took her a minute to wonder why, her brain a thick and sluggish thing. Before she could figure out what was wrong, the blackness of unconsciousness pulled her under again.

23

Chicken Queen

There was beeping. It annoyed her.

That was the first real coherent thought she was able to process. Where the hell was that beeping coming from? Who the hell had thought that was a good idea? Was it her alarm? Was she late for work?

Galina tried to lift her arm and couldn't. That sent a bolt of panic through her, which should have done something—made her move, leap to her feet, jerk upright in bed, *something*. Instead she lay wherever she was like a dead fish. What the hell was wrong with her? Why couldn't she feel anything?

She managed to open her eyes. They felt dry and gummy, her eyelids as heavy as wet snow. Taking a minute to focus, Galina slowly looked around the room. White and steel and industrial greeted her. *Hospital.* The word floated to the top of her mind, like algae on a lake. She was taking entirely too long to process things.

She tried to turn her head, then realized it was well beyond her in her weakened state. She had to settle for what she could.

"Galya?" Andrey's voice whispered. He sounded exhausted.

His face hovered above hers. Galina had never been so happy to see anyone in her entire life. His jaw was covered in stubble, his eyes were dark and shadowed from lack of sleep and worry, but he was beautiful. "Andrey?" She licked at dry, cracked lips.

He kissed her softly, his hands clutching at her. "Сладкая."

"What happened?" There were gaps in her memory. She had no idea how long she'd been unconscious.

He lifted her hand to press kisses on each of her knuckles. She saw an IV taped to the back of her hand. "You were stabbed. It was a silver blade."

"Maksim," she gasped, remembering her meeting with him in the hotel.

Galina looked around nervously. She hated hospitals — if she was afraid of anything, it was being stuck in one, unable to escape as she was poked and prodded and experimented on. She shifted, trying to push herself up. Then she realized she was wrapped up in plastic tubes and monitors and wires, and her mind blanked. She began to bat at the tubing.

"What are you doing?" Andrey pressed her hand down on the bed gently. "You need to rest."

Galina shook her head. She couldn't rest in a hospital. "What I need is to get out of here." She pushed weakly at his hands.

"Galya," he warned.

"Andrey, I can't stay." Her voice rose higher as she began to feel panic skim along her nerves. The beeping was going to drive her crazy.

"What are you talking about?" Andrey asked, voice tired and rough. He brushed hair from her eyes.

Galina subsided back into the bed, exhausted. All she wanted to do was sleep, but she couldn't, not here.

"I hate hospitals. Like *hate* hate them." She couldn't say she was scared. Galina hated being afraid. "I have always been…*concerned* that someone would find out, you know, what the family was, and they'll lock me up and do experiments on me."

"You're afraid of hospitals." His voice was soft, almost loving.

Galina tossed her head weakly on the pillow, even hating to just hear it said out loud. She closed her eyes, feeling exhaustion sweep over her. Just the few minutes she'd been awake had tired her beyond imagining. Her limbs felt heavy and numb; she suspected the silver still hadn't worked its way out of her bloodstream yet.

"Please, Andrey," Galina whispered, managing to twitch her fingers. Her eyes pleaded with him.

He ran a hand through his black hair. His blue eyes were clouded, tired. He nodded once. "Very well." Andrey clasped her hand. "Nik can handle the paperwork of discharging you. I will need to make sure my house is ready for you." He stood up to leave.

"Your house?" Galina asked, voice weak even to her ears.

"My house." Andrey leaned down, brushing hair away from her face. "It's the only place I can keep you safe. No arguments, Galya."

She managed a small smile. "I wasn't going to argue. I just never thought this would be the way I got to spend a night at your place."

He gave her a tired smile in return. "I will need to make some calls to make sure everything is prepared for your arrival." Andrey looked down at her fondly. "I'd tell you not to go anywhere, but it looks like we're in no danger of that."

"Just for that," Galina began, eyelids growing too heavy to lift, "I'm going to drag myself out of here…by my teeth." She felt his lips graze her forehead before she knew nothing more.

The sheets she lay on were much softer than those of her hospital bed. The pillows were plumper. The scent of the room was no longer medicinal; rather, the smell of…vanilla cookies?…tickled at her nostrils, along with something sharper, more herbaceous. Galina flexed her fingers, feeling pain spark along her nerves. The silver was still moving through her.

She moaned. Wasn't she supposed to be feeling better by now?

"She's this way." Andrey's voice came to her from somewhere else, nearby but not in the room.

The door to her room opened, revealing Andrey and a heavy set, squat woman wearing a nubby cardigan with chickens embroidered on it. Her iron grey hair was pulled back in a bun, her dark skin wrinkled like a raisin. "Mama Yaga?" she whispered, attempting to push herself up on elbows that wouldn't support her.

The full lips split into a wide smile. "Yes, child, that is my name these days." She looked up at Andrey, who was holding her bag. At least, Galina thought it was her bag; last time she checked, Andrey didn't have a tote bag with chicken tracks sewn all over it. "This young man was most insistent that I come right away." She shot Andrey a dark look.

"It's silver poisoning. She was stabbed," he tried to explain before she shushed him.

"I have eyes. They may be old, *boychick*, but they still work." Mama Yaga stood over her bed and softly brushed the hair from Galina's eyes. "Your young man says that you do not care for hospitals." She winked at Galina. "Smart girl not to trust them."

Galina stared up at Mama Yaga, amazed by the presence of this woman. She was a force, a howling vortex of power that filled the space around her. Galina understood now why everyone went to Mama Yaga for healing, for spells, for potions. "Can you help me?" For the first time, she wasn't ashamed that her voice shook. "It really hurts."

"Of course, my dear." Her hand was gentle on Galina's forehead. "But know this: often the cure is more painful than that which it is supposed to help."

Galina hesitated. She thought she could handle pain, but the silver inside her made her wonder. The stab wounds hurt more than she thought possible. Was there something that could hurt worse than that? Was it something she really wanted to attempt?

A knock at the door interrupted them. Konstantin stormed in, not waiting for Andrey's approval. All eyes turned to him. "I said I was not to be disturbed!" Andrey shouted, his voice a roar.

Konstantin winced, but held his ground. His handsome face was flushed, his clothing wrinkled and torn, and his normally perfect hair was a matted mess. He leaned against the doorjamb, breathing heavily, his arm pressed tight against his side. "Alexei…" he began, then had to stop to gulp for air. "He's got Irina."

"WHAT?!" Galina tried to push herself out of bed, but all she managed to do was sit upright for a few seconds before falling back in bed. "She's supposed to be at the safe house with you!"

"You were already out of it when this happened. She stole my car when I was on patrol. I took off after her, but even at my fastest, I'm no match for a car. I called someone to come and get me and tried to get her scent again."

Galina glared at all of them, but Andrey headed off her angry words. "I called Viktor at the motel and told him to watch Alexei."

Konstantin dropped into a chair, exhaustion set in the line of his shoulders. "Irina went to Alexei's club. I didn't get there until after they'd already left." He shook his head, and then looked at Galina. "Some of the men there said he was bragging about your unfortunate run-in with a silver knife."

Galina nodded. It didn't surprise her in the slightest. She wondered when Maksim had thrown his lot in with Alexei. Her brother must really be feeling threatened to try something like this.

Andrey's jaw clenched in rage. "Son of a bitch." He took Galina's hand in his. "What else?"

"Irina apparently came in to the club, loaded for bear. The old guard are not all that impressed with Alexei's stability, and his behavior tonight didn't help. He and Irina left. Once I found out all I could, I came here."

Galina looked at Mama Yaga and nodded once. The old woman began to take bags and jars of herbs and other less wholesome things from her tote. Galina interrupted Konstantin before he could begin his tale. "Call Nik. See if he can run interference. I don't think Irina should be alone with Alexei."

"Already called him," Konstantin said. Andrey went over and pried at the forearm Konstantin held against his side. "He's heading over to your father's place."

"What's this?" he asked his bodyguard.

"One of Alexei's guys jumped me when I was leaving the club. I took care of him, but he got a lucky hit."

"Drink this," Mama Yaga said, pressing a tall glass of something brown and foul smelling into Galina's hand. The old woman helped her to sit up. "All of it," she warned, having noticed Galina's less than excited look. "Once you have, I'll put poultices on your wounds to draw out the rest of the poison."

Galina lifted the glass to her lips, grimacing when she got a nose full of the nasty smell. "All of it?"

Mama Yaga looked down at her, a slight frown on her lips. Galina smiled at her weakly, and then sighed, answering her own question. "All of it."

Galina took a huge swallow and gagged, nearly spitting it back into the glass. One look from Mama Yaga convinced her it would be less painful to drink the horrible tasting stuff than to defy the old witch. She chugged it down, tears streaming down her face. When the glass was empty, Galina sagged back against the headboard of Andrey's bed.

"That young idiot over there," Mama Yaga said, indicating Konstantin with a nod of her head, "has a slash along his ribs that he needs help cleaning." She waved for Andrey to attend to him. "I will take care of your mate." When Andrey looked like he was going to protest, she raised one grey eyebrow. "What on earth made you think that was a request?"

Galina nodded. Andrey needed to see to Konstantin, as much as she might wish him to stay close to her. And she suspected that Mama Yaga had a reason for sending him away. "I'll be fine," she assured him, although she wasn't entirely sure she would be. "Go."

When he had helped Konstantin into the bathroom, Galina stared at Mama Yaga. The old woman was spreading a white paste onto clean cloths. When she turned to begin unwinding the dressings from Galina's wounds, Galina asked her, "Why did you really send Andrey away?"

Mama Yaga smiled a smile without mirth. "Not much gets past you now, does it?"

"Why?" She gritted her teeth as Mama Yaga began to drape the cold cloths over the deepest of her knife wounds.

"I have a question for you, and you are the only one who can answer it." She paused to situate another cloth. "I can give you something for the pain, but it will put you out for at least twenty-four hours, if not longer. And I won't be able to give you a restorative for full health until it wears off." She wiped her hands on a clean towel tucked into her belt. "But if you choose not to take the pain medicines, you will feel everything. There will be no unconsciousness for you."

Mama Yaga looked down at Galina, who could do nothing more than lie still and pray for this to end. "Which is it, girl? You must decide soon."

Galina thought of Nik and Rina, of Konstantin and Andrey, and everyone else who was in danger while Alexei still held power. She was the only one who could challenge him, but first she had to heal and be at full strength. Nik didn't have time for her to swan around in bed and recuperate, not if what Konstantin said was true. And Konstantin wasn't one to lie about things when it came to Nik.

"No drugs," she said firmly. "Not even if I beg."

Mama Yaga's lips lifted in an unwholesome smile. "I imagine you don't beg anyone for much of anything." She placed more poultices over her stitches.

Galina squirmed uncomfortably against the bed, trying to hold still, but unable to manage it completely as burning heat began to race through her. "I'm getting hot," she whispered, suddenly very, very afraid.

Mama Yaga put her face near hers. "The medicine you drank will burn the poison from your blood. The poultices I'm wrapping over the wounds will pull out the rest. It won't take long—my potions work quickly."

"How will I tell when it's over?" Galina asked, already feeling like her nerve endings had been dipped in acid.

"The pain will stop."

"That could mean I'm dead too, you know."

Again that unpleasant smile. "Oh, I know."

That did not make Galina feel even a little bit better.

Galina opened eyes that were still tacky with dried blood. Once the pain had finally begun to subside, Galina suspected she had slipped into an exhausted sleep. Her throat felt raw and painful, but she knew that was to be expected after all of the screaming she'd done. Mama Yaga had not been exaggerating about how painful her cure was. There were a couple of times where Galina had thought about dying and that perhaps it would have been easier. But she wasn't ready to give up, not on herself and not on Andrey. So she'd screamed her head off and hung on with teeth and claws while the silver's poison was purged from her system.

She looked down at her body on the bed, expecting to see it covered in red. She remembered blood leaking from her nose and eyes and ears, as well as her mouth. Black ichor had flowed out of her stitched wounds, staining the poultices Mama Yaga had wrapped her in. But instead, she was swaddled in soft white sheets. Andrey's dark head rested on the mattress next to her hip. The skin beneath his eyes looked bruised from lack of sleep and worry. His even breaths stirred the fringe of the blanket where his cheek rested.

Galina smiled fondly. This was the man she was going to marry, the man she *wanted* to marry. She wanted to bicker with him about his inability to pick up his shoes, grow old with him, have wild, mind-blowing sex with him. She wanted to love him the rest of her days. Resting her hand lightly on his head, Galina slid her fingers into his soft black hair. It felt smooth and lush beneath her fingertips. She could have stroked his hair for hours.

Andrey stirred, eyes opening. He blinked slowly, taking his time coming to full awareness. He kept his head still beneath her hand, so Galina continued to run her fingers through his hair, massaging his scalp. "Good morning," she murmured, giving him a smile.

"I think it's closer to midnight," Andrey replied, closing his eyes and sighing as she palmed the back of his head. "I'm glad to see you awake again."

His voice was light, but Galina knew he'd been worried for her. He hadn't left her side the entire time she'd been fighting to rid herself of the toxic silver. He'd held her hand and whispered words of courage and support in her ear. She couldn't remember exactly what he'd said, but she'd understood the feeling behind it. He'd encouraged her to fight.

He lifted his head, pulling away from her hand. "How do you feel?"

Galina cocked her head, taking stock. She felt…good. Great, actually. There was no pain anymore. She peeled up one of the poultices and saw nothing but mostly healed scars. She was tired and achy, but the silver that was poisoning her system seemed to be completely gone.

"Okay. Better than okay, really." She rubbed a hand to her hair. It crackled. "Although a shower would probably go a long way to making me look vaguely human again."

Andrey leaned forward and kissed her hard, his hands resting against her jaw line. Without words, he spoke of his devotion to her, and without words she answered him. Galina melted into him, wishing they had all day to revel in each other.

He broke away after a few moments. "I should get Mama Yaga."

"Wait," Galina said, clutching at Andrey's hand to stop him from leaving. "How's Konstantin?"

Andrey gave her an exhausted smile. "He's good. Mama Yaga patched him up."

"Any word from Nik and Irina?" she asked.

Andrey didn't answer her. He kissed her palm before leaving to get the healer.

Galina felt clear headed for the first time in what seemed like days. How long since she'd been attacked? Alexei wasn't waiting for her to recover. He'd be trying to make alliances and secure his position. And why had Irina suddenly decide to leave the safe house to, of all things, confront their grossly twisted brother?

She looked over to the side table where Mama Yaga had set up her things. A stuffed chicken stared back at her. Galina rolled her eyes. Above her bed, hanging from the light of the ceiling fan was a collection of dried chicken feet.

Sometimes the woman took the chicken thing a little too far.

Andrey returned with Mama Yaga. Konstantin and a battered looking Viktor brought up the rear. Kon gave her a smile when he saw her awake. Andrey took his usual place next to her on the bed and brushed hair back from her face. "Сладкая," he murmured.

"Touching," Mama Yaga interrupted. "Now get out of the way so I can check on her."

Andrey moved out of the way reluctantly so Mama Yaga could do a cursory examination. She looked at Galina's eyes, checked her tongue, asked her to lift her arms. Galina did as she was bid, wondering exactly how this was supposed to determine anything, but kept quiet. You didn't backtalk Mama Yaga unless you'd suddenly developed a really strong need for corn.

She peeled away each of the poultices, making approving clucking noises as she did so. "Worked better than even I expected," she said as she removed the last one. "Well done, *girlchick*."

"You mentioned a restorative," Galina reminded her. She needed to get up and out of bed so she could find Irina and Nikolai.

"I'm surprised you remembered. But yes, I can mix one for you." She lightly patted Galina's head.

"Do so, please." When Mama Yaga left, Galina swung her legs out of bed, to a chorus of protests from everyone else in the room.

"Get back in bed!" Andrey ordered.

She looked up at him and quirked an eyebrow. "Really, with Konstantin and Viktor watching? I didn't know you liked an audience." Galina grinned at him wickedly.

"Galya," he growled, not the slightest bit embarrassed at her words. "You need to rest."

"I need to find out what's going on with Alexei. I didn't just go through five kinds of hell so I could swan about like an eighteenth-century consumptive while the rest of you go charging in like the cavalry." Galina looked at the concerned faces of those around her. "I'll make you a deal. I'll stay in bed until Mama Yaga comes back with her potion, if you'll fill me in on what's going on. Deal?"

"Deal," Kon agreed before Andrey could protest again.

Andrey took the chair he'd been sitting in the entire night on her other side. Galina sat back against the pillows. She looked over at Viktor. "Why aren't you watching out for Irina?"

Viktor bristled at her tone, but Galina didn't really care if she'd hurt his feelings or his pride. He was supposed to love her sister; more importantly, he was supposed to protect her. What the hell was he doing here?

"Nik sent me away." His eyes blazed blue, anger making them almost shimmer. "I couldn't get her away from Alexei at the restaurant—he had too many guards. I even tried to get through to her in wolf form at your father's house, but no dice."

"Nik said he had it in hand," Kon interrupted. "You know he won't let anything happen to Irina."

Galina crossed her arms, but there was nothing she could do until Mama Yaga came back with her restorative. It made her teeth itch. "What else have I missed?" she snapped.

Konstantin began. "Alexei blowing up a couple of Andrey's warehouses for shits and grins." Andrey threw his friend and bodyguard a dark look. "What? She asked. And that's where he started."

Galina swiveled her gaze to Andrey. "How bad?"

"No one was badly hurt," he said, a storm brewing in his blue eyes. "I lost some smuggled product, but he didn't get what he was after."

Galina knew he meant Bullet. "What else?"

Viktor piped up again. "He's trying to turn the families against Andrey. And with him here, watching over you, there hasn't been any-one to counter him. I don't think many people are buying it though."

"I'm not worried about that," Andrey said. "I have enough people that Alexei doesn't know about who are backing me. He's only dig-ging himself a deeper hole."

"What the hell was Irina thinking, leaving the safe house?" Galina looked back at Konstantin. "Did she give you any indication she was thinking of running?"

Kon shook his head. "None. We ran, practiced shooting, talked—you know, the usual. I don't know what lit a fire under her ass." At Viktor's low growl, Konstantin said, "Calm down, Vik. It wasn't an insult."

"Did Nik tell you what she was looking for that got Alexei so angry?" Galina asked.

And that's when Galina remembered her last phone conversation with Irina, lamenting the fact that she hadn't been able to find any dirt on Alexei. She'd griped because she hadn't been able to get close enough to him to find anything. And if there was one thing Irina was capable of, it would be getting past Alexei's defenses.

"Oh, crap." She shook her head. "I know what she's doing. She's looking for some proof that Alexei arranged to have Papa killed."

Viktor looked ready to pounce on someone and use them as a chew toy. "We need to get over there!"

"And we will." Galina had had enough handwringing. If things with Alexei were going to escalate further, she wanted it to be on her terms. "Andrey, call the heads of the family and tell them I'm calling a meeting at Papa's place. Moonrise. They should all meet at the Circle."

She looked at Konstantin. "Let Nik know what's coming. He's going to need to let everyone through." Next up was Viktor. "I'm going to need a list of every bodyguard, streetman, and underling likely to remain loyal to Alexei. I need a purge list. Get on it."

Mama Yaga took that moment to enter the room. Galina was grateful for the break. There was no doubt that the car bomb had been deliberate, but she'd been hoping to be wrong about who'd ordered it. It was one thing to think your brother was a psychotic douchebag, but to have it proven true was quite another.

Pressing another tall glass of questionable liquid into her palm, Mama Yaga ignored the charged silence in the room. "Drink it all. But understand that if you're hit with silver so soon after your recovery, no amount of elixir will help you."

Galina nodded. "Does it taste as bad as the last one?" she asked the older woman.

Mama Yaga grinned. "Worse. But the results are worth it." She tilted the glass up to Galina's lips. "Especially if you plan to challenge your brother."

Everyone stared at the wise woman. She scoffed. "Oh, like I don't know what's going on with every family. I do more than think about chickens, children."

"*Na zdorov'ye!*" Galina tipped back the glass and finished every drop and then clutched at her throat, coughing. "Do you make anything that doesn't taste like crap?" she asked Mama Yaga.

24
Sibling Rivalry

Galina sat in the Maybach beside Andrey, bouncing her foot nervously. Konstantin rode in the car behind them, along with several of Andrey's best men. Another car full of them and Viktor brought up the rear.

Andrey's hand on her knee stilled her foot. She looked over at him with a grin. "Remember the last time we were in backseat of a car?" she asked.

A laugh rumbled deep in his chest. "I do." He pulled her closer. "One of the best nights of my life."

"And mine." Her hands slid up his chest. "Want to go again?" she asked, leaning forward to whisper in his ear.

"You were suffering from silver poisoning less than twenty-four hours ago." He kissed a line of heat down her neck.

"And I feel fine now." Galina hiked her skirt up and pulled herself onto his lap. "Better than fine, actually." She rocked against him until she felt him grow hard against her.

"What is it with you and cars?" Andrey asked, laughter making his eyes dance. His fingers climbed up her thighs until his hands grabbed her hips. He moved aside her panties.

"It's not cars," she told him, before she lowered her mouth to his. "It's close proximity to you that does it."

When she let him up for air, he said, "I'm flattered."

She caught a gasp between her teeth as his finger slipped inside of her. She rocked against his hand, bracing her own against his shoulders. Galina leaned against him, dropping her head down as he slid a second digit inside of her. She hummed as she moved against him, feeling the sweet rush of heat climb up through her stomach and across her chest.

"You feel amazing," Andrey murmured, sucking her earlobe into his mouth. "I've missed you."

Galina sighed, wishing they dared do more. She wanted him inside of her, wanted to feel his naked body rubbing and pressing against her own. Andrey added a third finger inside of her. She arched against his hand, grinding her clit into his palm, needing the roughness. He knew what she needed and thumbed the greedy nub of flesh, making her cry out in pleasure.

Her toes curled inside of her heels as she felt her orgasm build. Heat flushed her chest and cheeks as Andrey's clever fingers and thumb brought her closer and closer to the edge. His mouth covered hers, his tongue thrusting into her mouth in time with his fingers. He swallowed her gasps as she stiffened in his arms, her climax rolling through her like a tidal wave.

"Better now?" he asked, removing his fingers and licking her juices from them.

She slid off of him, laying her head against him. "Mmmm hmmm. That certainly took the edge off."

He pulled her tight against him. "Let me fight him."

Galina reared up to meet his gaze. "I can't." She put a hand to his cheek. "And you know why. It has to be me. This is Sudenko business more than anything else. Now that Alexei's gone off the rails, there's nobody but me. Nik doesn't want to run the business."

"You'll have to challenge your *brother*. And win." Andrey's eyes were a dark with concern for her.

"Do you doubt I can do that?" Galina tensed, waiting for his answer.

He chuckled. "I know you can take on anyone and anything, Galya. And that you will win. I just wish it wasn't against your brother." He lifted her chin so he could kiss her lightly on the mouth. "You will do what must be done, of that I have no doubt."

Curling up next to him, Galina asked in a small voice, "Do you think Irina's okay?"

"Nik is with her." Then Andrey's face turned thunderous. "And if she is not, you will not be the only one Alexei will answer to."

She thought of Viktor riding with Andrey's men. There would be no stopping him if Irina had come to any harm. Not that she would be particularly interested in stopping him.

This was her family. Galina would do whatever she had to in order to see them all safe. Even if that meant killing her own brother to do so.

The car pulled up in front of her father's house. Through the tinted windows of the Maybach, she could see the cars already parked around the circular drive in front of the main house. Almost everyone would be out in the challenge circle. Galina smiled, a small vicious thing. Let Alexei be surprised by her presence in front of everyone. Let him know that his assassin — if Maksim could be called something so lofty as assassin — had failed. She had to admit that it was in Alexei's style to half-ass his attempt on her life. He really didn't see her as a threat.

Good.

That would make things that much easier for her when she challenged him for head of the family.

That car stopped. Galina squeezed Andrey's hand one last time, then slid out of the backseat once the driver opened her door. She waited while Andrey got out, and then turned to see the rest of their entourage disembarking.

Nikolai was already waiting for her. He enveloped her in a warm hug, both for support and to whisper, "Rina's okay, just a little banged up. But big brother is a slavering mess." He let her go.

Andrey put his hand on the small of her back. "We're ready."

"Get everyone to the circle. Nik and I will get Rina and meet you there." She gave him an encouraging smile when he rubbed her back.

"Uncle Petyr is waiting inside," Nik said. "So's Maksim. He's on Alexei's crew now."

Andrey spun, ready to sprint inside. Galina pulled him back. "It's okay," she told him, squeezing his hand. "We'll deal with him later. Let me get Irina."

Andrey stopped, scowling. "Fine. But I'm going to rip his guts out when this is all sorted."

Galina squeezed his hand before climbing the porch steps to enter Papa's house. It would always be Papa's house, no matter who lived in it. She sniffed. She could smell Irina faintly, but the scent of wolf overpowered much of anything else she might get. Where was Irina?

Alexei's guards occupied the front entryway and stairs. Guns appeared as if by magic and everyone one of them was pointed at her. Galina stopped in the threshold of the house, a slow grin spreading across her face. All of her brother Alexei's bodyguards stared at her, as if she was about to devour their souls with a side of chili fries. They were nervous. Off balance.

They were afraid.

"What the fuck do you morons think you are doing?" Nik barked, his voice going Alpha. It was something he did rarely, allowing the tone to slip into his speech.

Some of the guns trained on her wavered. One man said, "Your brother gave orders…"

Nikolai cut him off with a scowl. "This is our father's house. His daughter is *always* welcome here, no matter what my brother orders. Do you idiots understand that? Now, GUNS DOWN."

Galina watched quietly as each and every gun was holstered. Most seemed relieved to do so. She noted the faces of the few who tried to fight the order. "Shall we go see Alexei?" she all but purred. "I can't wait to see his face."

Galina preceded Nikolai into the living area of the house, stopping in front of the closed door of the large parlor situated behind the stairs. She could hear muffled voices, but none of them were Irina's. "Where is she?" she asked Nik.

"I moved her to her old room," he answered.

Galina led the way upstairs. Nik followed. "Alexei wanted to keep her tied up his bedroom, but I moved her. I didn't think it was a good idea to have her that close to him. I told her to lock the door and stay put."

"I should smack him on the nose with a rolled up newspaper. Made of titanium," she muttered. She stopped in front of Rina's room, reared back with her leg and kicked the wooden door right next to the lock. The wood splintered with a low crunch. Nik put his should against the door, shoving it the rest of the way open.

Irina sat up on her bed, hair tousled, looking twenty years younger. She blinked sleepily, as if the noise from the door had woken her up.

Galina ran to her sister. "Are you okay?" She offered Irina a hand, pulling her to her feet. Galina inspected her sister carefully. There was some bruising on her face and scrapes on her body, but nothing looked permanent. Before Irina could do more than squawk, Galina pulled her into a tight hug.

"Ow!" Irina hissed as Galina squeezed too hard against her bruises.

"Sorry." Galina said, backing up.

"I'm actually doing pretty well, considering," Irina told her, smiling bravely around the split in her lip. "I blacked Alexei's eye and broke his nose."

Galya laughed, shocked, by the proud tone of her sister's voice. "You did what?"

"I hit him," Irina said, nodding. "A lot. Viktor taught me *systema* and I used everything I could remember. And then I improvised and hit him in his stupid wolfy face with a log. But I think Viktor would have approved of that, too."

"What the fuck are you doing in here?!" Alexei's voice boomed from the now broken door.

She had to give it to her eldest brother. He only blanched slightly when he saw her face. Galina had been hoping her appearance here, in the pink of health, would rattle him more, but she'd take the little she could get right now.

Uncle Petyr stood right behind him, a frown furrowing all the wrinkles in his face, giving him a bulldog-like expression. "Galina?"

She let go of Irina and gave her uncle a hug. "But Alexei said you'd been stabbed."

"Oh, I was," she said smoothly, giving Alexei a small smile. "I got better."

She took a step toward her oldest brother. "And as for what the fuck I'm doing here," she gestured to the rope now decorating the floor of the bedroom. "I think that's fairly obvious too. But you always were a little slow. I've come to get Irina and challenge you as head of the family." She wrapped her arm around Irina and began to walk down the hall to the front door. "If you'll all follow me?" She threw her request over her shoulder as if she were inviting them to a picnic. "The other families are waiting."

Galina heard Petyr ask Alexei what he thought he was doing, imprisoning his own sister. Alexei didn't even try to answer him;

her brother just snarled as he pushed past the older man and tried to catch up. Nik blocked him so he stayed well out of Galina's way.

The guards at the door bristled when they saw her and Irina. Galina growled low in the back of her throat, an Alpha threatening violence if her commands were not obeyed. They may not have been her men directly, but Alexei was no Alpha and she was. It probably scrambled their very tiny brains.

"And now that we're out of Alexei's hearing," Galina said, turning to her sister and punching her lightly in the arm. "Why on earth did you leave the safe house?"

"I had to do something to help," Irina said, rubbing her arm. "I couldn't just hole up in the woods while the people I loved risked themselves for me. I'm Alexei's weakness. If I showed up, unannounced, in a place Alexei was comfortable, I knew he would make a scene, come off looking crazy. And when, he, predictably, flipped the fuck out, I knew if I protested that I didn't want to go back to Papa's house, that's exactly where he would take me. I had his laptop open and running less than an hour after we got here. I found all kinds of e-mails between Alexei and some Italian guy who planted the bomb. I found schematics for Papa's car Alexei downloaded from the net. But he caught me. He probably erased it all, but I doubt he's smart enough to wipe his hard drive. I mean, he wasn't smart enough to delete e-mails in which he explicitly planned his father's murder."

Irina stared at her, voice a harsh whisper. "Who does that by e-mail, Galina? A crazy person, that's who." Her sister laughed and shook her head. "So I'm assuming that you got my message?"

Galina raised an eyebrow. She hadn't even checked her phone. "What message?"

"What?" Irina groaned. "I thought that was why you showed up! I sent you an audio recording of Alexei ranting at me after he found me snooping through his computer. He went off how ungrateful I was, about what he'd done to get me out of my engagement to Andrey. He basically confessed to the whole thing. I was hoping the text went through before he smashed my phone."

Galina looked at her sister like she'd grown a second evil head.

"What?" Irina asked.

She smiled at Irina, ridiculously proud. "I turned my back for five minutes and you turned into a Bond girl, one of the smart ones that doesn't get killed as soon as she sleeps with James." Galina dug through her bag for her cell phone.

"I go to the all of the trouble of coercing a confession out of our brother, and you don't even check your phone?" Irina asked.

"I've had a lot going on, Rina, it's not like I had time to check my voice mail."

"Oh, yeah." Irina paused. "What was that Uncle Petyr said about you being stabbed?"

Galina waved away the question as she opened the text and pressed "play" on the audio file. Alexei's shouting was tinny, but clear enough that Galina could make out everything he said. Galina could feel her breath hitch as she cradled the phone in her hand. This would do it. This would be enough to convince the other families that Alexei was unsuitable to lead, that she had every right to challenge him.

They arrived on the fringes of the circle. Galina saw the knots of people demarcating the other families. A few of the bodyguards turned and signaled their bosses, who in turn signaled others. By the time her group arrived, a space had been made to allow them to join the circle. Low mutterings passed down the line of the assembled men.

Maksim stood with the rest of Alexei's crew, staring at her in speechless shock. His gaze skipped from her to Andrey, who was staring at him as if he was already imagining how his blood tasted on his tongue. She sneered at him. The Caviar Prince seemed one step away from pissing himself in fear. Galina turned her attention to the rest of the assembly.

Suddenly, Irina went still beside her. She was staring, wide-eyed, at the man directly across the clearing, almost a head taller than all of the other gathered wolves. And that was the moment that Galina realized that in the tumult of the last few hours, she hadn't yet told Irina that Viktor was alive.

"Viktor?" Irina whispered, her hand creeping up to her throat.

Galina glanced nervously around the circle at the sheer number of werewolf Mafioso. "Uh, Irina…"

But Irina was off. "Viktor!" Irina streaked past bodyguards and old men to launch herself at her not-quite-dead lover.

He staggered under the impact, but wrapped his arms around her tightly, lifting Irina off her feet. The crowd went silent as Irina claimed Viktor's mouth in a kiss so fierce that Galina could practically feel the heat from across the clearing.

"What the fuck is this?" she heard Alexei mutter behind her.

Galina shared a grin with Andrey, who crossed the grass to stand beside her. The silence broke as many heads bent together, exclaiming and whispering over the shock of Ilya Sudenko's sweet human daughter making a shameful spectacle of herself with a poor, unconnected Beta. Galina looked over her shoulder to see the monstrous sneer pass across Alexei's face at the sight of Irina in Viktor's arms. He stepped toward them, but Nik held him back.

Irina let Viktor up for air just long enough to rear back and slug him with everything she had in her. The werewolf's head snapped backward from the force of her blow, but his smile was blinding. Galina heard Andrey chuckle next to her even after Irina spat, "Don't you *ever* do that to me again, do you hear me?"

"Thank you all for coming," Galina began, pulling the focus from her sister's reunion with her beloved.

Silence filled the yard. All eyes were fixed on her. She stepped away from Andrey and Irina, standing alone before all of them. Galina knew that she had to do this herself. It was the only way. But that didn't mean she wasn't nervous about challenging her brother to single combat.

"I've invited you all here to bear witness." Mutterings began, sweeping through the circle of people. She plowed ahead. "I, Galina Sudenko, do hereby challenge my brother, Alexei Sudenko for leadership of the Sudenko family."

Alexei looked murderous. The mutterings around her exploded, all shock and indignation over Irina's behavior forgotten as shouts began to ring back and forth across the open space.

"Nonsense!" Alexei scoffed. "A woman has no right to challenge me. Everyone knows females can't run the business."

Petyr interrupted. "That is not the case. A woman has every right to initiate a challenge. It has happened in the past when Ykaterina Grenko challenged her husband." The shouting settled down, Petyr's words calming the more excited of the group.

"This is ridiculous." Alexei stalked up to her, trying his best to intimidate her through height. He looked ludicrous since he was only an inch or two taller than her. "What cause does she have?"

"I don't need a cause to initiate a challenge, or are you unfamiliar with the rules, Alexei?" She waited a beat before continuing. "But if you must have something, then I challenge you for the murder of our father, for the attempt on my life, and for the abduction of our sister—these are my reasons for challenge."

Galina watched as Alexei's nostrils flared in rage. She hoped this would unbalance him further. He made stupid mistakes when he was angry.

"And just in case there is any doubt that I have cause to challenge my brother." Galina raised her arm, phone in hand, and pressed play. Alexei's enraged voice rose to life, echoing through the trees as he explained his "efforts" to Irina.

"Do you think it was so easy? Getting Papa out of the way? Do you know what I had to do to end this farce of an engagement to that Rom mongrel? Do you think I wanted to have Papa killed? No! But I did it, for you, Irina. So we could be together. I killed Papa for you!"

Alexei howled in rage, barely audible over the rising crest of the crowd's voices.

Petyr nodded, holding up his hands for quiet. The list of accusations against Alexei and his own confession were too much for the crowd to take. Galina heard a few of them calling for Alexei's blood.

"And who will be your challenger?" Petyr asked.

Galina smiled slowly, feeling it creep across her face like fog. "I will."

Again Petyr held up his hands for silence as the other wolves responded, still capable of shock, somehow. Alexei was grinning like a madman, obviously unconcerned about her challenge. He thought she wouldn't know how to fight. She was counting on his being overconfident.

"Galya," Petyr said softly, drawing close to her, "this is madness. Let Nikolai handle this."

"No, Uncle," she told him, shaking her head sadly. "This is between me and Alexei. He's the one who stuck a knife in my back."

"A woman does not fight!" he scolded.

"This woman does." She turned back to Alexei. "I'm going to change."

"Why don't you do it here?" he taunted.

There were a number of reasons why she wouldn't change in front of the group of men gathered. The most important was that she needed these men's respect when she took over as head of the family and it was hard to do that once they'd seen her naked. And she really liked the dress she was wearing; she didn't want to shred it.

Galina gave Alexei her most infuriating smile. "Because I think everyone should be focused on the fact that you're a murdering coward and not on my naked breasts. Even if they are fabulous." She walked away to a small copse of trees that Papa had planted decades ago for just such a reason.

Andrey followed her. Before she could do more than remove her coat, he grabbed her roughly and kissed her. His mouth pressed hard against hers, demanding, wanting. She opened her lips beneath his, feeling his tongue slide against hers. He kissed her breathless, so deeply and desperately that she wobbled unsteadily against him.

"Let me fight him," he demanded, breaking away from her mouth.

"You know my answer to that already," Galina answered, kicking off her shoes.

Andrey's hands on her shoulders stopped her from undressing. "I can't lose you." His voice was soft, pitched for their ears alone.

"You won't," she assured him with a confidence she didn't feel. Galina knew only that she would never be able to live with herself if Andrey was hurt fighting her battles. "Do you really think I could stand losing you?" She held a hand to his cheek.

"Be careful," he said, moving his head so he could kiss her palm.

"Watch my back?" She finished undressing quickly.

Andrey grinned, his eyes never leaving her as she triggered her change. "When the back is as lovely as that, of course."

Galina padded toward the circle slowly, taking time to adjust to her wolf senses. It took her a few minutes to get used to four legs instead of two, a lower center of gravity, and how alive everything looked and smelled. Her senses were in overdrive, her thoughts scattered.

Her sensitive ears picked up gasps as she stalked into the circle, Andrey behind her. Galina didn't spend a lot of time in wolf form and hardly anyone here—outside of Nik, Alexei, and Rina—had ever seen her as an animal. Her coat was thick and white, her eyes the same icy jade as when she was human. She was large for a wolf, even larger than most males.

Alexei had changed in the circle and he now growled when he caught wind of her scent. Galina ignored him for the moment, taking a turn around the area to inspect for things not visible to the human eye. When she was satisfied everything was to her liking, she sat at the edge of the circle and waited.

"To the death?" Uncle Petyr asked once more as soon as Alexei calmed down.

Galina nodded her big wolf's head.

Galina stared at Alexei, also in his wolf form. He was no larger than she, but he did outweigh her. Her coarse white fur bristled as they circled each other. "To the death," Uncle Petyr cried out, and the entire assembly called out their agreement.

They wanted blood? That was fine with her; so did she.

Alexei snapped at her, his blocky head lunging at her front legs. Galina jumped back lightly, feeling out his speed. He snarled, snapping again. She lunged in return, nearly catching his front leg in between her teeth. She'd held back her speed, not willing to give away one of her strengths to him. Instead she pulled back, letting him think he was in control.

Alexei always made mistakes when he got cocky.

He rushed her, hoping to bowl her over with his superior mass, but Galina dancing out of his way, making a high barking noise as she did so. It was a taunt, a sound designed to humiliate at the same time it egged him on. She heard her brother growl with frustration and he leapt forward again, this time snapping at her hindquarters.

Instead of jumping away, Galina spun. Ducking her head low, she lunged at Alexei's throat. He jerked back, pulling his head away from her. She kept at him, teeth closing on fur but nothing else.

Alexei rushed her, his greater weight bowling Galina over. She scrambled to her feet, feeling his teeth dig into her flank. Galina lashed out with a paw, smacking him in the head. Her claw grazed across his eyes and he jumped backward.

She hadn't meant to hit him in the eye, but she would take it. Blood ran down her leg from the gash Alexei's teeth had left on her. Galina tested her footing to make sure her leg would bear her weight, feeling relief when it did.

Alexei paced before her, rage vibrating through him. Galina watched him cautiously, knowing how dangerous he was in this state. His eyes held nothing but hatred when they met hers. She wondered when things had gotten so bad between Alexei and the rest of them. He'd always been a bully, but when had they missed the chance to help him? How had they missed the signs of what a monster he was becoming?

Galina felt a sadness spring up inside of her. It was too late to help him now, even if he would allow it, which she doubted. She had to end this — for Nik and Rina, for Andrey, for the family business.

She had to end him.

Alexei growled, then attacked. Rather than bracing for him, Galina rolled with it as he smashed into her. He fought to pin her, his teeth aiming for her throat. She turned her body to the side, closing her jaw around his foreleg and bearing down.

Her brother howled in pain. Galina kept biting, feeling the crunch of bone beneath her teeth. Alexei fell off of her, backpedaling to get away. She opened her jaw, the taste of Alexei's blood filling her mouth. She wanted to spit it out but couldn't.

They circled again, Alexei moving slowly. He did his best to not put weight on his injured leg. Galina suddenly wished it could have been different between all of them, all those years ago. Back when they were kids, before their mother's death and Elena's. She wanted to turn back into her human form so she could talk to him, tell him so.

But his gaze burned into her, and Galina knew that there was no going back. Alexei would never forgive her for this. He would kill her if he could.

She feinted on the side with his bad eye. He had to turn if he wanted to see her. Galina changed direction, only to find herself snout to snout with him. He slammed into her, ignoring the damage to his foot. She dropped to her side, off balance, knowing she'd made a mistake.

But Alexei's teeth and claws didn't cut into her. Galina looked and saw him snarling, his gaze pinned to Rina as she passionately kissed Viktor.

Galina used his distraction to her advantage. He leapt toward Viktor, intending to kill him, but she'd already guessed his purpose. Crashing into him, Galina brought him to the ground. Before he could get to his feet, she was on him, jaws closing around his throat.

"Galya! *Stop!*" Nik shouted. "You can't kill him! He's still our brother!"

Galina looked up at her brother from over the fur of Alexei's neck. She relaxed her hold slightly. What the hell was Nikolai thinking?

Alexei pulled free, changing as he did so. Human again, he staggered to the pile of his clothes. Galina stared at Nikolai, wondering why he would interfere with the challenge.

"Galya, look out!" Irina screamed, jumping into the fight circle. Viktor threw his arm around her waist and hauled her back.

Galina caught sight of Alexei with a silver knife in his hand, just like the one that had been used by Maksim at the hotel. Mama Yaga's voice flashed through her head. *"If you are pierced with silver again, you will not heal."*

Galina felt her leg muscles bunch in a powerful predator's twitch. Everything seemed to move in slow motion. Andrey was lunging at them, trying to interpose himself between her and the knife. Konstantin was shouting, his hand going inside his jacket for his gun.

She leapt forward, feeling something hot zip past her fur as she did so. Galina saw a red hole open up in Alexei's forehead, and then she was crashing into him, two hundred pounds of pissed off shewolf bearing him to the ground with her teeth in his throat. Without hesitation, she ripped upward, tearing through flesh and muscle. Hot blood slapped her muzzle.

She spun, claws digging into Alexei's shuddering body. Irina stood, gun in hand, staring down at her brother with a grim expression. Her sister's eyes were hard, like chips of smoky topaz. Irina had shot Alexei, right between the eyes. No hesitation. Kon was right. She was a hell of a shot.

There was a moment of quiet before pandemonium hit. Alexei's loyal followers pulled weapons of their own, or burst into the clearing on four paws. Galina met them head on, Andrey, as a great black wolf, by her side. Konstantin and Nik were also there in wolf form, snapping and tearing at anyone foolish enough to threaten their pack.

Viktor had also changed, but he stayed close to Irina, who now had both of Viktor's guns. The Rom contingent fought at their leader's side, while those without an immediate interest sat back and watched the carnage.

Galina slammed into one of Sergei and Alexei's lackeys, a dun colored wolf with all of the finesse and initiative of sponge mold. He bared his teeth, dewlaps rising over his fangs. She snarled back, head dipping down so she could bite at his hindquarters. They rolled in a flurry of snapping jaws and growls.

Galina saw her opening and went for it, her jaws closing on his exposed stomach. Thick blood filled her mouth, meaty and smoky and *hothothot*. She heard the pained whine he gave before she ripped him open.

Andrey raced past her, his eyes on Maksim. The younger man scrambled away, still in human form, but that didn't keep Andrey from bowling into him. The Circle echoed with Maksim's sharp scream as he disappeared beneath a wall of black fur.

Another wolf, a large grey, stalked her, eyes watching her for any sign of weakness. But before he could lunge, he collapsed to the ground, a bullet wound staining the fur over his neck. He flopped over in a burble of red. Galina threw a lolling grin of thanks at her sister, and then looked around for her next opponent. This wolf she recognized as Timur, the man who Alexei had sent to attack her in the parking garage. Irina was taking aim at him, but Galina slashed him across the throat before her sister got a shot off.

There were more, so many more. And Galina's pack took them all, until all was left was a pile of furry bodies on the ground and the quivering exhalations of the dying. The other wolves, both on two and four feet, were backing away, heads lowered, hindquarters nearly dragging the ground, tails quivering and tucked between their legs. The fight was over. Galina made sure none of her pack was injured, relieved to see no one was.

Uncle Petyr stepped into the circle, careful not to walk on any of the bodies. He stood next to Galina, resting a hand on her furry back. "By right of challenge, I proclaim Galina Sudenko the new head of the Sudenko family."

They waited a moment for objections. Galina looked around at the faces of the other families and saw shock and awe and a burgeoning respect. And a little bit of fear there too.

When no one dared to raise an objection, Galina tilted her head back and raised her wolf voice in a howling ululation of triumph. After a moment, Andrey, Nik, Konstantin, and Viktor joined in. And Irina lifted her guns in the air, yelling, "This is what you can accomplish when you stay in a form with thumbs, bitches!"

25

Hot Water

Galina had turned the *Volk Organizatsiya* upside down. She was the first female to ever run a family. The last week had been spent having meetings, cleaning house, and consolidating her power. After the carnage at the challenge circle, most of the other families were content, at least for now, to wait and see where she led.

Irina had also finagled the jewelry shop she had run for Papa for herself. Galina was more than happy to give it over to her sister, so long as Irina offered her a deep discount on the lovely custom pieces she designed.

There was still so much to do. But Nik was beside her, serving as advisor. He was actually getting to do more than clean up Alexei's messes and he seemed truly happy for the first time in ages. For that alone Galina was grateful.

Andrey had booked them a penthouse suite in the finest hotel in Seattle as a present to both of them. They had the whole weekend to themselves with orders only to be disturbed in the event of the Apocalypse. They didn't even have to get out of bed if they didn't want to.

She planned to test that theory. But first, she wanted a nice, hot bath.

Galina breezed into the suite with barely a glance at the opulent furnishings and finishes and headed straight to the bathroom. "Order us something to eat, would you please?" she asked Andrey as she threw off her clothes.

The tub was a huge clawfoot monstrosity that could easily fit three people. She filled it with scalding hot water, ready for a nice long soak. Inspecting the sample bottles of bath unguents and gels, she found a rosemary mint scented bubble bath and dumped that in to the frothing water. Then she stepped in, not even waiting for it to completely fill.

Sinking into the steaming water, Galina sighed in contentment. Irina was safe, Viktor was alive, and Andrey was here with her. She was head of the Sudenko family. Things had suddenly gotten so much simpler. She smiled, resting her neck against the cool edge of the tub.

"Food will…" Andrey began, trailing off when he saw the pale expanse of her skin beneath the bubbles and water.

Galina cracked open her eyes with a sly smile. "Join me?" She extended her hand to him.

Andrey stripped quickly. She watched, a lascivious grin crossing her face. He was utterly gorgeous: all dark hair, silvery eyes, and strong muscles. The long muscles in his thighs flexed as he stepped into the tub. His lean hips sank below the water as he lowered himself slowly into the bath.

Galina ducked beneath the water, slicking her hair back before popping up. As the water level rose to the top of the tub, she reached around Andrey to shut off the tap. When she did so, he kissed her wrist, tonguing the underside of it gently. She slid forward, wrapping her legs around his waist.

Andrey lowered his dark head to hers, his lips tracing her jawline from just under her ear to her chin. Galina sighed, running her hands down the flat planes of his chest. Her head dropped back and Andrey pressed hot kisses down the length of her throat.

Galina dug her fingers into his hair as his rumbling growl sent a rush of heat racing through her. Andrey nuzzled her breast, taking a nipple into his mouth. He kissed the hardened peak, swirling his tongue over it until she gasped and tightened her thighs around his waist. "Mmmmm," she hummed in pleasure.

He hitched her higher up so his mouth had easy access to both breasts. Galina sucked in her breath, her mind spiraling into a lust-filled haze. "Have I mentioned how much I appreciate your mouth?" She gasped, feeling her pussy twitch in needy spasms.

Andrey slipped a finger inside of her, teasing her moist folds. Galina dug her fingers into his slick shoulders. "You could stand to mention it more," he said with a grin. He worked another finger inside of her, scissoring her open until she was aching with need.

"I wouldn't want you to become complacent," she said, and then kissed him deeply. All she wanted was sensation and the feeling of him inside her, filling her up. The masculine scent of him mixed with the rosemary and mint of the bath made her senses reel. The hot water and Andrey's hotter hands made her flush with the heat of desire.

She needed him like she needed the air she breathed. The bathtub was her entire world, with Andrey at its center.

"Oh, really?" he asked after she let him up for air.

When he removed his fingers, Galina squirmed against him, chasing after the pleasure he'd denied her. He lifted her up, his hands spanning her waist, and guided her down on his cock. She cried out in mindless pleasure as his shaft speared her, but when she tried to grind down on him, to take him deeper, Andrey held her still.

She made a mew of distress in the back of her throat. His strong arms kept her where he wanted her, allowing him to control the pace he entered her. "Andrey," she whispered, fingernails scoring lines on his shoulders, wanting him to move faster. "I can't…"

"You can. And you will," his voice dark with lust. There was the command of an Alpha behind his words.

Galina's brain snapped to attention, her own Alpha will aroused. She pushed against his chest, arching over the arms that held her. Her wet skin made it hard for him to hold her and she slid from his grasp.

Andrey was after her in a second, his hands slipping around her. One hand nestled in the hair at the nape of her neck and Galina snapped her teeth together. "Let go," she commanded in her own Alpha voice.

His forehead pushed against hers as they fought each other in a battle of wills. Galina was even more turned on than she had been before, her body aching with the need for him. But she wasn't going to relent. Andrey would have to work for her surrender.

Water sloshed out of the bathtub as their bodies clashed together and then apart. Galina bit at Andrey's lips as he tried to kiss her. He growled, his fingers tightening against her scalp. He stood, dragging her up with him.

Galina snarled at Andrey, but followed his lead, knotting her fingers in his hair and yanking his head backward. Now it was his turn to bare his teeth, his eyes glowing silver. He grabbed her in his free arm, lifting her up and stepping out of the tub. His other hand tightened around the back of her neck.

She swung in his grip, wrapping her legs around his waist and trying to throw him off balance. A deep growl rumbled out of Andrey's chest and Galina's pussy clenched in desire. Her fingernails scraped at his scalp as she felt his cock twitch against her belly.

Andrey walked forward, despite the painful angle Galina held his head at. Before she could do anything else, he slammed her back against the wall. His hand at her neck kept her head from striking it, but it still hurt. Her grip on his hair loosened in surprise.

His mouth slanted over hers, hard and bruising. His kisses left her empty and aching. She thrust her tongue into his mouth, tangling it with his as their teeth clacked together. Galina felt his hands move from her waist to cup her ass, spreading her open. His lips swallowed her moan, all the while demanding more and more from her.

Galina became a creature of pure desire. She didn't think about right or wrong, about family, about Alexei's death or the family business. She couldn't. All of her focus was bent on one thing: Andrey and the way he was making her feel. She wanted his cock inside of her, his hands on her body, his mouth everywhere and she never wanted him to stop making her feel the way she felt right this minute.

He shifted her body slightly so that he was lined up with her entrance. Andrey entered her with one smooth thrust, making her cry out into his mouth as he buried himself in her up to the hilt. Galina clutched at his shoulders spasmodically, her thoughts blowing apart like a nuclear blast as his tongue in her mouth matched the rhythm of his cock thrusting inside of her.

Andrey pulled his head away from hers, his eyes hooded as he watched her. His strong fingers kneaded into the flesh of her ass, pulling her cheeks further apart. Everything he did felt incredible. It was like she was one giant string, and Andrey knew just how to pluck it.

His eyes watched her, intent on her face. Galina had no idea she could ever feel this way. She'd had sex before, but never like this. This went beyond sex, into another realm entirely.

Andrey changed the angle of his thrusts and everything turned to heat and light inside of her. She cried out with each stroke as his cock bumped against her g-spot. She stared at him, seeing his face alight with a kind of lustful determination at seeing her so undone.

Galina felt her orgasm building inside of her, spiraling around her pelvis and up into the base of her spine. She rocked her hips against his, reveling in his strength and power.

Andrey quickened his pace. His voice was hoarse with need as he ordered. "Say. My. Fucking. Name."

Galina leaned her head against the wall, unsure if she could even form words. But she would try. He slammed his hips into her again, making sparks shoot through her entire body. "Andreyev," she gasped. "Andreyev Lupesco."

"And who am I?" he growled.

"My match." Her eyes rolled back in her head at the pleasure he was giving her, striking her g-spot over and over. "My mate."

"Damn right."

He kissed her deeply, smothering her scream as her orgasm slammed into her like a meteor hitting the earth. His own followed soon after. Galina clung to him as his release coursed through her.

Andrey carried her over to the bed. Galina was still wrapped around him, shivering from the aftershocks of her climax. She felt like she had been taken apart and remade into something better, stronger. She couldn't explain it; all she knew was that she would follow this man into the fires of Hell and back out again if it meant having him in her life.

She protested weakly when he slid out of her. Andrey chuckled and she pulled far enough away so she could see his face. She felt a bone deep exhaustion settle over her, but she didn't want to let him go.

"I imagine that this is similar to what I looked like in the car after the ballet," he murmured, his lips curving up in a fond smile.

"дьявол," she whispered. She'd called him a devil in Russian.

"Сладкая," he replied. "I love you."

Acknowledgments

Gia: Thanks to my partner in crime, Jacey Conrad, for embarking on this adventure with me. I couldn't ask for a better collaborator. Thanks to vodka for making all of this possible. Thanks to Arizona. We're really, *really* sorry. And thanks to you, the readers, for taking this journey with us. We hope you enjoy it!

Jacey: Thank you to Gia, my evil snark twin, the only person with whom I would want to co-write these books. Thanks go to M., for introducing me to Gia. You have no one to blame but yourself. And to the readers who enjoy giggles with their naughty reading, welcome home.

About the Authors

Jacey Conrad is a sushi-loving, pop culture nerd living in the South with her high school sweetheart. She delights in horribly made mutant shark movies and watching Sean Bean die in his various cinematic incarnations. To keep up with Jacey on twitter, go to:

twitter.com/JaceyConrad

Gia Corona (aka Molly Harper) loves boots, boys, and bourbon, not necessarily in that order. When she's not actively stalking Michael Fassbender and his abdominals, she's watching questionable television or reading comics. You can find her at:

twitter.com/Gia_writes

New Adult Romance

Three Daves by Nicki Elson
Streamline by Jennifer Lane
The Shades series: *Shades of Atlantis* & *Shades of Avalon* by Carol Oates
The Heart series: *Beside Your Heart, Disclosure of the Heart* & *Forever Your Heart*
by Mary Whitney
Romancing the Bookworm by Kate Evangelista
Flirting with Chaos by Kenya Wright
The Vice, Virtue & Video series: *Revealed, Captured, Desired* & *Devoted*
by Bianca Giovanni
Granton University series: *Loving Lies* by Linda Kage
Missing Pieces by Meredith Tate

Paranormal & Fantasy Romance

The Light series: *Seers of Light, Whisper of Light* & *Circle of Light* by Jennifer DeLucy
The Hanaford Park series: *Eve of Samhain* & *Pleasures Untold* by Lisa Sanchez
Immortal Awakening by KC Randall
The Seraphim series: *Crushed Seraphim* & *Bittersweet Seraphim* by Debra Anastasia
The Guardian's Wild Child by Feather Stone
Grave Refrain by Sarah M. Glover
The Divinity series: *Divinity* & *Entity* by Patricia Leever
The Blood Vine series: *Blood Vine, Blood Entangled* & *Blood Reunited* by Amber
Belldene
Divine Temptation by Nicki Elson
The Dead Rapture series: *Love in the Time of the Dead, Love at the End of Days* &
Love Starts with Z by Tera Shanley
The Hidden Races series: *Incandescent* & *Illumination* by M.V. Freeman
Something Wicked by Carol Oates
Chronicles of Midvalen: *Command the Tides* (book 1) by Wren Handman
Saving Evangeline by Nancee Cain
Twice Upon a Kiss by Jane Susann McCarter
From Russia with Claws by Jacey Conrad and Gia Corona

Romantic Suspense

Whirlwind by Robin DeJarnett
The CONduct series: *With Good Behavior, Bad Behavior* & *On Best Behavior*
by Jennifer Lane
Indivisible by Jessica McQuinn
Between the Lies by Alison Oburia
Blind Man's Bargain by Tracy Winegar

www.ingramcontent.com/pod-product-compliance
Lightning Source LLC
Chambersburg PA
CBHW020405120726
47904CB00002B/708